NEVER DOUBT A DUKE

The Never Series
Book One

By Maggi Andersen

© Copyright 2020 by Maggi Andersen
Text by Maggi Andersen
Cover by Wicked Smart Designs

Dragonblade Publishing, Inc. is an imprint of Kathryn Le Veque Novels, Inc.
P.O. Box 7968
La Verne CA 91750
ceo@dragonbladepublishing.com

Produced in the United States of America

First Edition May 2020
Print Edition

Reproduction of any kind except where it pertains to short quotes in relation to advertising or promotion is strictly prohibited.

All Rights Reserved.

The characters and events portrayed in this book are fictitious. Any similarity to real persons, living or dead, is purely coincidental and not intended by the author.

ARE YOU SIGNED UP FOR DRAGONBLADE'S BLOG?

You'll get the latest news and information on exclusive giveaways, exclusive excerpts, coming releases, sales, free books, cover reveals and more.

Check out our complete list of authors, too!

No spam, no junk. That's a promise!

Sign Up Here

www.dragonbladepublishing.com

―――

Dearest Reader;

Thank you for your support of a small press. At Dragonblade Publishing, we strive to bring you the highest quality Historical Romance from the some of the best authors in the business. Without your support, there is no 'us', so we sincerely hope you adore these stories and find some new favorite authors along the way.

Happy Reading!

CEO, Dragonblade Publishing

Additional Dragonblade books by Author Maggi Andersen

The Never Series
Never Doubt a Duke
Never Dance with a Marquess
Never Trust and Earl

Dangerous Lords Series
The Baron's Betrothal
Seducing the Earl
The Viscount's Widowed Lady
Governess to the Duke's Heir
Eleanor Fitzherbert's Christmas Miracle (A Novella)

Once a Wallflower Series
Presenting Miss Letitia

The Lyon's Den Connected World
The Scandalous Lyon

Also from Maggi Andersen
The Marquess Meets His Match
Beth

Chapter One

Dountry Park, Keswick Cumbria
Late February 1815.

"Nellie, you must see this article!" Nellie's sister, Marian, her green eyes wide, rushed into Nellie's bedchamber, clutching a newspaper. "It's about the duke!"

"I don't know why you have those scandal broths sent to you. Let me see." Nellie almost snatched it. Thirsting for any information on the man she was to marry and had yet to meet, she quickly perused the item concerning the Duke of Shewsbury. "Oh, dear Lord!" She thrust the paper back into her sister's hands as if it burned her.

"It shows Shewsbury is human." A gleam of amusement and affection lit Marian's eyes. She plopped down onto the sofa, waking Peter, Nellie's beloved King Charles spaniel. He sleepily licked her hand.

"Does it? A brute and a rake, more likely." Nellie picked it up from the table where her sister had cast it. *"A certain duke whose estate is in Leicestershire, but shall remain nameless…"*

"It may not be Shewsbury," Marian interrupted as she fondled the dog's silky ears.

"It's hardly the Duke of Rutland, he has a brood of children and breeds racehorses." Nellie continued to read, *"…seems to have had some trouble with his French mistress. This writer was passing a certain elegant establishment in Mayfair when he sighted said duke, descending the steps to* the road with a comely lady over his shoulder, one hand on an unmentionable part of her anatomy, the other holding a canary's cage. Smoke could be seen wafting from an upstairs window. As I watched, captivated, the duke was addressed in voluble French as she pounded her fists on his back. He set her down none too gently to hail a passing hackney. Placing her and the canary's cage in the carriage, he then gave the jarvy directions, and slammed the door, running back, apparently, to stifle the flames. Might their affair be at an end?

"This..." Nellie's voice hitched, "...coming right on top of that other newspaper article describing how he took a member of the press outside Parliament by the scruff of the neck and savagely shook him."

"Not a dull man by all accounts," Marian observed.

She glared at her sister. Marian refused to take this seriously. Perhaps because her own husband could be relied on to behave badly on occasion. Nellie suspected Marian enjoyed it.

"Surely, Papa doesn't expect me to marry a brute!"

"Papa needs an injection of funds after that stock exchange debacle, but I doubt he'd sacrifice you. He and the old duke were friends, so he must know the family well."

"I must speak to Papa. Mama is talking of purchasing new liveries for the footman, hiring more staff, and having the drawing room and the guest bedchambers repainted. I can't let them spend a fortune to make us look prosperous for the duke's visit if I don't intend to marry him."

The newssheet clutched in her hand, she went downstairs and knocked on her father's study door.

Papa hunched over a stack of letters on his desk, a glass of brandy beside him, while the smoke from his cigar drifted around the room.

He glanced up from a letter he held and smiled. "What do you have there, Nellie?"

She approached the desk and held the paper out. "This can only refer to Shewsbury." He took it from her and read it while Nellie leaned against his desk and fidgeted with his silver pounce pot. "It must be the duke. He's a rake, Papa. Surely you don't wish me to marry such a man?"

He reached across and removed the pot from her nervous fingers. "This is little more than a scandal rag. I don't believe a word of it."

"But what about the item in the newspaper? The one that said Shewsbury attacked a journalist in the street?"

Her father tossed the paper down onto the desk and leaned back in his chair. "I don't believe that, either. There will be a story behind it, mark my words."

He gestured to a chair. "Sit down, Nellie. Stop hovering over me. I know Shewsbury. He's a serious and thoughtful man, as his father was before him. I am confident you will make a fine match."

She sank onto the chair. "But the mistress, Papa!"

"I dislike discussing a man's mistress with my daughter." He cleared his throat. "Men do, on occasion, take a mistress. Charles was heartbroken, and his father told me after he suffered a broken engagement. I imagine that was the reason. And it's all I will say on the matter."

In Nellie's opinion, that only made things worse.

"Where would you be now, daughter, if I'd let you run away with that Irish poet without two pennies to rub together?" her father asked. "And what did the fellow do when I had words with him? He scurried off to Ireland. A fortune hunter. Good thing I discovered it in time and put a stop to it." He frowned. "You weren't thinking clearly, Nellie."

While no actual plan of elopement had been in place, she had been left heartbroken and angry with her father. At eighteen, one's first love carried a good deal of importance. And for a while, she continued to make excuses for Walsh, until she was finally forced to admit he was a coward, and his feelings for her did not run deep. He'd needed no prompting to leave her and return home. But the hurt remained and tore at her confidence. She would never trust her heart to another man again.

Her father smiled at her, pleased as punch with the arrangement.

Shewsbury was a wealthy duke, after all. He pointedly picked up the letter he'd been reading when she came in.

Nellie left the chair. Unlike many fathers, he had given her the opportunity to find a husband of her choice. It was not his fault that she had failed to do so.

"I will agree to marry him *if* I find him acceptable, Papa."

"I have no doubt of it. Now, Nellie, leave me to this correspondence."

She slowly mounted the stairs, the newssheet scrunched in her hand. It appeared she would have to marry the duke. She did not believe the portrait her father had painted of Shewsbury. But she could hardly let her father down when his financial future now depended on their union. She just hoped for a tolerable marriage and a husband busy with his own matters, who wouldn't ask too much of her.

⇶⫷

A MONTH LATER, Nellie studied her reflection in the Cheval mirror. She gathered the violet-gray muslin folds of her dress at the waist.

"I am nothing like her."

"Like whom?" Marian peeped over Nellie's shoulder, her eyes questioning.

"Drusilla, Marchioness of Thorburn."

"Oh, Shewsbury's ex-fiancée. No, you're not. I saw Drusilla once in London. She looked as if she'd blow away in a slight breeze. You have breasts and hips." Marian put a hand on her own rounded hip. "Belfries approves of mine. Says he prefers a woman with a bottom. Something to grab hold of." She raised her eyebrows. "Surely you don't wish to be like her."

Nellie drew in a breath. "Of course not. It's just that I'm not his type. I am neither an exotic creature like his mistress nor a slender waif." What she feared most, she struggled to express even to Marian.

"Although it won't be a love match, I do want a husband to approve of me. I want us to be content together and have children. But if I find it impossible, I won't accept him."

"You would go against Papa's wishes?" Marian asked in mock horror.

"I have explained it to Papa. If the man is a brute, he won't insist on it." She shrugged a shoulder. "Apparently, Shewsbury loved Drusilla. I can't help wondering what happened for the engagement to end."

"Perhaps her father married her off to the old neighbor in a greedy land grab," Marian suggested. "Do you remember Shewsbury wasn't the heir at that time?" She turned Nellie toward her and smoothed a stray wisp back into her upswept hair. "But it's in the past, surely."

"Drusilla is exquisite. So fine-boned. But that's not the point."

"I'm struggling to see the point." Marian smiled. "You're just anxious, dearest. And it's not surprising."

Nellie sighed. "He didn't choose me." She gave a hard tug to rearrange the sash, which never sat well beneath her ample breasts. "I know my worth as a woman, Marian, but I fear we will not suit."

"You can't be sure of that, Nellie. And you don't have time to dwell on it. He'll arrive at any moment. The house groans with guests and their servants. There's a distinct air of expectation."

"And there's the article I wrote against foxhunting," Nellie added, leaning forward to pinch some color into her pale cheeks. Should she resort to rouge? Mama would have a fit. "Shewsbury must be told if we are to marry. If I don't tell him, he might discover it, and I shall be subjected to his ghastly bad temper."

"He's unlikely to hear about it," Marian said as she glanced over at the untidy desk piled high with books and papers, quills, and an inkwell. "Unless you intend to write another."

Nellie shrugged. "I had planned to do more. There is a groundswell of opposition to fox hunting."

"Well then, I expect you'll learn how the duke feels about it," Marian said prosaically. "But a groundswell hardly describes the few people I've encountered. Fox hunting has gone on for hundreds of years. Didn't you say it began in ancient Egypt?"

Nellie frowned. "Yes, but it was because of the law passed in 1801, which allows common land to be enclosed and makes it difficult for hunters to shoot rabbits, that fox hunting became a despicable, so-called sport." She shook her head. "I don't like secrets in a marriage, and I shall have to tell him."

"There are always some secrets within marriage. It's inevitable. Might it be prudent to wait for a better time?" Marian glanced at the clock on the mantelpiece. "And we are late."

Nellie sighed. Shewsbury would never understand her aversion to foxhunting. "Papa and Mama had an arranged marriage. Papa says very few in Society marry for love. Love is only for the lower classes because no money is involved."

"Your marriage to the duke is to honor the pledge Papa made with the old duke. Never mind that it was years ago, and the duke has since passed away. Men are funny that way. A gentleman's honor means a lot. Not always practical, but there it is. Turn around and let me take a good look at you."

Nellie obliged.

Marian smiled. "You look wonderful in that. He will be struck dumb."

Distracted, Nellie smoothed her skirts. "A man of his ilk will disparage my interest in poetry. We have absolutely nothing in common."

Marian grabbed her arm and steered her toward the door. "Is that so important?"

"Well, of course it is!"

"Mm. In the bedroom, certainly."

"Oh, the bedroom. Mama attempted to explain all that to me. It sounded embarrassing and uncomfortable. I wanted to put my hands over my ears, but I didn't wish to upset her when she clearly wasn't enjoying telling me about it. I prefer your version, although you put me to the blush, Marian."

"You must admit my version of events sounds more fun. And I rather think the duke… Oh, we must hurry, Nellie. We'll be unforgivably late, and I can't wait to clap eyes on him. Surely you feel the same, and that article about his mistress is rather titillating."

Nellie eased her tense shoulders. "Titillating is hardly the word. It's positively unnerving. The man is an obnoxious brute!"

"Listen! There's the duke's coach," Marian cried, flying to the window. "Father will be furious."

"All right," Nellie said breathlessly. "Into your basket, Peter!"

Peter merely yawned and rested his head on his paws.

"Really! That dog is most dreadfully spoiled," Marian observed. "He should be outdoors."

"Lilly will take him for a walk."

Marian shrugged, "You have a very obliging maid. Mine would protest and say it was a footman's job."

They left the bedchamber and hurried along the corridor. Nellie paused in the gallery to gaze down into the great hall. Hinkley had just admitted a gentleman who handed him his hat and gloves. His short-cropped hair shone inky black in the light from a tall window.

Their parents' voices rose in welcome as they greeted Charles Glazebrook, His Grace, the Duke of Shewsbury.

"You should be there to welcome him."

Nellie's fingers gripped the banister rail. "I needed time to compose myself."

"And are you composed now?"

"Not entirely."

"*Goodness*, but he's tall. Look at those shoulders," Marian observed thoughtfully. "He could easily carry a woman."

"I'll bet she was as hipless as a gazelle," Nellie said through her teeth.

"Don't gazelle's have hips?" Marian asked, her attention on the hall below.

Nellie watched from behind a column. "He looks as if he owns us," she murmured. It was the way he walked. He seemed to prowl across the marble floor.

The duke accompanied her parents toward the staircase leading to the drawing room.

"He is to prop up Papa's finances, so maybe he will," Marian said as they made their way to the stairs.

Nellie's chest swelled. She intended to be a reasonable wife, but he would never own her heart. She shivered, recalling another item Marian had found in *The Times,* which described the duke as an uncompromising negotiator in the House of Lords, who reduced his opposition almost to a state of helpless rage. Her sister had garnered every scrap of gossip she could about the duke, details which only served to further alarm her. She'd assumed there would be a mistress but still felt unprepared. He looked like a man who would want regular… She wrestled her mind away from the subject.

Shewsbury was a member of the Quorn Hunt, a Melton man, his estate in Leicestershire was where the oldest and most famous of the fox hunting packs were found. And renowned for his sporting prowess. Marian, scouring the journals, discovered the duke also excelled at fencing and boxing. With a First in mathematics at Oxford, he was known to have a meticulous eye for detail in everything he undertook and did not suffer fools gladly. It all served to make Nellie very tense.

She went over what she'd learned about him in case it might enter the conversation. The widowed duchess still lived and was in residence at Shewsbury Park. The old duke's eldest son and heir, Michael, had died from consumption a year or two before the duke; and Shewsbury's much younger brother, Lord Jason Glazebrook, had married Lady Beverly last year.

The footman opened the door for Nellie and Marian. Surrounded by guests, Shewsbury stood near the fireplace at the far end of the long drawing room her mother had recently repainted porphyry pink, to set off the white columns and the carpet.

Nellie had to agree with her sister's assessment. He was elegantly but appropriately dressed for a country drawing room. He was undeniably attractive, his well-built frame set off by the excellent tailoring of his blue tailcoat, his muscular legs encased in light-colored pantaloons. She couldn't find fault with his appearance at least, for everything about him, from the simply tied knot of his cravat to the discreet gold fob and seal that decorated his blue and cream-striped waistcoat, was tasteful and restrained.

"He is worth looking at, I must say." Marian murmured.

Her sister sounded impressed, and it was not easy to impress Marian without first engaging her in conversation.

They had hesitated near the door. It seemed bad manners to wander over to him. "I wish Papa would introduce us. I want to get this over with."

"Get what over with? You are to marry him, aren't you?"

"He might plan to back out." But she didn't really believe he would. The fact that he had come had probably sealed both their fates.

When His Grace's frankly appraising gaze rested on Nellie, she grew nervous, unsure what his look had meant.

He turned back to speak to her father.

She stood upright, waiting for Papa to finish introducing the duke to their friends and neighbors.

Shewsbury hadn't glanced at her again after that first swift appraisal. "He doesn't want this marriage any more than I do," Nellie said in an undertone to Marian.

The house party was arranged for them to get to know each other.

Even this early in the proceedings, she feared it wouldn't go well. Everyone knew, of course. All the guests were glancing toward her.

"Nonsense, Nellie, you always tend to see the worst in every situation. In time, he is sure to love you," her loyal sister said. "How could he not?"

Nellie fondly squeezed her sister's arm. "I hope we can at least be civil to each other. But there's quite a lot about him I dislike already. Still, if he doesn't ask me to marry him, it won't be the end of the world, will it?" There were few men who liked a bookish female. It was almost as bad as having smallpox scars.

Kealan Walsh had. He'd composed a poem to her eyes in iambic pentameter. Violet pools of mystery. Although she doubted there was much that mysterious about her, she had enjoyed his attention, his declarations of undying love. She'd fancied herself in love with him, too. And she had enjoyed the picture he painted of their life together at the time. A poet's wife, assisting him with his work, had been very appealing.

There would be no such discussions of poetry with Shewsbury. Nellie felt frustrated with the duke already, even though, to be fair, he had yet to speak to her, let alone censure her.

Marian laughed. "How can you be sure he won't come to love you. It took weeks for Gerald to show much interest, and another two months before he declared his love and proposed to me."

"Mmm… still," Nellie said. "Surely a man would prefer to choose his bride, not have one thrust upon him." And she wished to do the same. What common ground could she find with a duke who could add up long lists of numbers without an abacus and spent his time boxing and fencing? She had no interest in any sporting activity, except for riding, and shuttlecock, perhaps. She couldn't imagine him on the other side of the net. It seemed too tame a sport. Her face burned. She wished she had her fan. How she abhorred being on display for the consideration of His Grace, like a horse at Tattersall's auction.

"Father is bringing him to you," Marian said in a solemn tone as if announcing a funeral cortege.

With a broad smile, their father paused to introduce His Grace to another guest, then advanced almost regally over the swirled patterned rose and gold carpet, to where she and Marian stood.

Papa had talked of this proposed union as if it had been decreed by the gods on Mount Olympus. He and the old duke had planned the joining of their families years ago. She suspected their agreement had been nothing short of a blood pact, which brought home to her with force that, except for dying, she would not escape marriage to Shewsbury. Unless he backed out of it. Now that his father was dead, he might. Her breath hitched. Papa would be crushed. She wondered again why it mattered so much to him, as it had never been properly explained to her.

"Chin up, Nellie girl." Marian murmured close to her ear.

"This dress is too formal. As if I'm trying too hard. I should have worn the embroidered muslin," Nellie whispered back, surprised that she cared at all what this man thought of her.

"It's perfect, the violet tones compliment your eyes."

A maid entered the room. "Lady Belfries, Nanny urgently requests a moment of your time in the nursery." Marian gave Nellie's arm a discreet squeeze and hurried away to attend to her unholy terror, two-year-old son, Frederick.

Abandoned, Nellie stood still, her hands clasped together, aware that the hum of conversation had quietened.

Her father and the duke stood before her. Papa seemed to have shrunk and begun to look old, his hair almost completely gray, she realized with a pang. Perhaps it was because he stood beside the duke, who was so vitally alive. "My dear, I am delighted to introduce His Grace, Duke of Shewsbury. Your Grace, my second-eldest daughter, Lady Cornelia."

The duke bowed. "Delighted to meet you at last, Lady Cornelia."

His voice held her attention, deep and composed.

"How do you do, Your Grace." Close up, the expression on his lean, aristocratic face didn't look especially haughty, but nor did he look overeager to meet her.

Nellie rose from her curtsey and could not banish the thought of the duke's handsome features, especially his attractive mouth. He exuded a sense of calm authority. It seemed at odds with the description of him in the newspaper article attacking a journalist. His serious, blue gaze roamed her face. Did he hope for someone more girlish? She was hardly a young debutant after two unsuccessful Seasons when she'd failed to find anyone she wished to marry.

"It was most unfortunate when our youngest sister, Alice, came down with the measles," she blurted, hating how awkward she felt. "It spread through the family and staff and condemned us all to the country until after Christmas."

"I hope your sister and those afflicted have recovered?"

"Oh, yes, everyone is in good health now, thank you. I trust your journey wasn't too arduous?"

"Not at all. I took the opportunity to visit a livestock market. There's a hardy breed of sheep to be found in this part of the country, Herdwicks, which I plan to introduce into my flock. It proved quite a successful venture. I purchased a ram."

"How fascinating." Perhaps he was here for his flock and not her?

He raised his black brows. "You have an interest in sheep?"

Dismayed to be caught flatfooted, she nodded. "Of course. Where would we be without them?"

She was sure she caught a glimmer of amusement in the duke's eyes.

At her father's frown, Nellie hurried on, "As this is sheep country, you've certainly come to the right place. There's a county show held in May." The particular reason which brought him here hovered unsaid between them.

"I will be sure to add it to my diary for next year," he said politely.

Suspecting he was merely patronizing her, a prickle of heat rushed up her neck.

"I hope you will join us tomorrow, Your Grace," her father said. "After breakfast, my guests and I plan to bag a few birds for Saturday's dinner."

"I should be delighted."

Nellie was relieved to avoid further scrutiny. Her father and the duke were now discussing guns and the killing of innocent wildlife. Something she'd always hated. The sound of guns booming through the woods made her cringe.

"Now, Nellie, I know you don't approve." Papa cast her an affectionate smile. "My daughter doesn't care for hunting, Your Grace. But what member of the gentler sex does."

The duke didn't comment, but she was sure he could name many women who did. She knew one or two herself.

Hinckley appeared at her father's elbow. "Her ladyship is arranging tea and a game of loo for the ladies in the parlor. Cards for the gentlemen are in the library, milord."

"Ah, yes, Hinckley. Perhaps you'll join us, Your Grace? After you've removed the travel dust from your journey."

"I will. Thank you," His Grace murmured. His gaze rested on her overlong. It made her take a steadying breath.

Nellie snatched her chance. "If you'll excuse me, Your Grace, I promised to help my mother."

"But of course." Shewsbury bowed.

"You can show His Grace over the estate after luncheon," her father said before she could beat a cowardly retreat. "As he has told me he wishes to see more of it." He frowned at her over his shoulder as he turned to order a footman to escort the duke to his suite.

Nellie escaped into the passage. A quick glance told her Shewsbury had turned to watch her as he followed the footman from the room.

Was he thinking she wouldn't suit? And what did she make of him? He'd given away nothing of himself. Apart from that slight look of amusement, which might have meant he mocked her, he had been quite formal and rather serious. She was sure they would bore each other to death.

"Well, how was it?" Marian asked, waylaying her on the landing. "I shall be seated next to him at the table. Conversation at dinner is always helpful when assessing a man's character."

"A lot of good it will do me, but please do. Papa wishes me to show the duke around this afternoon. I imagine we'll ride to the pastures to view the sheep."

Marian giggled. "I can think of better things to do in a pasture."

Nellie frowned at her. "He is sure to make his excuses and leave. He won't even stay to dine, let alone spend another two days here."

"There you go again." Marian tutted. "I'll wager my coral-beaded reticule, which you admire so much, against the shawl with the silk fringe you bought in Piccadilly last year, that he will not only be here at dinner, but he will stay until Monday."

"It's a bet," Nellie said, not entirely sure whether she wanted him to stay or not.

"You're lucky he's good looking. He might have resembled the Duke of Culchester with a paunch and three chins," Marian said before she hurried back to her recalcitrant son.

"Well, looks aren't everything," Nellie called after her. She must read up on Herdwicks before she and the duke rode this afternoon. It would be something to talk about, but even if she studied the subject, she feared her contribution would dry up in a matter of minutes.

She hurried to her bedchamber to tidy her hair. *Dear heaven*. Was he a rake and a bad-tempered bully, as those newspaper items Marian found had suggested? If she disliked him, it might be wiser to discourage him. But if she did, would Papa ever speak to her again?

EVEN DURING THE journey to Cumbria in the ducal coach, Charles had been in two minds as to what to do concerning Dountry's daughter. His brother, Jason, had told him the little he knew about Lady Cornelia. The lady was a bluestocking by all accounts, favoring the company of poets, and had been often seen in the company of Walsh, an Irishman. That alone gave him pause. Charles had made inquiries. The fellow was now in Ireland. So nothing had come of their relationship.

His marriage to Lady Cornelia had been arranged by his father and Dountry. The joining of the two families having been decreed long before any progeny had been born. The lineage was all Charles heard in his father's last two years on this earth. After his elder brother, Michael, died, it had taken on even greater importance. Charles struggled to adopt the same heartfelt belief. For when men died young or lived a mere threescore years and ten, what did it really matter in the scheme of things?

Charles had been heartsick at his brother's death, followed so quickly by that of his beloved father. For the years prior, Charles had envisaged himself never marrying, engaging a succession of attractive mistresses, and involving himself in his estates and the House of Lords. And it was not until his younger brother, Jason, fell in love and married that Charles had begun to hope he, too, might find a degree of contentment within marriage. Not love, for he would never risk his heart again.

Charles's mood lifted when he'd met the gaze of the tall blonde woman in violet-gray across the Dountry's drawing room. While he was engaged in conversation with Dountry, one half of his mind questioned if she might be his intended. The weekend would prove to be difficult if she were not, for in his estimation, she eclipsed every other woman in the room.

He chose not to look her way again, while keenly waiting for her long-winded father to introduce them. Then, when he finally met her, she fulfilled his expectations. She was not one of those insipid debutantes found in London during the Season who giggled a lot. Although not a beauty in the classical sense, Lady Cornelia was unusual and undeniably attractive. He likened her to a mythical woman, statuesque, a long graceful neck revealed by upswept hair of honey-gold, and eyes that reminded him of violets in the misty woods at Shewsbury.

He discarded his initial plan to cry off, compelled to discover more about her. She intrigued him. He'd expected to be feted, for her to greet him with flirtatious eagerness, and was relieved when she did not.

Charles had never envied Michael, nor wished to be duke, and as a second son, had not been groomed for the role. Nor was he prepared to turn his life upside down. His future wife must understand that. While he knew he must expect a certain amount of pomp and ceremony and had far more responsibilities and duties to perform, he had kept his friends and lived in the manner which suited him. And that meant retiring to the country whenever he could, where he involved himself in the running of his estates and saw to the needs of his people.

After luncheon, which was an informal buffet where he could only view his intended from afar, he retired to his suite where his valet buffed a pair of riding boots with his own special polish until they shone like mirrors. Charles's brown coat and riding breeches had been laid out in readiness.

Once his valet had run the brush over Charles's shoulders, he sat and put up his foot. "Are they looking after you in the servants' hall, Feeley?"

"Aye, that they are, thank you, Your Grace." Feeley pushed the boot up Charles's leg. "A pretty young maid will soon have me needs in hand."

Charles eyed his Irish valet, his one claim to disorder in his life, and he rather enjoyed him. Feeley could charm the clothes off any wench he fancied and often did. "None of that here, Feeley, if you please. I don't want any embarrassing issues to arise with my prospective in-laws." He paused.

After three days spent in the lady's company, he would be better able to judge if they would suit. His father had taught him that nothing should ever be undertaken without serious consideration. Charles heaved a sigh. His father hadn't been thinking clearly during the last year of his illness. Had he not considered Charles's sentiments as death grew closer?

Feeley slid the other boot over Charles's stockinged foot. "If you wish, Your Grace," he said, sounding regretful.

"I do, Feeley."

He cast a sly glance at Charles. "Then we'll be stayin' 'til Monday?"

"We will." Charles stood and reached for his hat. The man was incorrigible but entertaining and a damn good valet. He had engaged Feeley when he was a mere second son and saw no reason to replace him with one of those top-lofty valets his friends seemed to rely on. "Find something innocuous to do in your free time, which will not set the household on its ear."

He walked downstairs, hat and crop in hand, and found Lady Cornelia waiting for him, walking up and down the terrace. The sight of her pulled him up. His first instincts about her were correct. She looked edgy and not at all happy to see him.

She greeted him briskly as she pulled on leather gloves. "It looks like rain, Your Grace."

He studied the wide expanse of blue sky. Only a few dark clouds lurked on the horizon. He tucked his crop beneath an arm and settled his hat on his head. "Quite a distance away."

"But driven by a strong wind. The weather here can be changeable. It rains a lot."

He raised his brows. "One might think you don't wish for my company, Lady Cornelia."

"I merely don't wish us to get wet, Your Grace," she demurred, the tips of her ears pink.

"I doubt it will bring on an inflammation of the lungs," he said, smiling. "Unless, of course, you are prone to illness?"

"I am not. Which part of the estate do you wish to see?" She ran lightly down the terrace steps to the lawn.

Lady Cornelia set off, and he strode after her. Her coltish stride carried her along at a fair pace. As if she wanted to escape him. But he was taller and easily kept up with her. "Where do you have in mind?"

"There are sheep in the eastern pasture. We'll take the bridle path."

Sheep? Was that irony he detected? As they strolled through the gardens, he studied her profile beneath her black riding hat: an elegant nose, a rounded chin, and wide mouth, her full lips firmly pressed together. Her figure, curvaceous in the tailored, rust-colored habit. Good child-bearing hips, his father would have said. When she finally deigned to look at him, Charles averted his gaze from the pleasing curve of her bosom. "I have many interests apart from sheep." He'd begun to wonder if she was determined to rebuff him. Should he back off now before this went any further? "And your interests, Lady Cornelia, what are they?"

She flushed and drew in a breath.

What on earth had he said?

"I enjoy reading and riding," she said, replying finally.

Her reaction surprised him, for both interests were perfectly respectable. Hadn't Jason said she was part of the London literary set?

"We need not view the flock, Your Grace. It was just that you mentioned your interest in the Herdwicks, and my father told me where to locate them," she said as they walked along the gravel drive.

"I don't believe I care to see them, but thank you. I saw enough of them at the cattle show in Cockermouth."

"Of course. As you know, Herdwicks are a very strong breed with long fleeces." She led the way over the carriage drive to the stable block. "They've been known to survive under a blanket of snow for three days while eating their own wool."

"Remarkable," Charles said, turning to her in surprise. "You have knowledge of this?"

She scrutinized him, her eyes suspicious. "Not personally. We would never treat our sheep in such a cruel fashion."

"No. Your father would not risk his valuable stock. Then where...?"

"I read about them in a farmer's magazine," she confessed, looking charmingly disconcerted.

"Ah." Had she looked it up? For him? After her dig at him about sheep, it was impossible not to tease her a little. And it might lighten the mood. "I find such a thing extraordinary. Is the journal in your father's library? Might I read it?"

"Of course." She glowered at him. Then a half-smile tugged at the corners of her mouth. "I shall ferret it out for you."

He smiled. "Thank you. That is very good of you."

"It is my pleasure." They walked through the archway into the stable yard and crossed the cobbles to enter the long stone building. The immaculate stable smelled of hay and horses. Grooms and stable boys straightened from their tasks to bow as they passed. Over twenty horses occupied the stalls. Curious, they poked their heads over the stall rail to observe them.

"Not all are ours," she explained. "Some guests have horses here. The stallion might suit you. Thor makes for a good challenging ride. Come and meet Barnes, our head groom."

Charles ambled after her. "Thor? God of Thunder? I imagine he will."

Barnes emerged from the tack room. "His Grace would like to see Thor," she said, "Could you bring him outside, Barnes?"

He bowed. "Certainly."

"Thor is my father's recent purchase. He has confessed it was an unwise one. He'd forgotten he is no longer a young man."

The groom hastened to open the stall door and slip a leading rein onto the large black horse.

They emerged from the shadowy stables into the sunlight again.

Led outside, the stallion reared up on its hind legs and whickered. Even Barnes, a muscular fellow, struggled to hold him.

"He's a bit excitable, Your Grace," Barnes commented unnecessarily. Charles turned to Lady Cornelia and arched an eyebrow, as the handsome animal of more than seventeen hands snorted and viewed him with suspicion, showing a good deal of white in his black eyes.

Charles took the reins from Barnes and ran a hand over the animal's glossy neck. "Easy, fellow."

"Poor Thor hasn't been ridden for a while," she said. "To be honest, there aren't many who care to ride him. I believe you are an accomplished horseman, but of course, if you prefer another…" She waved her hand to indicate the stalls.

Was this some sort of test? Or revenge for teasing her? "I like a challenge, Lady Cornelia," he said and enjoyed her blush.

"Saddle him, Barnes," he ordered, tapping his riding crop against his thigh. "And Lady Cornelia's mare, if you will. I shall not require you to accompany us," he added, noting her surprised look and even deeper blush.

CHAPTER TWO

THOR BEGAN HIS dance of protest once the duke had mounted, rising on his hind legs to throw His Grace off. Nellie felt a little guilty at having suggested the animal, but Shewsbury's strong grip on the reins soon settled the bad-tempered stallion. She admired his ability and the firm but quiet way he showed the horse who was in charge. He looked very much at ease in the saddle as he rode beside her bay over the grassy parkland.

He had seen through her attempt to impress him with her knowledge of sheep. And teased her into admitting it. She had deserved it, she supposed. Marian would laugh when she told her.

They entered the woods along the narrow bridle path, the sunlight dappling the trees. Shewsbury followed. It was cooler here and quiet, but for the clip-clop of the horses, the creak of leather and the chirp of birds. Her tight shoulders eased. This was her place. She breathed in the woodland scents so familiar to her, violets, damp earth, the lichen on the trees. Was she to leave it and the peace it offered her for a turbulent marriage? For she doubted the duke would be an easy man, and the life she was to live quite demanding.

"Cumbria is a picturesque county," Shewsbury observed, the low-pitched modulated tones of his voice undeniably attractive. "The lakes are magnificent."

"The home of poets." Nellie wished the man didn't unsettle her with so little effort on his part. "Coleridge lived here in Keswick with Wordsworth and his sister for a time. Writing their wonderful poetry, no doubt."

"Inspired by the natural world around them."

While they continued along the path, he offered no further comment. Not a subject which interested him, apparently. Kealan Walsh would have been quoting Wordsworth by now.

"You have a great interest in poets, Lady Cornelia," he said unexpectedly. "Would you include any close friends among them?"

Nellie stiffened. Had he heard about her intention to set up a literary salon? Or did he refer to Walsh? Her father would be furious if he walked away because of the poet. And unfair, for nothing untoward had happened between them, except for two chaste kisses on the balcony at Mrs. Burton's ball.

"Only acquaintances, Your Grace," she called back. "I imagine you find Cumbria different to Leicestershire."

"Yes, but the Midlands are not without charm."

They emerged from the woods and reined in where a stream wound its way, tumbling over rocks, to join the river farther on. On the opposite bank, sheep grazed in a meadow, their black faces and white coats stark against the verdant grass.

"You have brought me to see the sheep, I see," he observed, a touch of humor in his voice.

Nellie raised her eyebrows. "It's rather difficult to avoid them. But if you've changed your mind about the Herdwicks, we could…"

Shewsbury dismounted.

Nellie clutched the pommel in her right hand and turned to view him. "Oh, you wish to stop here? I thought we might ride over to…"

He tossed the reins onto a bush, walked across to her, and reached up his arms. "Allow me to assist you to dismount."

She stared at him. What did he intend? To pick daisies? Or ravish her? Really, she should have insisted on the groom coming with them.

What was wrong with her? She wasn't often slow-witted.

His strong hands encircled her waist and lifted her down as her breath fluttered in her chest. Once she found her feet, she tucked her crop beneath her arm and stepped back from him with the pretense of ordering her long train. She felt the strength of his big warm hands on her waist. The man was so alarmingly masculine and unpredictable. Why had he ordered Barnes not to accompany them? While it would be utter folly to fear that Shewsbury might ravage her on her father's land, especially when he had come here at Papa's request, he did make her wonder what he might do next.

He turned away and rested a foot on a rock. While she eyed his noble profile, he stared into the water.

"Good trout fishing here?"

"My father has some success in the smaller pools." So one could add fishing to his sporting activities. A wife might never see him. She searched for a topic of conversation. Really, this was quite awkward. "An archery contest is to be held tomorrow if it's fine. I trust that will be to your liking."

"Certainly."

"And perhaps a game of croquet on Sunday?"

"Indeed."

She puffed away a wisp of hair floating before her eyes. He was becoming annoyingly monosyllabic. When he turned back from his contemplation of the river, his thoughtful gaze on her made her fidget with her crop. "Shall we go on, Your Grace?"

"Lady Cornelia." His eyes settled on her mouth as he approached her. "Let us not beat about the bush," he said, distracting her with a hunting phrase.

"I beg your pardon?" What was she? Fair game?

"If you would prefer to call a halt to this engagement, you have only to say so. I will shoulder the blame, of course."

Shocked, she stared at him. Then the onus must rest on her. His gentleman's code was admirable, she had to admit, although it was as Marian said, not always sensible. Did he want to honor his father's wishes or not? As he'd offered her a way out, should she take it? Her father would be up in the boughs and would never forgive her. Oh, dear, poor Mama. All that money spent on the house and gardens. And it was too soon to judge, for she hadn't had time to… "I…" Her voice strangled in her throat. "I'm not sure, that is to say…"

"You have yet to make up your mind?" He removed her crop from her hands and threw it on the grass.

She stared up at him wide-eyed, her heart pounding. "Your Grace?"

He took her by the arms and drew her toward him. Surprised, she didn't resist and allowed his hands to slide around her waist. He pulled her closer, her breasts resting against his chest. Not prolonged or fiercely passionate, the soft touch of his mouth on hers remained after he released her.

"Well, really, Your Grace," she murmured with what remained of her breath. What lay behind the kiss? If it was to put her off balance, he certainly achieved it.

"Do you wish to marry me or not, Lady Cornelia?" His handsome eyes darkened as if daring her to defy him. "Or do you have some other fellow in mind?"

"I do not," she said quickly.

She resisted the need to run her tongue over her lips. Hardly the proposal a girl dreamed of. More of a demand, really. The picture in her mind of him carrying his mistress over his shoulder made her unsteady. He was not the right man for her. She felt it in her bones. They would never understand one another. But when he kissed her, her body tightened in the strangest way, and she would not have objected had he kissed her again.

Marian said that this was the most important thing. While Nellie believed there was a lot more to marriage, she did admit it was an attractive aspect of it. As her pulse slowed, she deliberated. To refuse him now would bring the matter to an end. But she was fooling herself. It would cause an enormous fuss to refuse him. And she didn't seem to want to. She took a deep breath.

"I will marry you, Your Grace."

He nodded. "Charles, or Shewsbury, if you prefer."

"My family call me Nellie."

"Nellie," he said as if savoring it on his tongue. His eyes seemed full of promises. She swallowed. He was devastatingly attractive. "Shall we walk?"

They followed the stream along the grassy bank, he taking her arm to help her over a puddle she could have easily jumped.

"Shall we tell your father to announce our engagement at the ball?"

"Yes." There was no turning back. Charles had not given her much of a chance to… No, he had offered her a means to end it. Would she rue this decision to the end of her days?

She waited for the ensuing panic at the sealing of a commitment, which would change her whole life. But she felt rather warm and calm. Could he tame her with one kiss? Was that the power of the man? *This wasn't love*, she reminded herself, *it was*, as Marian had explained to her, *merely desire*. Her mind refused to let go of the touch of his mouth claiming hers, his masculine scent, the strength of his arms, his commanding presence. *His commanding presence?* It was like a smack of cold water.

He would ride rough-shod over her. She must give up her opposition to fox hunting. Being married to a renowned advocator of the sport would effectively silence her. Suppose he discovered that article Walsh had helped her publish, stating her stance on the cruelty inherent in the hunt? Her pulse beat hard in her throat, and her steps faltered.

Shewsbury saw her stumble. He took her arm and assisted her

over a rocky patch. As if she were a poor, helpless female who could never help herself. Well, she must show him she wasn't one.

Nellie's initial panic subsided. It was most unlikely he would come across the article, for it appeared in a lesser-known periodical and under a male pseudonym, but still, she couldn't agree with Marian. Married couples should be honest with each other. She steeled herself.

"I don't intend to ride to hounds."

He raised his strong black eyebrows. "Did you have a bad experience?"

"I have never hunted foxes. I don't approve of killing animals for sport, and furthermore, I have…"

Shewsbury had raised a hand to shush her. "Shall we leave that discussion for another day?"

According to the newspaper, Shewsbury shook a man so hard he'd fallen to his knees in the street. Must she be wary of his temper? Better, perhaps, if she became more familiar with him before mentioning her article. Might they one day discuss it reasonably, and in a kinder light? Somehow, she doubted one who hailed from the shires would agree with her.

They walked on. Despite her concerns, she was curious about this tall man at her side who matched his stride to hers as they crossed the ground toward a copse of willows, the branches trailing in the stream.

The smell of mud and mold and the sound of rushing water rose up to greet them. He stopped beneath the delicate tracery of leaves and pulled a leafy stalk from a branch to wave away an inquisitive bluebottle buzzing near her hat. "I believe you'll approve of Shewsbury Park."

Aware of his closeness, and unsure of his intentions, she stepped back, swiping at the persistent insect. "I'm sure I will."

"My mother plans to move into the dower house after we wed. She has requested that you come to Leicestershire to meet her before the wedding. Parish affairs keep her engaged, and she seldom visits

London."

"I can't wait to meet her." Did any potential daughter-in-law really mean that? Mother-in-laws could be so difficult. She thought of Marian's, who gave her no end of concern. Nellie wanted to like her mama-in-law and hoped they might become fond of each other, but she was aware that in a mother's eyes, no woman ever measured up to their sons.

"My brother, Jason, and his wife are to come to London for the wedding."

"How delightful. You will be seated next to my elder sister, Marian, Lady Belfries, at dinner. Marian is an amusing conversationalist."

Nellie was suddenly quite eager to find out what her sister thought of him.

"Indeed? One always hopes for a lively dinner companion and so seldom gets one."

How arrogant. She would love to take him down a peg or two. "Perhaps they don't put you next to the right people."

"That could well be so. They are obviously of the view that I'm a sober-minded fellow."

"Perhaps they expect it from dukes," Nellie said.

He cocked an eyebrow. "Shall we return to the horses? Anywhere we can gallop?"

She pointed. "There's a straight run through the trees." It was extremely doubtful that she could beat him on Clover, but she would like to. She often galloped her mare here and knew every inch of the ground.

"Right. I want to see what Thor can do."

They mounted and trotted their horses over to a long stretch of grass bordered by trees. Nellie nudged Clover into a canter while Charles urged Thor forward. The stallion took off like the wind. Clover was a lazy horse but stirred up by the stallion, was soon not far behind him.

Ahead of them, a raven rose from the grass with a sharp cry. Thor suddenly began to sidle and buck. As Charles fought him, Nellie urged her horse on. Clover reached Charles and galloped past him. Nellie was unable to resist casting a mischievous grin in his direction.

Charles settled the thoroughbred down and came thundering after her.

Nellie leaned forward. *"Go, Clover!"* She reached the end of the gallop where a thick copse of trees blocked the way and reined in, beating Charles by a whisker.

Charles pulled Thor up. "Enjoy your good fortune, Nellie. It will be the last time you beat me on this horse," he said, amusement in his eyes.

She lifted an eyebrow. "Can you be so sure?"

He chuckled. "He's a bit flighty, but a splendid animal." He edged Thor alongside her mare. "We have some fine mounts at Shewsbury Park. You can have your pick."

Nellie murmured a thank you. She repressed a shudder. They would ride to hounds there.

"Tell me Thor's history while we ride," he said. "If he's not ridden often, your father might agree to sell him to me."

Trotting their horses through the trees, Nellie told him all she knew about the stallion, which wasn't a great deal. He listened without comment. She couldn't deny Charles looked good in the saddle. In fact, he made most of the men she'd met seem less virile. Of course, it was his self-assured manner. A duke would have his wishes fulfilled with no more than a look. No one would ever dare refuse him. He'd been confident she wouldn't either. Uneasy, she caught her lip between her teeth. If she allowed him to bend her to his will, she would be miserable. Her spine tingled. While it would never be a love match, it might not be the dull marriage she had feared.

⤜⤜⤜✺⤛⤛⤛

CHARLES DREW IN behind Nellie's mare when the bushes narrowed the path. She was a woman of strong opinions. She'd flashed those beguiling eyes at him as if daring him to disagree with her. Her aversion to foxhunting posed a few problems, which he would deal with later. He approved of the teasing laughter in her eyes when she'd ridden past him.

It appeared that she enjoyed gentle sparring as much as he did. He approved of her bottom, too, as he assisted her back onto her horse, and how she'd felt in his arms. Her full lips when he'd kissed her had been sweet and soft. He would have liked to kiss her more deeply, to hear her sigh and respond to him. He'd seen enough to know she would, and in that moment, knew at least in this, they would be good together. Physical attraction certainly made marriage more agreeable.

He and Dountry had already agreed on a satisfactory settlement. All in all, not a bad decision. The ledgers balanced, and all parties were satisfied or would be in the near future. He smiled slightly at his unintended double entendre and drew his horse alongside hers. "Let's visit those Herdwicks, shall we, Nellie?"

"As you wish, Charles." He caught her smile as she turned her horse's head and led the way.

It surprised him how much he enjoyed his given name on her lips. *Intimate.* He allowed himself to dwell for a moment on the pleasure they would experience together.

The sheep were as expected. The lambs cavorted on the grass. He'd suggested they come to give them more time together, and it confirmed his opinion. Nellie was amusing, poised, and intelligent. He liked how confident she was. No clinging vine. She wouldn't impinge too much on his life or make outrageous demands on him. While involved with her own duties, the charity work, and so on, she would fit seamlessly into the routine of his days, while he continued to pursue his interests.

When they returned to the house from the stables, four ladies who were ambling along the garden paths paused to watch them.

"We are being observed," Nellie said in an undertone. "My father did try to keep the possibility of an announcement quiet, but these things have a way of slipping out." She smiled. "The servants are worse gossips than we are."

"It hardly matters now," he said. "Everyone will soon know."

He saw her chest rise and fall sharply.

"Let's give them something to talk about." He took her hand in a firm grasp, and they climbed the steps to the terrace. He smiled down at her as a ripple of conversation floated toward them on the breeze.

As his duchess, she would attract attention wherever they went. He considered her a good choice. He knew of several successful marriages where love was not the glue that kept a couple together, but rather friendship and understanding. He preferred that to the explosive love matches, which burned out fast and messily, or worse, faded into indifference.

He and Nellie parted in the hall. He would wash and change before they told Dountry.

Charles ascended the stairs to his bedchamber. So he was to marry. He had made up his mind to marry Nellie at first sight, which was unlike him. He usually gave a good deal of thought to a matter before proceeding. He forced his mind back to the time when his older brother, Michael, had rallied and enjoyed a brief period of good health. Hopeful talk of his marrying Nellie's sister, Marian, to secure an heir had been revived.

At that time, Charles had become informally engaged to Drusilla. Although no announcement had been posted in the *Morning Post*, it was common knowledge amongst the *ton*. When it appeared, Charles would not be next in line, his prospects were suddenly diminished in the eyes of Drusilla's father. He decided the Marquess of Thorburn, whose lands joined his own, was the better prospect. Charles had thought Drusilla would fight for him, but she did not. He had struggled with the loss of hope, and his dreams and been bitterly angry and hurt. Then he'd watched his brother grow ever paler and sicker. Michael slipped away without fuss, and the family plunged into mourning for a beloved brother and son. Not long afterward, their father, his heart broken, sickened and joined Michael in the Shewsbury vault.

Charles, determined never to fall in love again, had taken a French mistress full of fire and charm, whose mercenary heart ensured he would never love her.

Chapter Three

In the library, Nellie's father beamed when given the news. He congratulated the duke and kissed her. After Charles had left them, Papa confirmed his view that Nellie was the daughter he'd always thought would marry well.

Nellie was glad Marian was not present. She had been permitted to marry the man she loved, but her choice was not a popular one. Gerald Belfries was not particularly wealthy.

"Marian and I believe Alice will be the beauty in the family, Papa," Nellie said.

"All my girls are beauties." He smiled at their mother beside him. "Like their Mama."

"Alice shows great promise," Mama said, "but she is still hoydenish. She must learn to conduct herself like a young lady. All you girls are spirited and intelligent." She patted his arm. "You take after your father."

Nellie left her parents behaving like a pair of lovebirds. Her father had been at pains to assure her that although their marriage was arranged, he and her mother loved one another. And there was every chance Nellie and Charles would come to love each other in time.

Marian awaited her in her bedchamber. "How was it?"

"I accepted him."

Her sister nodded. "You approve of him then?"

Nellie took a deep breath. "One would find it hard not to, I suppose," she said. "He's attractive, and he rides superbly...but..."

Marian's eyes widened. "But what?"

"He kissed me."

Her sister nodded appreciatively. "After you accepted him."

"No. Before."

"He is a rake?" Marian's eyes narrowed. "He behaved improperly? Grabbed you and mauled you?"

"No, it wasn't like that. I had trouble making up my mind, so..."

"He kissed you and made up your mind for you. I like him already." Marian chortled. "And as you've accepted him, I gather you didn't mind the kiss."

Nellie frowned at her. "Charles will always want to have the upper hand. I shall have to fight for everything I want and probably won't get it." Nellie shrugged and frowned at Marian's expression. "He said he would take the blame if I refused to marry him. But of course, I couldn't. Papa depends on this marriage."

"Oh, Nellie. I pray he makes you happy."

Nellie put her arm around her sister's waist. "Thank you, dear. But I imagine Charles and I will disagree on many things."

"Charles?"

"Yes, he invited me to call him by his given name."

"Well, he can't be too stuffy."

"I tried to tell him about the article I wrote about foxhunting, but he cut me off in the most autocratic fashion. No doubt, he disdains such a view. He'll be angry if he learns about it before I can find the courage to tell him." She smoothed her dress with both hands. "He is sure to anger me, too, at times."

"Welcome to marriage," Marian said dryly.

"I must go and tell Alice, although the whole house, from the kitchens to the stables, knows by now."

In the schoolroom, her tall, willowy, fifteen-year-old sister was complaining of missing out on all the entertainment.

"When I have my Come-out, will you hold a ball for me at Shewsbury Park and invite loads of eligible gentlemen?" Alice's big blue eyes were alight with visions of a rosy future.

"Indeed, I shall," Nellie promised.

"The duke is *so* handsome. I peeked at him through the drawing room door."

"You will meet him when you take part in the archery contest. You can make a game of it. You are quite skilled with your own bows and arrows."

"Oh, good." Alice gave a gusty sigh. "Are you both madly in love?"

At Alice's age, Nellie had dreamed of falling in love at first sight. It was part of growing up, after all, and she disliked quashing Alice's girlish dreams. "Shewsbury and I have only just met," she said with an amused shake of her head. "So how could we be in love?"

"People do fall in love at once. Why, I just read a novel where…"

"And what novel might that be, Lady Alice?" Her governess, Miss Dale, looked up from her desk at the end of the room. "I trust your father will not disapprove of your reading material?"

Alice tightened her lips and looked mulish. "I found the book in the library."

Nellie doubted that was where she'd discovered it. "It can't be anything too shocking," she said to Miss Dale. She suspected Alice found one of Marian's gothic romances left behind after she married. What harm could it do? One should enjoy an unrealistic view of life, if only for the brief time allowed to a young girl before real life intruded.

Was it possible to fall in love at first sight? Charles could make her heart beat faster with a look. That was not love but physical desire. It was more important that they become good friends. Or might they not even remain on good terms?

"I'm sure His Grace fell desperately in love when he first set eyes on you, Nellie," Alice said, breaking into Nellie's thoughts.

Nellie smiled. "Thank you, poppet."

Charles did not seem the sort of man to utter overblown emotional speeches. Unlike Kealan Walsh, who had declared his adoration of her supposed charms, hand over his heart, as he read aloud his verses. But then the thought struck her that Charles might well have been that way with his former fiancée. If the poets were to be believed, a man only ever loved with such intensity but once.

"The duke has chosen me to be his duchess. It is quite an honor. I'm sure love will follow in time," she said. While Nellie didn't believe it, she wanted Alice to hold onto her dreams.

"An honor!" Alice gasped. "How very dull. As if you're something he might place behind glass in his trophy room. Will he lock you up in the attic in Shewsbury castle after you've given him an heir?"

Nellie's laugh sounded brittle to her ears, for something similar, although a little less dramatic, had occurred to her. "The ruins of the old castle remain on the grounds," she said to guide the conversation into safer waters. "The mansion was built in the last century. I believe it has a very fine park." Nellie smiled. "You only find such things in novels, Alice. The duke would not be so cruel, but if he does, you will have to rescue me."

It was quite possible that Charles would take another mistress after she gave birth to his heir. She must guard her heart. Divorce would be out of the question, for she would be ruined socially. But no eyebrows would be raised at a discreet separation, or even if she took a lover. Nellie despised the idea. She would rather create her literary salon and immerse herself in books and poetry.

Their marriage might be for financial reasons, but she would hate it if Charles strayed. She wished she could be sure of the man she was about to spend her life with. The *Haute ton* lived by their own rules, and few benefited women. At least the archaic practice of dueling had fallen into disfavor. Their brother, Nathaniel, had been wounded defending a woman's honor when barely more than a youth. Thankfully, he had survived with merely an arm wound when the lady's husband took pity on him. Now married to Eliza, who was not the lady in question, Nat was the proud father of a three-year-old daughter, Julia.

"Shall I come and see you when you're dressed for the ball?" Alice asked.

"I depend on it," Nellie said. "You must give me your opinion."

"Your gown is *so* beautiful," Alice said with a wistful smile. "It's like gossamer. White satin and gauze with those pretty lilac silk flowers. I shall have a gown just like it one day."

"An even prettier one." The ballgown had not been Nellie's choice. Although she wasn't inclined to spend hours poring over lady's fashion magazines the way her sisters did, she knew what best suited her figure and looked forward to choosing her wardrobe. Marriage did offer some agreeable benefits.

She eased one of Alice's thick braids over her shoulder. Her pretty sister's hair was a paler blonde than her own, and her features were more delicate. "Your first Season will be here before you know it. And you will be such a success."

"I do hope so. I can't wait for the parties and the balls." With a dreamy expression in her eyes, Alice danced across the schoolroom rug.

"Lady Alice, we have a French lesson from four to five o'clock." Miss Dale made a point of looking at the watch on her bodice. "If you will excuse us, Lady Cornelia?"

Nellie left the schoolroom and made her way down to her bedchamber. Miss Dale, who was now in her sixtieth year, had been the family governess for Marian and herself. She'd accepted no nonsense from them, either. When she was a duchess, Nellie was sure Miss Dale would address her in the same manner.

Peter ran to her when she opened the door. Nellie picked him up and hugged him. A duchess! It brought with it such responsibilities.

There would be little time for herself. Everything she did or said would be written and talked about, she supposed.

Some years ago, the Duchess of Devonshire held a fashionable literary salon, but Nellie did not wish for that amount of notoriety. She hoped for something more discreet, a gathering of a few devotees of prose and poetry. To be at the heart of intellectual discussion. Poets and writers would be invited to read their latest works. But would it even be possible now? Although Charles seemed not quite as arrogant as she had feared, something about him warned her that he would resist too many changes to his life.

The relief on her father's face when he'd learned the news gave her great pleasure. Her father appeared to like Charles. But was he a good judge of the man? He could be the worst rake in society for all they knew. And a bully to boot. But to be honest, although she couldn't discount their differences, there was that heady pull of attraction. Whether it was enough for a satisfactory life together, time would tell.

Dinner was held in the claret-papered, gilded dining room for the family and house guests. On the vicar's arm, Nellie trailed after her parents into the room. Charles sent her an intimate smile. As if they had a secret. That he was a passionate man sent a shiver down her spine. It distracted her from the man seated next to her, who described in detail his last trip to London and the play he'd seen.

The footmen served fragrant pea soup followed by turbot with oyster sauce, while Nellie discreetly continued to watch her fiancé. Seated on his left, Marian engaged him in conversation. Her sister could bring out the best in any man. At twenty-six, she was pretty, favoring their father with her brown curls and green eyes, while Nellie and Alice were like their mother.

Their brother, Nathaniel, who at twenty-five was between Nellie and Marian in age, flirted with Lady Hattersley. As he leaned his blond head toward her, the lady simpered, while opposite them, Lord Hattersley appeared bored.

Nellie glanced at Nat's wife, Eliza. She was talking earnestly to the vicar. Did she accept her husband's flirtatious ways? Or was it something that tore them apart? It was disturbing how a man like Nat, who loved his family, went from flirting to affairs. If the tales which reached them were true. She glanced back at Charles seated beside her father. Could she uphold the pretense if he were unfaithful? Her throat tightened, and she reached for her wine. She must never fall in love with him, for how vulnerable she would then be to hurt.

Whist and faro followed dinner, but the evening ended early, as the shooters were to be up with the dawn.

Nellie mounted the stairs with Marian. "Well, what did you make of him?" Nellie asked. "You seemed to get on well."

"He has a good sense of humor," Marian said as if that was of great importance.

"He can be a bit pompous," Nellie said a trifle unfairly. "One expects that of a duke." She was still smarting from her thoughts during dinner.

"I didn't find him so. Is it true of all dukes?" Marian laughed. "The Duke of Wellington might well be arrogant in men's company, but when asked if he had affairs, he said 'A lot of that.'" She laughed. "I found him vastly entertaining and an accomplished flirt."

"We were talking about pomposity, not rakishness," Nellie said with a frown. "And he is a rather poor example. He is Irish."

Marian peered at her in the flickering light from the wall sconce. "What bee has got into your bonnet?"

"I don't think I could bear it if Charles took a mistress. He might still have the French one."

"It looked very much as if the affair was at an end to me. He might have no intention of taking another mistress."

"Many men do. Our own brother, for instance."

Marian's eyes narrowed. "I wonder if Eliza knows. It's surprising if she doesn't. There was gossip last Season about him and someone.

Well, whether Eliza does or not, Nat needs Papa to give him a good talking to."

"Papa doesn't seem to want to. And anyway, I doubt that would help. Nat has always been so inclined."

"But it's time he grew up and realized his actions hurt those he loves," Marian said. "Not all men are like that, dearest. I am quite sure that Gerald is not. He is too lazy to pursue other women. And too exhausted."

Nellie giggled.

"You must stop concerning yourself with something which may never happen. At least give Charles the benefit of the doubt."

"Yes, you're right, of course." Her throat tightened. "I don't know why I fear it so much. I suppose I am of a suspicious nature."

"No, dearest, you're not. You're just nervous, as most brides are." Worry darkening her eyes, Marian gave her a hug.

Nellie kissed her cheek and said goodnight. She made her way to her bedchamber. Was she wrong to expect him to be faithful?

―――⋅⋅⋅―――

WHEN CHARLES RETIRED for the evening, his valet, Feeley, awaited him in his bedchamber. He assisted Charles out of his coat. "May I offer my congratulations, Your Grace?"

"You may, thank you, Feeley." Charles thought of his bride-to-be as he pulled off his cravat and unbuttoned his waistcoat. She had been a delightful surprise.

Feeley took the clothes Charles held out to him. "The servants were all aflutter about it in the servants' hall. Could talk of nothin' else."

"Mm? I imagine so." Charles pulled his shirt over his head and threw it to his valet, then turned his attention to his pantaloons. Seated, he pulled off his shoes and stockings.

"The can of hot water has just been brought up. Shall I fill the bath?"

"Please."

Charles settled into the warm water. He lathered a piece of soap and washed his hair.

"There was much talk about Lady Cornelia tonight." Feeley poured water over Charles's head. "Everyone is very happy for her."

"Yes?" Charles pushed wet hair out of his eyes with both hands and took up the washcloth.

Feeley turned to lay out the nightshirt Charles chose to wear when away from home. "Lady Cornelia is very much liked," he said over his shoulder.

"Mm?" Charles leaned back and closed his eyes. A vision of Nellie floated into his mind. How soft her mouth was against his, her husky laughter when she beat him on Clover, that overfed mare of hers. He enjoyed the intriguing glimpse of her seductive playfulness. It was very appealing how she unconsciously stirred a man's lust. He was sure a civilized and pleasurable marriage awaited him.

"And there's a maid here," Feeley said, holding the towel. "Lilly, her name is. Very pretty, she is."

Charles opened his eyes. He pushed an errant wet lock of hair back from his forehead. "Feeley, have you forgotten my instructions?"

"No, Your Grace. But it will be difficult as I'll see her again after you're married. Being the duchess's lady's maid and all."

Charles stood and stepped out, dripping water onto the hearth tiles. He took the towel from his valet and began to dry himself. "Your future employment is hanging by a thread right now, Feeley."

"I am listening, for sure I am, Your Grace," Feeley said, far too meekly for Charles's liking.

Chapter Four

The men were out with their guns by the time Nellie opened her eyes. Lilly drew back the curtains, and the early morning sun filtered in. It failed to remove the chill from the room. Nellie pulled up her blankets and flinched at the gunshots echoing from the woods as she sipped her chocolate and ate a slice of toast.

When Lilly took Peter down for his morning walk and to feed him, Nellie donned her dressing gown and slippers and sought her sister in her bedchamber. Still abed, Marian declared her husband woke her far too early before rushing off to join the shooting party.

"At least we have the day free," Nellie said. "Except for Nat, who isn't taking a gun out. He prefers to play shuttlecock."

"He has always been mad about the game. Mainly because he beats us." In a lacy peignoir, Marian put down her cup, yawned, and stretched. She looked rested and so content, she made Nellie a little envious. "Do you think you might warm to Shewsbury?"

Nellie fiddled with the ribbon on her dressing gown. "I have found nothing to disturb me about him so far."

"Well, that's damning the fellow with faint praise." Her sister giggled as she took a sweet roll from the plate on the tray. She lavishly spread butter and sweet blackberry jam onto it, then bit into it with a sigh of satisfaction.

"I need time," Nellie protested. It was because the man was so attractive. When his blue gaze observed her last evening, she found it difficult to think. "We have differences to overcome."

"What men and women haven't? We are different animals. They are out having a lovely time with their spaniels and their guns and will come home all muddy and contented with their birds for the table. Like primitive huntsmen killing a boar to feed their womenfolk."

Nellie laughed. "How you do go on. You know I hate animals killed for sport, but I know there's a purpose behind it. The birds cannot be allowed to over-breed, for they will run out of food. Rabbits must be controlled. I don't deny foxes cause problems, but fox hunting is unnecessarily cruel."

Marian threw back the covers and rose. "Let's not get onto your pet subject. It is too early." She rang for her maid. "I plan a leisurely bath, after which, I will see you downstairs. Papa asked me to invite some of our guests for a stroll to the lake. You should come, too."

"I suppose so, although I will be fending off subtle inquiries about my engagement."

"Some not too subtle, I fear." Marian paused as her maid entered. "A bath, Becca, send for hot water."

"Yes, my lady."

Nellie nodded to the maid and left her sister to her ablutions. What would she wear?

In her bedchamber, she asked Lilly to take out the primrose muslin with the embroidered vandyke trim around the hem. The color flattered her, and she wished to look her best, although she doubted she'd see much of Charles today.

After their promenade to the lake, the guests arrived back at the house for luncheon. Nellie was exhausted from fending off their questions, but they all took it in good part when she smilingly rebuffed them, confident, no doubt, that her father would announce the engagement at the ball.

She almost welcomed the game of shuttlecock with Nat, Alice, and

Marian after luncheon to escape further scrutiny.

Nat and Alice were partners. They declared a win after a particularly hard thrust of Nat's sent the shuttlecock into the middle of the rose garden. With a satisfied smile, he took Eliza's arm and led his wife, who had been watching them, off for a stroll in the shrubbery.

"He's a disgrace," Nellie muttered, angrier with him for his flirtations than his overbearing play. She called to Peter, who was sniffing at a bush.

"I know. I doubt it would do much good to mention it. Our brother is a man now and will not take kindly to a dressing down from his sisters on a matter such as that. Let's walk," Marian said. "We might meet the men coming back. I haven't heard a gunshot for a while."

With Peter on a lead, they ambled along the bridle path through the trees, the smell of gun smoke reaching them on the breeze. They soon met the beaters pulling a barrow filled with birds. The men followed, laughing together, guns resting on their shoulders, the dogs at their heels. Peter yapped, and Nellie picked up her nervous dog.

At the head of the group, Charles walked beside Gerald, Viscount Belfries, Marian's solidly built husband. A good head shorter than Charles, Gerald had curly brown hair, heavy sideburns, a roguish manner, and patent disregard for convention. Nellie liked him for his warmth and sense of humor, but especially because he adored her sister. The men hailed them as the gamekeeper whistled the dogs to heel.

"I see you had a successful day," Marian said when they reached them.

Her husband slipped an arm around her waist and kissed her cheek. "No one shall go hungry. The staff will partake of the feast tomorrow, too."

Charles crossed the path to walk beside Nellie. He reached over to give her dog a pat. "Who is this?"

"Peter," Nellie said as the dog obligingly licked his hand.

"Peter the Great," Marian amended.

Gerald guffawed. "Is it a real dog?"

"None of your rudeness, thank you," Nellie said with a grin.

"How have you spent your day?" Charles asked.

"Marian and I played shuttlecock against Nathaniel and Alice."

Marian wrinkled her nose. "Nat enjoys getting the better of us. The game ended when he hit the shuttlecock into the rose garden. We've lost several that way. No one wishes to be pricked by thorns, so we must wait for the gardener to retrieve them."

Charles chuckled.

"Do you play?" Nellie asked him, struggling to imagine him indulging in anything quite so trivial.

"When I was home, and before Jason was up at Oxford, we got in the odd game. It's been years." He smiled down at her. "Pity there's no time. It must wait until we are in Leicestershire." They approached the house. "Ladies, I shall see you again at dinner." With a slight bow, Charles left them to bathe and change his clothes.

"Well, he seems a good fellow," Gerald said approvingly. "He's a dashed good shot."

"Then he must be a good fellow." Marian winked at Nellie.

"None of your cheek, my lady." Her husband grabbed her hand. "Shall we go and see how our son fares? I wonder if he has left anything unbroken in the nursery."

Nellie smiled as they wandered off. Theirs was such a loving marriage. Might she and Charles have the same?

At dinner, Charles sat beside the widow, Lady Arabella Forrester, who all but fluttered her eyelashes at him.

Nellie picked at the fish on her plate, vaguely aware that the sauce was Cook's triumph. On her right, her brother, Nat, ogled Lady Hattersley across the table. Nellie feared he was intent on pursuing the lady, as he appeared to be attracted to older women. On her left, the vicar talked endlessly of parish matters. Neither of her dinner partners managed to banish Charles from her thoughts. She glanced again in his direction. Goodness, did Arabella just lay her hand on his sleeve?

After platters of veal collops, roast chicken, a leg of lamb, and an array of fresh vegetables from the garden in delicious sauces were removed, footmen put cheese, nuts, tarts, and puddings on the table.

As Nellie ate her custard, the vicar launched into another topic concerning the need for repairs to the church roof. Nellie composed her features into an expression of interest and watched as Arabella, in her low-cut gown, leaned close to Charles, her eyes wide, as if pearls of wisdom fell from his lips. The dinner seemed interminable. Relieved when the last course finally ended, she rose with a warning frown at her brother. He raised his eyebrows in surprise.

She and the other ladies left the men to their port and cigars.

Seated on the sofa in the drawing room, Nellie drank coffee with Nat's wife, Eliza, as they listened to the Mozart piece played by the three-piece orchestra set up in the corner of the room.

"We never have time to talk, do we?" Eliza's brown eyes searched Nellie's. "I suppose it's going to be even more difficult in the future."

Might Eliza know of Nat's affairs? Nellie pushed down her anger at her brother. "We can talk. Do you want to come up to my bedchamber later?"

"No. Nat will wonder where I am. We leave for home after the ball."

She gazed into her sister-in-law's anxious eyes. "We can have a good coze in London."

Lady Forrester entered the room and approached them.

"Yes, that will be good, Nellie." Eliza stood, and with a nod at the lady, left them.

"May I join you?" Arabella Forrester indicated the seat beside Nellie.

"Please do," Nellie said, wishing she wouldn't.

"It was a splendid dinner. I did enjoy it. One doesn't always find interesting dinner partners, does one?"

"Not always."

The red-haired woman unfurled her fan and waved it slowly before her face. She nodded toward newly married Lady Brixton, who was busy arranging her shawl about her arms.

"Amelia Brixton should never wear that particular shade of yellow," Lady Forrester said with what Nellie suspected was feigned sympathy. "Canary is a difficult color to wear, is it not? It makes her look quite bilious."

"I imagine she finds it pretty," Nellie said.

"Brixton's mother chooses her gowns. Spiteful, jealous woman."

"I'm sure Amelia would refuse to wear it if she didn't like the color. After all, she is a married woman now."

Lady Forrester's laugh had an edge. "Freedom cannot be found in marriage, Lady Cornelia. Rather the opposite."

While wondering what kind of marriage Lady Forrester had endured, Nellie said, "Amelia looks content enough."

"One might hope so. Her handsome husband was obliged to marry her when facing bankruptcy."

Nellie frowned, not wishing to be drawn into nasty gossip, especially with the lady in question on the other side of the room.

Arabella leaned forward with that look of a conspirator that Nellie so disliked. "I have been told there is a wager in the betting book at Whites that Brixton will take a mistress before the end of the Season. He is shopping for one."

Across the room, Lady Brixton chatted brightly to Mrs. Bainbridge. She smiled in agreement with something the other lady had said, her light brown curls bobbing. Might she be happy and madly in love? She found herself hoping Arabella was wrong.

Nellie put her coffee cup on a footman's tray. "Inadvisable to believe all you hear, surely."

"Men are untrustworthy creatures, Lady Cornelia," she said with a warning lift of her brow.

"Some women are also, Lady Forrester," Nellie said, relieved when the door opened, and the men entered.

Charles appeared. Nellie's heart gave a thump when he moved with easy grace into the room.

Lady Forrester rose from the sofa with a gracious nod. She joined acquaintances gathered at the other end of the room.

Beyond his slight bow to the widow, Nellie was pleased to see Charles's gaze did not follow her. He cast Nellie a lazy smile and joined her on the sofa. She liked his smell, citrus soap, starched linens, and cigar smoke. When he reached forward to take a glass of wine from a footman, his muscled thigh touched hers before he tactfully edged away.

"There's to be no dancing tonight?" he asked after the last strains of the concerto faded, and the musicians consulted their music sheets.

"Not until the ball."

"Pity." His eyes swept over her face.

Something sensual and heated lay behind that one word. Her imagination took flight, and she was suddenly too warm. She struggled to find an innocuous topic to discuss. "On your final evening with us, Mrs. Bosworth is to perform *Tornami a vagheggiar* from Handel's *Alicina*."

Amusement lit his eyes. "A lady with a remarkably large voice and a figure of equal stature."

Nellie smothered a laugh, smiling back at him. She enjoyed his subtle wit.

He glanced up at the portrait of her paternal grandmother over the fireplace.

"My grandmother, Elizabeth," she explained, eager for a distraction. Dressed in the fashion of the last century, her grandmother's large creamy bosom was on display in the low-cut purple gown. Known to be a beauty, she wore the family sapphires, her blonde hair dressed high with feathers.

"You take after her," he said. "Your eyes are a similar color and shape." He studied her, then looked again at the portrait. "And her chin, perhaps. She looks to be a lady with firm opinions."

Was that condemnation? She raised an eyebrow.

His eyes widened. "Don't glare at me. It was a compliment."

Was it? Men did not like opinionated women. "I can't say if I do resemble her. She died when I was a young child, but I've always admired her. She was a lady with varied interests."

"How so?"

"She was a friend of the Duchess of Devonshire and a member of her literary circle."

"Indeed."

Did he disapprove? She would be proud to be favorably compared to her grandmother. But before she could discover what his opinion was, the guests drifted to the library, where the card tables had been set up.

She and Charles were soon inveigled into a game of whist, and there was no further opportunity that evening for them to converse.

Most of the next morning, her father and Charles were holed up in his study. In the afternoon, Alice joined Nellie, Marian, and Charles on the terrace.

"Your Grace, I should like to introduce my sister, Alice, to you," Nellie said.

Charles bowed. "How do you do, Alice."

"Your Grace." Rising from a pretty curtsey, Alice blinked up at him. "No one mentioned how tall you are."

Nellie stiffened. Her sister was so unpredictable. What would she do or say next?

Charles laughed. "I hesitate to ask in what manner I was described to you, Lady Alice."

"You weren't described to me at all. No one ever bothers to tell me much," Alice said frankly. "Are you good with a bow and arrow, Your Grace?"

"I consider myself tolerable. I have been warned that you excel at the sport."

"I practice a lot. I have not much to amuse me while waiting for my Come-out."

"I quite understand," he said in a sympathetic tone. "Life does tend to drag when you're waiting for something important to happen."

"And after you make your debut, it speeds up far too much," Marian said in a dry tone.

They made their way to the far lawn, a wide swathe of green ringed by elms, where the archery targets had been set up. Guests stood about with their bows, chatting.

"Really, Alice," Marian said. "You have your music and French lessons, not to mention dancing and riding. You are hard-pressed to find a moment to read as I know you like to do."

"That is true," Alice said thoughtfully. "Although I have been enjoying a very interesting book, *The Castle of Wolfenbach*, and it is ever so exciting."

"My goodness! That was one of mine," Marian said. "I doubt you should be reading it. It sent chills down my spine. It's a wonder you can sleep."

"Oh, no." Alice shrugged. "I am made of sterner stuff."

Charles's amused gaze met Nellie's.

"You have the honor, Lady Alice," he said when it was their turn.

Stepping forward, Alice withdrew an arrow from her quiver. She took aim, her blonde head close to the bowstring with her eyes fixed on the target. The arrow flew straight and true and found its mark dead center of the bull's eye.

"Good shot, Alice," Nellie cried.

Marian smiled at Alice. "Remarkable."

"I see your reputation is well earned, Lady Alice." Charles turned to Nellie. "I believe it is your turn, Lady Cornelia."

Nellie moved forward. As she took careful aim, she was aware of his eyes and those of the gathering upon her. Her hand shook. When released, the arrow struck the outer rim of the target. She cringed, and her cheeks grew hot.

"Oh, bad luck, Nellie. Nowhere near your best," Marian murmured, fitting an arrow to her bow. Her aim was better, but her arrow still struck well left of the bull's eye.

Charles placed his arrow into the bow. It twanged as it left the bow and hit the center target right beside Alice's.

Everyone clapped.

Charles and Alice were well in front by the last round. When his final shot failed to find the bull's eye, and as everyone else taking part had not come close, Alice was declared the outright winner. They all trooped back to the house for afternoon tea.

"Charles deliberately let Alice win after her second shot fell a fraction short," Marian said as they went to their bedchambers to tidy themselves. "I thought it exceedingly generous of him."

"If he did, it was indeed kind of him," Nellie admitted. "I'm pleased Alice is no shrinking violet and has firm opinions for one so young. But her lessons in grace, deportment, and conversation haven't brought about a significant change in her demeanor. Perhaps I should have a talk with her."

Marian raised her brows, a slight glimmer in her green eyes. "Are you sure, dearest? When she is so very like you at that age?"

"Men are not the enemy. One does not have to outsmart them or better them at every turn," Nelly said firmly. *But hadn't she been eager to beat Charles when they galloped?*

"She won't feel that way in a year or two," Marian said. "Men are such fascinating creatures. One tends to grow fond of them."

Nellie couldn't suppress a grin. "Did you hear Alice tell Charles she would allow him to win next time?"

Marian paused, a hand on her bedchamber door. "Yes, he was still chuckling when he entered the house."

Nellie approved of his laugh, which was deep and rich, although she saw no reason to mention it. Marian needed little encouragement to sing his praises. And while she was tempted to agree with her, she didn't want to chance fate. "He is bound to have habits I dislike."

"Like Sir Michael Kettering, who sucks his teeth?"

"Oh, Marian, I wish you could take this seriously."

With a glance down the corridor at a maid with fresh linens over her arm, Marian took Nellie's hand and drew her into her room. She shut the door. "Are you afraid to risk your heart?"

"What? No! This will not be a marriage like yours, Marian. Charles is not in love with me. Nor I, him."

"Because of that business with Kealan Walsh?" Marian persisted. "You were in love with him and very unhappy when Papa warned him off."

"And he went away like a lamb," Nellie finished for her. Walsh was better at writing poetry than fighting for what he wanted. Or hadn't he wanted her enough? That possibility had hurt her deeply at the time. They had been quite close, penning verse together, and writing that article for the journal.

"More like a dog with its tail between its legs," Marian said. "In this, I am in full support of Papa!"

"I didn't love Walsh. I know that now." She had never felt true passion for the man himself, only his words.

"Yes, thank heaven. He's returned to Ireland, has he not?"

"I believe so."

"Good riddance."

THE EVENING FOLLOWED much like the last, with an excellent meal, good conversation, and a game of billiards. Little time to speak to his betrothed, however. It was still early when Charles made his way to his bedchamber. The ladies wished for their beauty sleep, and the gentlemen, after several glasses of port, found their way to bed.

As he undressed, Charles thought about his newly acquired family. He had yet to warm to Nathaniel. He seemed an arrogant fellow with a shy little wife. But he liked Nellie's youngest sister. Lady Alice was an outspoken woman, already displaying a good deal of charm. He hoped she wouldn't be taught to behave like the debutantes he'd met. Most of them simpered, and were too flirtatious, while seemingly afraid to express any opinions that had not been schooled into them. Marian, Lady Belfries, was a good soul. He enjoyed her company, and she was obviously very fond of her sister. Her husband was a companionable, good-natured fellow.

Charles looked forward to spending more time with Nellie in London. Tomorrow, their engagement was to be announced at the ball. The pressure he'd been under since his father demanded he make good on this family obligation, eased. No turning back, now. His mother would be happy. She had been urging him to marry and produce an heir.

CHAPTER FIVE

THE MORNING OF the ball dawned fine, but dark clouds hovered some miles away on the horizon, and Nellie could smell rain on the breeze blowing through her bedchamber window. She hoped the bad weather would hold off on this special day. Charles and the evening ahead loomed large in her mind. Their engagement was the first step toward their life together.

She looked forward to the freedom marriage would give her. She doubted Charles would ask much of her. So far, he had not said or done anything to give her pause. Was he the unflappable man who deposited his mistress in the hackney? Or the brutish fellow who punched a journalist? He was certainly the man who had loved a woman and suffered heartbreak when she married another. Maybe Nellie would never know him well. They might not see much of each other after the honeymoon. He was, as Marian said, extremely attractive. Trouble was, other women thought so, too. They would have a busy social life together, but apart from that, they could pursue their own interests.

Smoothing her hair, she hurried downstairs to have breakfast.

Nat had already ridden out with the guests when Nellie and Marian were called to assist their mother. Preparations for the ball had begun weeks ago, but there were still many last-minute things to be done. The back stairs rang with the feet of footmen as they delivered breakfast trays and hot water to late risers. Upstairs, maids were busy answering bells.

In the kitchens, Nellie delivered her mother's message to Cook. As Cook bustled about, issuing orders to kitchen and scullery maids, she assured Nellie the ices would be placed in the cool room in the cellar once they were brought in from the icehouse. Nellie found their housekeeper, Mrs. Pritchard, in the butler's pantry talking with Hinkley, while he gave a final polish to an elaborate silver tureen.

"Please tell your mother that she must not concern herself. Everything is under control," Mrs. Pritchard said.

Their efficient housekeeper brought the enormous staff at Shewsbury Park and the running of the ducal London house to mind. So daunting, in fact, that Nellie pushed it hurriedly from her thoughts.

It was past noon when she entered the dining room, where a buffet was set up for the guests. An array of hot and cold dishes had been placed on the white-linen tablecloth beside a stack of gold-banded plates and sparkling silverware. Footmen roamed the room, offering iced champagne or wine to the diners.

Chatting with guests, Nellie filled her plate, then took a seat at one of the tables set up around the room.

Charles entered the dining room. He'd spent the morning riding over the estate with her father and had since changed into a moss-green coat with brass buttons and light-colored, thigh-hugging pantaloons. He was his usual immaculate self. But his hair, damp from his bath, curled over his forehead and nape, which sent a surprising thought through her head. What would he look like naked? Quite splendid, she was sure. She grew warm, wondering what had happened to her mind, and reached for her glass.

He joined her, his plate piled with food. "How are you, Nellie?" His gaze roamed her face. "Dealing with Thor this morning has given me an appetite. And your morning?"

"I'm assisting my mother with some last-minute tasks. Where did you ride to with my father?"

"Up Haystacks. It's a wonderful view of the fells and the lake from there." He buttered a roll. "Nice countryside. Very enjoyable, despite Thor trying to throw me off when my attention was elsewhere."

"Didn't my father offer you another mount?"

He sliced into the ham. "Thor is now part of my stable. Your father sold the stallion to me."

"Then it is to be hoped that Thor will prove a good purchase."

"He will."

He was so confident. Masterful persuasion seemed to be inherent in his nature. She couldn't help thinking of it in terms of their relationship. She'd begun to realize her own needs. This intense feeling Charles seemed to evoke in her was not a desire to be mastered, but to give as well as receive. As with their earlier horse race, she wanted his respect. She wanted to matter in his life. Her life had offered few ways to express herself. As a duchess, she would have choices. It was exciting.

"You're in a pensive mood," Charles said, forking up some potato. "Are you thinking of the ball tonight?"

"Yes. Are you?"

His sultry gaze met hers. "I am."

Nellie found herself trembling.

"May I join you?" Lady Forrester stood at their table with a plate of food.

"Please, do," Nellie said as Charles climbed to his feet.

A footman hurried over to assist her.

Once seated, the widow turned to Charles. "Did you enjoy your morning ride, Your Grace? I saw you atop that tall black horse. Impressive."

Nellie wondered if she meant Charles or the horse.

"I did, thank you," Charles said. "I've been telling Lady Cornelia how much I admire the fells."

"I have yet to view them. You must tell me more."

While Charles described the beauty of the landscape, Lady Forrester listened intently. Nellie mused about life. If only women could be offered the same opportunities as men. They had so little power over their lives. Some sought underhanded methods to obtain what they wanted, as she suspected Arabella Forrester might. And some were left dissatisfied, like her sagacious Aunt Bea, who could only educate herself from books when she'd yearned to attend university and study mathematics.

Unable to listen to more of Lady Forrester's gushing conversation, Nellie put down her napkin. "You must excuse me, my mother has some things for me to do."

"You would be wise to get some beauty rest, Lady Cornelia." Lady Forrester leaned toward her in an undertone, as if Charles could not possibly hear. "You do not want to appear tired on such a special evening." Her voice dripped sympathy, but her blue eyes seemed calculating. "Dark shadows under the eyes are to be avoided. Should you require assistance, I shall send my maid to you. She has an excellent remedy."

"How kind, but please don't bother."

It was true, Nellie hadn't slept well these last few nights. But she suspected the widow was pleased to have Charles to herself. Nellie fought not to show her displeasure, for it was the height of rudeness to flirt with Charles, and under Nellie's very nose. Arabella didn't fool her for a moment. She attempted to take advantage of the situation. It was no secret that the joining of two old families lay behind this arranged marriage. Perhaps she saw a role for herself as Charles's mistress and might even have read the article in the newspaper about him and his French mistress.

Charles stood and drew back Nellie's chair before the footman could leap into action. "I hope you find time to rest this afternoon, Lady Cornelia."

"I will, thank you." She climbed the stairs, frowning at a disturbing thought. Did Charles want her out of the way so he could continue his conversation with Lady Forrester?

Marian came into her bedchamber as Nellie donned a dressing gown. After she dismissed Lilly, she related to her sister what had occurred with Arabella Forrester.

"Shewsbury is not a fool. He would hardly cause a scandal here," Marian said.

"There's nothing to stop him from making an arrangement for the future." Nellie tied the ribbon bows down the front. "Even a clever man cannot be entirely relied upon to behave well where a beautiful, wily woman is concerned." She joined her sister on the chintz settee, the tea tray on a table in front of them, and opened the caddy.

Marian took the cup of tea from her. "You're not ready to trust him yet. That's perfectly understandable."

Nellie stirred sugar into her cup. "I'm not blind to the advantages Papa sees in marrying one of us into the Shewsbury family, but why did the old duke wish it?"

"It was a schoolboy agreement. Apparently, they were at Eton together. The duke's firstborn son was to marry a daughter of Papa's. Should the good Lord see fit to bless them."

"Michael was the firstborn. There was talk of you marrying him."

"Yes, at one point, but he was too ill. Then, of course, he died."

"So, if he had not been ill, you would have been the one to marry a man you did not love."

"Yes. I have been blessed to be allowed to choose my husband, even though Papa disapproved of him. I wished the same for you." Marian sighed. "But I can't say I've seen any sign that the duke is anything other than a decent man."

Nellie thought a decent man could succumb to a determined beauty as easily as a rake could, but it sounded sour, and she refrained from mentioning it. "I am so glad you're here," she offered. Her sister always buoyed her up. She had missed Marian's company most dreadfully since she'd married. "I hope you're right about him. It's all so horribly rushed."

"You can get to know each other better in London before the wedding."

Nellie nodded thoughtfully. "Hopefully, we shall still like one another when we meet at the altar."

Marian took a sip of tea. "I adore you, dear sister, but sometimes I wish you weren't so serious and complicated."

Startled, Nellie laughed. "Am I?"

"Don't think so much. Take things as they come." Marian put down her cup and saucer and rose. "Now, please rest. It's not long until dinner."

Nellie lay down, but the excitement of the coming evening banished any hope of sleep. She threw off the cover. Rising, she peered into the mirror. Perhaps she should consult Lady Forrester's maid for help to banish the tiredness from around her eyes.

After a lavish formal dinner where Nellie, seated once again at a distance from Charles, watched him hold the attention of everyone within earshot, they retired to dress for the ball.

At eight o'clock, Lilly was on the floor at Nellie's feet with needle and thread, sewing on a silk violet which had come loose from the elaborately decorated hem. Lilly bit through the thread and stood. "It's secure now, my lady."

"You'll ruin your teeth doing that," Nellie observed. She moved to the mirror and turned before it as a white satin slipper poked from beneath her gown. Pearl and diamond earrings caught the light, and similar jewels glittered on her wrist and at her low décolletage.

The door opened, and her mother entered, resplendent in swathes of pale blue silk, the family sapphires on display at her throat and ears. One quelling look at Peter, and the dog deserted the sofa and curled up in his bed on the carpet. "Dismiss your maid, Nellie. There is something I must discuss with you."

Nellie hoped it wasn't another attempt to describe what happened between husband and wife in the bedchamber. She nodded to Lilly, who gathered up her sewing paraphernalia, placed it in her basket, and slipped from the room.

"You look wonderful in that shade of blue, Mama."

"Thank you, my dear." Mama examined Nellie's gown, turning her this way and that. "Madame Bonnet has done well. You will have the duke at your feet."

Nellie didn't believe that for a moment. The cool, composed duke would prefer she be at his feet. She looked at the ceiling, wishing Marian hadn't given her quite so much information about what couples got up to. She adjusted the bodice, which showed a good deal of her chest. "Do you really think so, Mama?"

"But of course. I very much want you to be happy." Her mother's violet-gray eyes, so much like hers, grew concerned. "I know you disliked the idea of not choosing your husband. But you resisted the interests of more than one suitor in your two Seasons. In a few short years, your idea of how you wish to spend your life could have led you to become a spinster. That would be such a terrible shame. And I am confident you will find contentment with Shewsbury."

Contentment seemed such a small, sad word. Horrified at how raw her emotions were, Nellie gulped back unwanted tears. "Oh, Mama. I fear I shall make a frightful duchess. I am not the right person for such a dignified position." She yearned to cast herself on her mother's breast and confess all her fears, that a man such as he might hurt her, wound her soul, but she held back. For what could her mother do but just be worried and upset for her? And Nellie was determined not to let her parents down.

"What nonsense." Her small mother reached up to arrange one of the fragrant violets tucked into Nellie's curls. "You have all the makings of a wonderful duchess. But it is well known that gentlemen dislike fiercely intellectual women. They want a wife committed to them and the raising of their children."

"Can't one be both, Mama?"

"Against your husband's wishes? It would cause great discord between you, Nellie." She sighed. "I am as keen as you are to see women advance in the world. But few bluestockings have happy marriages. It seems that for now anyway, a woman has to choose. Happiness in the home, or disunity if you should seek a life beyond it."

"Grandmama managed it, as did the Duchess of Devonshire, Mama."

"Yes, but their marriages were not great successes."

Nellie had heard it said that her grandfather was a rake. But she doubted he was unfaithful because of her grandmother's penchant for literary circles. She was more inclined to believe her grandmother had sought those interests to fill her empty life.

"It seems so unfair," she murmured.

"Life isn't always fair, Nellie. But we can try to make it better for our loved ones rather than embark on more worldly matters society is not yet ready to accept. A woman has the rewards of motherhood and charity work, too, my dear. That can be most satisfying."

The door opened, and Alice's head appeared, eyes wide.

"Come in and see how lovely Nellie looks, child," Mama said. "We must go down soon." She turned back to Nellie with warm approval. "When we enter the ballroom, the duke's eyes will be upon you. Don't forget to smile."

Nellie nodded. Her mother had just poured cold water on her dreams. She feared her features were too stiff to smile.

⋙⋘

CHARLES WAS PLEASED. He now had a challenging new stallion for his stables. And that ram would prove an excellent investment. As he chuckled with Marian over a political cartoon, they'd both seen in the *Times*, which had Napoleon riding backward on a donkey, a collective gasp spread through the ballroom as the butler announced Lord and Lady Dountry and their daughter. Charles's blood heated, and all thoughts of horses and rams vanished. Nellie looked beautiful! With a shy smile, she walked through the room as a low buzz like a hive of hornets rose among the guests. Had his father been aware of how attractive she was when he'd insisted on this marriage? Charles was prepared to give him the benefit of the doubt. He met Marian's observant green gaze, excused himself, and strode over to greet Nellie. The guests obligingly parted to allow him through.

"Lady Cornelia." He raised her gloved hand to his lips, and for a moment, you could hear a pin drop.

Nellie smiled up at him. As it was required of him to marry and produce an heir, he was confident he could not have chosen better. Was it only days ago he had considered seeking a tactful means to end talk of an engagement?

"Your Grace, Nellie, will you join me?" Lord Dountry showed the way to the dais. Gathered before the guests, he cleared his throat. "Thank you all for coming to share this auspicious occasion. Lady Dountry and I are delighted to announce the engagement of our daughter, Cornelia Elizabeth, to His Grace, Charles Anthony Glazebrook, Duke of Shewsbury! We welcome the duke into our family and wish every happiness for their future together."

"The best kept secret in Keswick," a male guest shouted. Laughter and loud clapping broke out from the three hundred guests gathered in the ballroom.

"The first dance is mine, I believe," Charles murmured close to her ear, breathing in the perfumed scent of her skin.

They were soon surrounded by guests, kissing Nellie, and offering him their congratulations. When the country dance was called, Charles offered his arm and led Nellie onto the floor for the first set.

"You look beautiful tonight," he said as couples began to form, and they waited for the music to begin.

"Thank you." She blushed becomingly and gave him her hand as they moved into the first figure.

"I claim the supper dance," he said before the movements drew them apart.

She smiled and nodded.

The lead couple called the steps, and any conversation ceased until they came together again. But with everyone in proximity watching them, he said no more.

Dountry waited when they left the dance floor. "I should like to introduce you to friends here tonight, Shewsbury. If I may." With a smile at his daughter, he drew Charles away.

Charles left Nellie to those waiting to speak to her.

When a quadrille was announced, Charles pushed through the crowd and claimed Marian.

Before the music began, Marian searched his eyes. "You might accuse me of sisterly devotion," she said. "And you would be right. But Nellie is a wonderful girl, Your Grace. As you shall no doubt discover."

"I have already," he said before the orchestra struck up and they were caught in the movements of the dance.

Chapter Six

Nellie had to force herself to concentrate as she performed the steps of the quadrille with Lord Beauchamp. On the other side of the dance floor, Charles danced with her sister. She thought he moved gracefully for an athletic man. They turned, and for a brief moment, his gaze fused with hers from over her sister's shoulder. Ellie's hand trembled, causing Lord Beacham to glance at her.

Charles intrigued her, that was the trouble, and his masculinity drew her to him. He was handsome in his superbly tailored black and white evening clothes. To free her mind from speculation fueled by Marian's colorful account of the marriage bed, which would have shocked their mother, Nellie attempted to settle her thoughts on prosaic matters. She couldn't help being pleased for her mother that the ball was such a success. Once the possibility of a union between Nellie and Charles had become more likely, Mama had toiled for months planning every detail of this ball. Because of her efforts, the occasion would be talked about for months to come.

Many had come tonight with the expectation of seeing Nellie engaged to the duke. Laughter floated in the air along with the candle smoke. The long room, its twin chandeliers ablaze, had been transformed into a perfumed garden festooned with garlands and hot-house flowers. In their new liveries, which replaced their sadly faded garbs, footmen carried trays of champagne and lemonade among the guests.

What a disaster it might have been if, for some reason, she and Charles had decided not to marry. What if she'd hated him on sight? He would not have considered for one moment she might refuse him. A thrill ran down her spine as she recalled how he'd wasted little time in claiming her. Was it because he liked what he saw? Did he approve of her?

Her steps faltered again. Nellie shrugged apologetically at her partner.

"You have good reason to be distracted," Lord Beauchamp said with an understanding smile.

"How kind, sir. I shall endeavor not to stand on your toes," she said with a laugh.

She was floating, feeling outrageous and so unlike herself. She'd begun to fear she would never be quite herself again.

Even her Aunt Bea, who rarely ventured out of her house these days, had come tonight. Nellie had watched when her father introduced Charles to her aunt. Charles had sat and talked to her for several minutes. She had listened intently and nodded with a thoughtful expression. Charles could converse on any level. And when he spoke, people listened. It might be expected of a duke, but it was also a gift he had that she approved of.

When the dance concluded, Nellie made her way to her aunt, where she sat holding up her pince-nez, observing the guests with a jaundiced eye.

"My dear, Cornelia." Aunt Bea smiled as Nellie kissed her papery cheek and took the spare chair beside her. "I have met your fiancé."

Lady Beatrice Ralston's branch of the family could be traced back to the signing of the Magna Carta. Bea considered few people other than royalty worthy of her respect. Even some royals were treated with the utmost contempt. George I was considered a German upstart, as were the subsequent Hanoverian kings. Nellie was careful not to mention the Prince of Wales, for she feared his latest antics would produce an apoplectic fit.

"Do you like Shewsbury, Aunt Bea?"

"I do. He gave me some very good advice about investments. He is very knowledgeable and precise. I suspect he prefers a well-ordered world. That is all very fine and good, as long as you don't allow him to demand the same from you." Her aunt waved her fan before her face, failing to stir the rigid curls of her gray wig. "You were a passionate child, Nellie, quick to love, and hate, too, when it was warranted. You've learned to temper your emotions, to be the dutiful daughter, but you haven't changed much." She nodded sagely. "You and the duke might be like chalk and cheese, but if you give full rein to your feelings, you'll loosen him up. And that makes for a passionate relationship." She patted Nellie on the cheek, the large diamonds on her gloved fingers flashing a spectrum of colors in the candlelight. "Men do like to control women. It's extremely tedious. As if we women haven't a reasonable thought in our heads. Makes me exceedingly glad Ralston passed away years ago."

Nellie was used to Aunt Bea's forthright speech, but she was also the wisest of souls. Nellie glanced over to where Charles talked to Mr. Penhurst, whose property ran with her father's on the west boundary. Penhurst was a keen hunter. He was always out shooting. No doubt he and Charles had much in common. She caught her bottom lip between her teeth. Her aunt was right. She and Charles were very different. She doubted he would ever fully understand her. It should not matter, and yet it did.

"Don't stand for any nonsense." Aunt Bea's gray eyes brightened. "It will be a battle worth winning."

Nellie laughed. "Thank you, darling Aunt Bea. I can always count on you for excellent advice. Shall I ask the footman to bring you a glass of lemonade? Or would you prefer coffee?"

Aunt Bea's eyes widened. "Champagne, my girl. How do you think I've kept my complexion?"

Nellie rose. "I'll give an order for a glass to be served to you, and perhaps a lobster patty? I tried one, and they are delicious."

Her aunt nodded her approval.

As Nellie went in search of a footman, Charlotte Liddiard, her second cousin on her mother's side of the family, intercepted her. "My felicitations, Nellie." She raised her heavy dark eyebrows. "His Grace is the catch of the Season. In fact, he has been for the past several Seasons."

"You make him sound like a prize trout." Nellie smiled. "But thank you."

Charlotte snickered. She was not one of Nellie's favorites among her cousins. Charlotte wasn't a happy person since the man she wanted had married someone else. Although Nellie felt sorry for her, she had witnessed how spiteful and jealous Charlotte could be. She had never been that way with Nellie. Until now, perhaps, for there was an unpleasant expression in her green eyes.

"Shewsbury is close to thirty, isn't he?"

"I believe so." Nellie wondered where this was leading.

She nodded with a knowing expression. "He has not sought to marry since his former fiancée was snatched from him almost at the altar. Her father wed her to a neighbor."

"Well, he has obviously recovered," Nellie said crisply, glancing around for a footman.

"One's first love is always so special. Don't you agree?"

"I don't know. Do you?" Nellie stared at her, surprised at her rudeness. Charlotte's mouth looked pinched. Nellie only wanted happy memories tonight. "Where are those footmen? Aunt Bea needs champagne."

Charlotte caught her arm as she stepped around her. "You haven't heard?"

"Heard what?"

"The Marquess of Thorburn died. He was gored by a buck when

out hunting. Drusilla is now a widow."

"My goodness. What a horrible thing to happen. When was this?"

"News is slow to reach us in the country, is it not? The funeral was held in Northumberland several weeks ago."

Nellie's heart sank. "Poor, Drusilla."

"Poor?" Charlotte laughed. "Thorburn left her rich as Croesus. She'll wear her widow's weeds, but I doubt that will stop her. Fanny, her personal maid, is my maid's sister. I get to hear all the gossip. Since their marriage, Thorburn kept her in the country. Drusilla has been a virtual slave to the old man. She cannot wait to return to London." Charlotte giggled. "Fanny said the marchioness is making a list of eligible gentlemen. She wants a virile lover until such time as she can decently remarry." Charlotte paused and eyed Nellie. "Shouldn't have too much trouble finding one. She's still young and very beautiful."

"I wish her well," Nellie said. "Now, you must excuse me. Poor Aunt Bea is waiting for her drink."

"Yes, you must attend to Queen Bea." Charlotte reminded her of a satisfied cat. "Fanny said Shewsbury's name was on Drusilla's list," she added as she turned away.

Nellie watched the spiteful woman move through the crowd as her mind whirled. Was there any truth to it? Could there still be something between Drusilla and Charles after all this time? Would he have asked Nellie to marry him if he'd known Drusilla was free?

<hr />

WHEN THE SUPPER dance was called, Charles went to claim Nellie. It took him a while to find her. He finally discovered her in an alcove, engaged in an intense conversation with Marian.

"My, you two ladies look serious," he said as he approached. "Have we run out of champagne?"

They both looked startled. Hadn't Nellie been aware it was their dance? Was she so unaffected by him?

"A ghastly notion." Marian recovered her composure with a grin.

Nellie laughed. "Papa has stocked enough in the cellars to sink a ship."

The dance floor began to fill. He offered Nellie his arm. "My praise goes to your parents. A delightful affair."

He led her onto the floor. "Has something occurred?"

"No. Mr. Braithwaite has lost his glasses. He's blind as a bat without them."

"Poor fellow."

"Poor us. He plays the violin."

He laughed. "Dear me."

"I see you have charmed my Aunt Bea," Nellie said as they waited for the first notes of the waltz. "It is not easy to do. She is very particular."

He smiled. "Your aunt likes to talk about money."

"She never concerns herself with society's dictates."

"I don't see why she should."

Nellie's eyes warmed. She was obviously fond of her aunt. "I am totally in awe of her. Aunt Bea believes that on reaching a certain age, a lady might do as she pleases." She laughed. "Perhaps it's an excuse to behave disgracefully in her dotage."

Her husky laugh captivated him. One of her many charms. He looked forward to discovering more of them, slowly, on their wedding night. "Your father and I have yet to fix the date of the wedding. It won't be easy to arrange. The prince's secretary must be consulted. He will wish to attend, as will the prime minister. The cathedral must be booked, or we won't be able to marry until next year. We must discuss the honeymoon. I fear it may have to be delayed because of the war."

"Yes, of course." Nellie broke eye contact, and he sensed an almost physical withdrawal from him. Surprised by the change, he wondered what had so concerned her and her sister that they shut up like clams when he joined them.

"I trust that meets with your approval," he said. "St. Paul's is something of a tradition in my family."

"Of course. I did expect it to be a large affair." She looked dismayed and hardly the excited bride. He had to admit it might be somewhat intimidating. "You will make a lovely bride, Nellie."

"Thank you, Charles."

"And I shall be there to lean on."

Her eyes searched his with a faint smile. "And I shall certainly take advantage of that, I assure you."

He chuckled.

They stood near the French windows onto the terrace. Torrential rain gushed down the windowpanes. "I had planned a stroll on the terrace in the moonlight." He hoped she would understand his romantic intentions. "But nature has other ideas."

There was no responding glimmer in her eyes. "Papa is certain it will clear before morning. He is seldom wrong about the weather."

"Lady Forrester tells me she and Mrs. Knight, and a few of the hardier guests who don't plan to spend the afternoon languishing at cards, have expressed a desire to see more of the estate." Perhaps they could slip away for a few minutes alone.

"Nathaniel will be only too pleased to escort them," Nellie said.

No chance for a tête-à-tête, then. He wondered what had upset her, for something clearly had.

"We might play croquet for an hour or so if the lawn isn't too wet. It's one of my favorite games," she said a little breathlessly.

The musicians struck up the waltz, and he took hold of her hand. He'd been looking forward to this since their kiss. He liked how she felt in his arms, her head just below his chin. Her slim hand settled in his, and with his gloved hand spread against the small of her narrow back, he breathed in her delicate perfume and swept her into the dance.

They moved well together, a good sign, he thought. "Jason always triumphed when we played croquet. Am I to fear your expertise?" he asked. "Roundly beaten by my bride-to-be? A man has his pride, particularly after your sister destroyed my confidence by beating me at archery."

She laughed. "You have little to fear from me. Will Lord Jason and Lady Beverly be in London?"

"They reside in Dorset. A reclusive pair, but they are not long married," he said. "My brother writes that they plan to come to London to meet you. In any event, they will be at our wedding."

She nodded and continued the dance in silence. Her gown was the perfect foil for her lovely figure. He was surprised at how pleased he was to be marrying her. But Nellie's feelings about the marriage, he wasn't so sure of. She wasn't shy or missish but rather cool. He smiled down at her, wanting them to begin on a good footing. A nervous bride-to-be? "We only have tomorrow, shall we go for a walk?"

"We might walk to the gazebo by the lake if it's fine. I'll ask Marian and Gerald to accompany us."

A chaperone? Did she fear he might kiss her again? He hoped she would welcome it if he should choose to do so. "Your father tells me he is opening your townhome. You remove to London within a sennight."

"Yes. My parents are eager to return after such a lengthy absence."

"I'll take you driving in the park. We might ride."

"Papa only keeps the carriage horses in the city."

He was aware that Dountry's finances were in difficulty. It was only temporary, Dountry had assured him. But Charles suspected he might be financing him in the future. "No matter. I keep a good stable and shall provide a mount for you."

"I would love to," she said, appearing warmer than she had a little while ago. "I miss riding when in the city."

He glanced at the rain and cursed beneath his breath. If they could be alone, he might discover what worried her. A thought came unbidden. Might there have been another man in her past? Someone Dountry disapproved of? Was he still in her thoughts? It wasn't that Charles was jealous. A man had to be deeply in love to suffer that excruciating emotion. But he dashed well didn't want some fellow prowling around his wife. Surprised at the direction his thoughts took, he sighed inwardly as the music slowed.

Chapter Seven

Nellie rested her arms on the windowsill of her bedchamber and gazed down at Grosvenor Square. The family had been in London for a week, and for most of it, the weather had been dreary. A stultifying week of accompanying her mother on morning calls, where the wedding was discussed over the tea tables.

The drizzle continued, the sky a washed-out gray, the trees in the park drooping with the weight of a recent deluge. Rain in the city was not like rain in the north. It didn't smell fresh and sweet as it replenished streams and revived the gardens and woodlands. It merely formed brown torrents in the gutters and splattered the carriages with sooty water.

Earlier, she'd taken Peter to the park, but hadn't remained there long. Ordinarily, she liked to walk in the rain, but not here where people hunched beneath their hats and umbrellas intent on reaching their destinations. Was that a glimmer of watery sun she spied between the clouds? Probably not.

Nellie turned from the window. The long afternoon stretched ahead. Marian and Gerald had gone to their Kent estate because his mother suffered from another of her ailments. Her sister declared them to be imaginary and attention-seeking, for her mama-in-law always rallied at the sight of her son.

She wandered the room, picking up books and discarding them

while thinking of Charles. He had suggested a carriage ride in Hyde Park, but so far, the dismal weather prevented it. She wished she didn't feel so absurdly disappointed. There was the Brocklehurst's soiree this evening, which Charles would attend. She hadn't seen him since the day he left Dountry Park. That Sunday, the rain kept them indoors, ruining their last day together. With the diva's performance after dinner, it had been impossible for more than a snatched conversation alone. Their parting had been formal with the whole family present to wave goodbye.

A maddening thought slipped uninvited into her head. Had Charles already encountered Drusilla in London? Nellie wished her cousin's news hadn't rattled her so much. She shrugged. *How vulnerable one was to be marrying a man who didn't love you.*

Despite her fears, it would have been pleasant to be out in a carriage with Charles this afternoon. The Brocklehurst's reception rooms this evening would be crowded and make conversation impossible. She wandered over to examine her pale blue muslin with white lace decorating the puffed sleeves and neckline, chosen for this evening, and the matching blue silk slippers Lilly had placed in readiness. It was decidedly missish, more for a girl of eighteen than a woman of twenty-two. Nellie was determined that once married, she would wear more dramatic silk gowns in rich colors, deep violet, gold, and crimson.

It wasn't like her to mope. She owed Aunt Bea a letter. Nellie sat at her desk with a sheet of bond. Picking up her quill, she dipped it in the inkwell and addressed the letter. She paused when no words came to her. Her mind filled with thoughts of Charles. His lean, handsome face. She wished she didn't find him quite so attractive. Sighing, she replaced the pen in the holder and then moaned in dismay at the smudge of ink on her finger.

The clip-clop of horses drew her to the window again. A smart, dark blue curricle had pulled up outside. She couldn't make out the livery of the groom in his oilskin coat and dripping hat, who stood at the horses' heads. Their footman rushed out with an umbrella and shielded its occupant from view as their visitor was ushered into the house. Her father was at his club. Mama had mentioned an afternoon caller, but Nellie hadn't paid much attention to who left their cards. They would be sent away, for Mama complained of a headache. She had drunk an infusion of feverfew and was resting.

As Nellie scrubbed at the stubborn ink stain with a piece of pumice, their butler knocked on the door.

"Lady Cornelia, the Duke of Shewsbury is here to see you."

Nellie's wet hand went to her hair as excitement and consternation filled her. "Is my mother still resting, Hinkley?"

"I believe she is, Lady Cornelia."

"Please ask the duke to wait."

As the door closed, Nellie whirled around. She wore a dreadful house gown of faded lemon. And Lilly had gone down to the kitchen to heat the iron, to remove creases from Nellie's evening gown. She whipped open the wardrobe and pulled out the first dress that caught her eye, Pomona-green cambric, which wasn't too crushed. Struggling out of her morning gown, she drew on the green, then attempted to do up the hook and eye at her nape. One would need to be a contortionist like the one she once saw at Drury Lane to fasten it. With a moan of disgust, she gave up and rushed to the mirror. Her upswept hairstyle had been slightly disarranged in the act of dressing. She could never manage her thick hair well. Tucking the untidy strands behind her ears, she left her room and rushed to the stairs.

When she entered the parlor, Charles turned from the fireplace, his greatcoat swirling around his polished black boots. She'd not forgotten how tall and imposing he was, but still, his elegance robbed her of breath. It only served to make her feel untidier. She resisted the impulse to hide the stain on her finger and hurried forward. "Charles, I didn't expect you to call. The weather is so inclement...."

He took her ink-stained hand, his eyes amused as he raised it to his lips. "The curricle hood is up, and I think the sun is at least attempting to shine. We shan't let a little weather keep us from our outing, shall we?"

"I am afraid I'm not really dressed…"

"You require a warm pelisse. But first, allow me." His hands on her shoulders turned her slightly, and his fingers, cool and sure on her skin, did up the hook.

"Oh! Yes. Thank you."

His citrus scent enveloped her, and she had to fight the urge to lean back against him. Her embarrassment at her appearance safely prevented her from succumbing. She waited a few seconds too long in breathless anticipation for him to slide his hands down her arms and turn her to him. To kiss her and declare his love for her.

But, of course, he didn't. He was merely neatening his untidy betrothed, who was unable to dress herself. Such a grand duchess she would make!

Her cheeks grew hot. "If you'll wait a moment."

"Take your time, Nellie, the park will still be there."

She took a deep breath to slow her racing pulse and went to get her pelisse, bonnet, and kid gloves to cover the cursed stain. Must he always be so…immaculate and composed?

They left the house. The rain eased as he escorted her into the curricle, taking care to make her comfortable with a rug over her knees. "Let them go, Reilly," he called to the groom. "You may await me in the stables."

"Oh, no! Please go to the servants' entrance, Reilly," Nellie called. "Tell Cook I said to give you a cup of tea and a slice of her pound cake."

"Are you encouraging my servants to adopt bad habits?" Charles asked as he expertly feathered a turn.

She stared at him, unsure if he was serious. "He looked thoroughly miserable. I don't believe it will spoil him too much to enjoy a cup of tea in comfort on such a day."

He arched a dark eyebrow. "Indeed. He can sit by the fire and warm his toes. It is spring, not the depths of winter. My grooms are used to all weather. They live in the stables. A little cold and wet toughens them up."

"The stables? Oh, you are too harsh!" Nellie cried. The corner of his mouth twitched. "You are teasing me," she said with a half-laugh.

"It's entirely possible." Charles glanced at her briefly before drawing in the reins as they approached a laden wagon trundling heavily along the road. "Actually, the stable staff live in very comfortable accommodations *above* the stables. I'm sorry. It was irresistible, and I enjoy seeing you flare-up."

"You do? That is horrid of you." Nellie doubted he was sorry, but she couldn't banish the laughter in her voice. "Enjoy it, for it will not happen again. How does the saying go? Fool me once, shame on you, fool me twice, shame on me."

He chuckled. "That sounds like a dare."

"You can take it as such," she said with a teasing smile. He would not like to lose, she decided. But neither did she.

They entered the park gates and proceeded to the South Carriage drive, busy despite the drizzle. Carriages circled, and riders trotted down Rotten Row. Heads turned to view them, and many hailed the duke. Two men of a similar age to Charles strolled over to greet them.

❯❯❯❮❮❮

NELLIE LAUGHED AT one of Lawrence Frobisher's witticisms. He had a repertoire of them for the ladies. It appeared Lawrence was better able to entertain her than Charles was. Damn it, but she was appealing when she laughed. Frobisher obviously thought so. Charles was torn between being captivated by that slightly abstracted air she adopted when wanting to evade him and a desire to have her really look at him as if she wanted him.

When she'd entered the salon to greet him with her dress undone and her hair in slight disarray, thoughts of her in his bed caused sudden heat to course through his veins. As he did up her gown, he fought the urge to pull her into an embrace and kiss her. Her neck seemed vulnerable, the skin velvety soft beneath his fingers. He almost pressed his lips there, but pulled himself up sharply, aware of where he was. He found it unsettling that it took so little for Nellie to light a firestorm within him.

Once they were married, things would settle down. He would have her nights, and she could spend her days writing poetry if she wished. Order would be restored.

"I like your friends," Nellie said as they left the park, and the curricle rattled along the street. Her cheeks were flushed, and her eyes sparkled. "Mr. Frobisher is most amusing."

"Yes, he can be on occasion." When a pretty lady pays him attention. *The damned roué,* Charles thought, but not without some affection for a friend of long-standing. Women always took to Lawrence.

"I had luncheon with your father today." He turned the horses into Grosvenor Street. "As you haven't mentioned it, I assume he has yet to tell you that the cathedral has been booked for late July."

She gasped. "Oh, so soon? I wonder what Mama will say."

"Unfortunately, it was the only date that fits in with everyone. Your father agrees. Unless we wait until closer to Christmas."

"Oh, no. Of course, we must accept it."

He eyed the frown creasing her forehead. "I am sure your mother will rise admirably to the occasion."

"Mama always does."

Foolish to feel offended because she didn't appear eager to wed him. "Yes, and should she like some assistance, my secretary is at her disposal. Prinny has offered his personal pastry chef, Marie-Antoine Carême, for the cake and the wedding breakfast."

"That is most generous of the Regent. Mama will be thrilled," she said. "I'm sure it will all be superb."

Charles smiled, pushing away his pique. "I have been fortunate to sample some of Carême's patisseries at the prince's table. His pastry sculptures made from sugar and marzipan are called *pièces montées* and are quite spectacular."

As if in anticipation, her tongue licked her bottom lip. "I do enjoy dessert."

Charles cleared his throat and took a firmer hold of the reins. "Then I assure you, you will not be able to resist these."

She laughed. "I have no intention of it."

He visualized feeding her one. Licking the sugar from those full lips and allowed his mind to dwell on other possibilities as he drew the horses to the side of the curb.

"Ah, there is Reilly," he said, turning to her. "Still remarkably hale and hearty."

She wrinkled her nose at him.

He chuckled as he helped her down and escorted her inside. Alone in the salon, they took seats by the fire.

Nellie rang for tea. "Mother is resting with a megrim. She will be very sorry to have missed you."

"I hope she recovers soon." He took the armchair opposite, crossed his legs, and studied her. The misty weather had made those stray wisps curl against her cheek. He studied his hands, resisting the temptation to reach across and tidy them. "When I am free to do so, shall we honeymoon in Italy? A friend, Baron Giordano, has offered us his villa in Venice."

"Visiting Italy has long been a dream of mine."

"We can travel around the country, visit Rome, Florence…"

"Oh, Charles!" Her warm smile embraced him. "How wonderful!"

He was gratified to have pleased her. "I have engagements which keep me in London for the rest of this week, but then I should like you and your parents to join me at Shewsbury Park. My mother writes she is unable to come to London at present. Something of importance keeps her in Leicestershire." Although he couldn't imagine what would be more important than meeting his fiancée.

"I look forward to meeting her and visiting Shewsbury Park."

A footman brought the tea. Nellie busied herself, preparing the brew. She added a slice of lemon to the tea, the way he liked it, and handed him the cup and saucer.

"Nellie?"

Her questioning gaze met his. "Yes?"

"Does becoming my wife make you nervous?"

Her hand shook slightly as she stirred sugar into her tea. "Perhaps a little. I never imagined myself as a duchess. It entails considerable responsibilities. But I am eager to embrace it. You have bestowed a great honor on me, Charles." She smiled shyly at him, "I am grateful."

He referred to becoming his wife. Might she have deliberately misunderstood him? He nodded, disliking her gratitude with unaccustomed vehemence. "Then there is nothing else that worries you?"

"No. Why would there be?"

A smile in her eyes, she offered him a plate of apricot tartlets.

"No reason, I suppose." He took one, urging himself to be patient. She was evading him again, slipping out of his grasp like a trout escaping the hook.

Chapter Eight

The Brocklehurst's overly perfumed reception rooms were always popular, and tonight was no exception. Guests crammed every corner. The hum of conversation almost drowned out Nellie's words as she spoke to a friend, Lady Mary Bellamy, whom she'd met in her first Season and who had subsequently married an earl.

Nelly kept an eye out for Charles. The long-case clock had just chimed the hour. Eleven o'clock, and he had not arrived. She examined her feelings. Was she disappointed or insulted? Worry was uppermost, she decided, for it didn't bode well for their future together that he cared so little for her to actually *attend*.

"Your fiancé is here," Lady Mary said, spying him before Nellie did.

Nellie's heart lifted when he strolled into the room. After greeting their hostess, he made his way toward her. All the women he passed turned to observe him. She accepted they were no less immune to his appeal than she was.

Before he reached her, a lady claimed his attention. Nellie became aware of a faint stirring in the room.

When Lady Mary excused herself and left Nellie alone, she faltered, her face stiff, her smile plastered on. Heads turned from her to the duke with unfeigned interest when his former fiancée, Lady Drusilla, the Marchioness of Thorburn, detained him in conversation.

Mourning clothes seemed to become her. She was even more waifish and slender. Talking animatedly, she gazed up at him with what Nellie considered a wistful expression on her beautiful face.

Nellie grew suddenly too warm and fiddled with her bracelet.

When she glanced up again, Charles said something that made Drusilla turn in Nellie's direction. He bowed slightly and left her.

"Sorry I'm late." When he reached her, he took her hand and raised it to kiss her gloved fingers. "My brother and his wife have just arrived in London. They are weary and have retired for the evening but express their eagerness to meet you."

"And I look forward to making their acquaintance." She sounded shaky. While Charles spoke of his brother and sister-in-law, all she could think of was Drusilla.

Nellie's cousin had told her the marchioness came to London to find a virile lover. Of course, Drusilla's first choice would be Charles. They were probably lovers years ago. Nellie scolded herself. That did not mean that he would wish to pursue the relationship again, especially after what happened between them. No, he would not...

"Nellie?" He raised his brows. "I don't believe you've heard a word I said."

She swallowed. "But of course I did. Do go on."

Humor brightened his blue eyes. "What was I saying?"

Her eyes narrowed, and she fell silent.

He studied her for a moment, then took her elbow. "Allow me to show you the garden. It looks delightful beneath lamplight."

He escorted her across the room, greeting people, and then out through the French doors. The terrace was deserted, the breeze cool on her hot face. Her anxious breath drew in the scented air from the tubs of spring flowers. Beyond the arcs of lamplight, the gardens appeared sinister, which quite matched her mood.

Charles's frowning countenance was all too plain in the flickering braziers along the wall. "What troubles you, Nellie?"

How could she tell him? She would sound like an unreasonable, jealous woman. Well, to a certain degree, she supposed she was. And a little annoyed at his ordering her about. "It's nothing, really. I was surprised to see a friend here that I believed to be seriously ill. I must go and speak to her directly."

His hand on her arm stilled her. "Not until you tell me what the matter is."

"I dislike being whisked off and questioned like one of your servants, Your Grace." Her tone was playful, but his frown remained in place.

"Are you happy to marry me, Nellie?" he asked, concern in his voice. "It's not too late for you to change your mind."

But of course it was. He was now compelled to marry her. In fact, probably always had been. As soon as the old duke decreed it, their future marriage would have been entered into White's betting book. Wagers would be placed on their union and even the date it might occur. She could never embarrass him, and her father, well, that didn't bear thinking about. And she didn't want to, it was only… "No, Charles, I…"

She took a deep breath and placed a hand on his silk waistcoat. His chest hard beneath her fingers, she almost moved back. "Goodness, Charles, we are out here in the moonlight. Alone. Is it not romantic? Kiss me."

The furrow between his brows deepened. Then with a soft laugh, he drew her to him and took her mouth in a kiss. This was not like their first exploratory kiss. It promised so much, her body responded with a throb of desire. He stole her breath, and she clutched onto his coat, her eyes closed as he gently traced the seam of her mouth and swept his tongue inside. It was so intimate and exciting, and she sagged against him. He tasted of brandy blended with his essence, his body strong and unfamiliar against hers. Wanting more, she reached up and boldly threaded her fingers through his silky hair.

He broke the kiss and pulled back with a soft groan, while his warm hands remained at her waist. She was glad of his support, for she needed to steady herself.

With a wry smile, he removed his hands and moved to a safer distance. "Nellie, if you employ that technique to deal with our disagreements, I doubt I shall win even one of them."

She flushed, still trembling from the heated embrace. Their explosive kiss had a surprisingly powerful effect on her body. Her initial sense of triumph at having aroused him to passion was dampened by fear he would respond to another woman, Drusilla, quite possibly, in much the same way.

He turned to the balcony and stared down into the dark gardens. "I've invited your parents to dinner at Shewsbury Court on Saturday. Merely a family affair with my brother and his wife."

"I look forward to it." Her pulse still thudded. She licked her lip. If he'd drawn her down into the shadows, she would not have said no. But Charles was quickly in control of his emotions. He turned to smile at her, then tucked her arm through his. "Shall we go inside?"

She feared her face was flushed as gazes settled on them when they entered the room. Charles escorted her to her friend, Caroline Faulds. After a brief introduction, he left them.

"Well, Nellie, what news!" Caroline said, wide-eyed. Her ordinarily pale face bore a healthy color. "And such a charming, handsome man."

"Yes...but Caroline, how *are* you? I am pleased to see you look extremely well."

Her hazel eyes sparkled. "Completely recovered." She raised her fair eyebrows. "I am ready and eager to participate in your literary salon." She frowned. "But now perhaps...?" She turned to view Charles's broad back across the room. "Will it still be possible?"

"Most certainly. And I am counting on you being there." Nellie sounded far more confident than she felt. "After all, the Duchess of

Devonshire…"

"Had great success, yes, of course," Caroline interrupted. "What about the poet Kealan Walsh? Wasn't he to be part of this venture?"

"I'm afraid not. Mr. Walsh has returned to Ireland."

"Oh. What a shame. He seemed so keen…" She shrugged. "Well, never mind. Imagine if Wordsworth read from his recently published work *The Excursion*," she said, her eyes glowing. "I should think you could persuade him. And dare we hope that Byron might entertain us with *The Corsair*?" She placed a hand on her heart.

Nellie laughed. "Indeed, that would be a coup. But it may be some time before my salon can begin."

"I understand. Do tell me about the wedding plans. Do they go well?"

Nellie had discussed certain aspects of them with her mother and could now reveal some of the details. She was pleased she could do so in a calm voice, while her pulse still raced from Charles's kiss.

Caroline stared. "St. Paul's Cathedral? I am agog and must confess to being a little envious."

"The Shewsburys have married there since an ancestor was awarded the Order of the Bath," Nellie explained. She would not disappoint her friend by confessing that she'd have preferred a simple ceremony. As it was, the grand affair terrified her.

"And what about you, Caroline? Do you have news?" Her friend, some six years older than herself and resigned to spinsterhood, eagerly launched into a description of her days, the plays she had seen, and her favorite book. When that was exhausted, Nellie promised to write. With a glance at the clock, she went to join her parents.

Her path through the rooms took her past Drusilla. As they had not been introduced, they did not acknowledge each other, but Drusilla's glance at her said it all: fierce determination to claim what she considered was hers. And if she couldn't marry Charles, she'd have him in her bed. Spiteful eyes took her in disdainfully. The confidence of an acclaimed beauty who could have whoever she wanted. And Nellie, as the wife of an arranged marriage, would hardly be a rival for Charles's affections.

Nellie thought of Charles's passionate kiss, the promise it held, and just smiled.

Drusilla abruptly turned her back. A glossy black ringlet dancing near her ear, she continued her conversation with the two men who had been fawning over her.

Later, curled up on the chaise longue in her bedchamber with Peter on her lap, Nellie wasn't quite so confident that their kiss meant anything to Charles. She had reached out with the need to draw close to him, and he'd obliged. Perhaps he'd later regretted she'd led him into an indiscretion. He was attracted to her. The knowledge warmed her, but how long would it last? Men, such as Charles, would seek variety, and she was a virgin with only a dim notion of what people did together. While Nellie considered she had much more to offer than what happened between couples in the bedchamber, she would make sure he was not disappointed. She must listen more carefully to Marian.

※※※

CHARLES DISMISSED FEELEY. Dressed in a banyan, he sat by a small fire with Plato's *Symposium* in his hands. Although it was a favorite of his, he had been unable to take in a word. He grinned and shook his head. He'd long suspected Nellie would surprise him. What he hadn't anticipated was his own loss of control. At a soiree? He hadn't succumbed to kissing ladies at parties since he'd been a green youth!

On returning home, he sought the calm of his study, then left after a few minutes, having failed to settle. Undoubtedly, there was a powerful attraction between him and Nellie, which he'd felt from the first moment of meeting her. Was this the way his life would be? At the mercy of his emotions? His much longed for peace, constantly disturbed? He wished he could embrace the episode wholeheartedly. But something held him back. Was it Nellie? What drove her to smile seductively and act that way? And make the extraordinary request for him to kiss her?

He went over their conversation, which preceded the kiss. While he couldn't pinpoint it precisely, he became convinced she intended her action to be a distraction. It was obvious she didn't want him to question her. What lay behind such a fierce need for secrecy left him completely in the dark. He put the book on the table and abandoned the chair, needing sleep. Jason would be up early to drag him out for a ride in the park.

Charles stripped off his banyan and put it over a chair for Feeley to deal with in the morning. Naked, he stretched his limbs, yawned, then slipped beneath the cool linen sheets.

He lay with his arm beneath his head. How contented Jason was. Might he wish for such connubial bliss? Beverly seemed a steady sort of young woman. A perfect wife for his brother. Nellie was different. He suspected that if she disagreed with something, she might refuse to obey him. This marriage could rock his orderly world.

He blew out the candle and stared into the dark. Drusilla came to mind. Her pleading eyes as she offered him her congratulations. She'd attempted to explain why they'd been unable to marry, how she could not dissuade her father from marrying her to Thorburn. Charles, embarrassed for the widow, said he understood, and left her, bringing the conversation swiftly to an end. They were in danger of becoming a subject of interest, which was unfair to Nellie. And what was the point in dredging up the past? Still, he admitted that seeing her again, so classically perfect that no women in the room, or indeed in London, could hold a candle to her, did conjure painful memories he'd fought hard to forget.

Marriage had changed Drusilla, and Michael and his father's deaths had changed him. Their lives took different paths years ago. He bashed the pillow and closed his eyes as thoughts of Nellie pushed Drusilla from his mind.

Chapter Nine

At a knock on her bedchamber door, Nellie put down the book she had been trying to read, and rose, disturbing her dog. Peter abandoned the sofa and jumped onto the bed.

She was surprised to see her sister-in-law so early this morning, and smartly dressed for travel, wearing a buff-colored carriage gown, and an Indian shawl over her shoulders. Beneath her smart bonnet, her face appeared strained and sad.

"May I have a word, Nellie?" Eliza asked. "You aren't preparing to go out?"

Nellie had a sense of foreboding. "I haven't anything planned for this morning. I'm to dine with Charles at Shewsbury Court to meet his brother and his brother's wife, but that's not until this evening." Nellie took her arm. "Do come and sit down, Eliza. It's lovely to see you. Shall we have tea?"

"No, please don't worry about the tea." Eliza's brown eyes were red-rimmed. "I don't know who else to turn to. I hate burdening you with my troubles when you must be so happy. I would have spoken to Marian, but she's not here in London."

"What is it, Eliza?" She patted the sofa when Eliza remained standing, her York tan gloves crumpled in her hands.

Her sister-in-law sat beside her and took a deep breath. "It's Nat. Yesterday at the Tighe's party, a woman warned me he is having an affair with Lady Hattersley. I was so shocked that I wasn't quite sure what to do about it."

"Oh, my dear." So Nat was up to no good again. Horrid for Eliza to have learned of it that way. *Save us from these interfering busybodies*, Nellie thought with exasperation. "People can be spiteful. Are you sure it's true?"

Eliza nodded, taking a handkerchief from her reticule, and blowing her nose. "He admitted it when I asked him. Said it was what men did, and it meant nothing. He only loves me." Her large eyes filled with tears. "That was supposed to comfort me. But it doesn't." A sob escaped her throat. "How could it? I love him and could never betray him. How can he do this and say he loves me?"

"I believe he does love you. But it does not excuse him for hurting you." Anger coiled in her chest as she placed an arm around her slim shoulders. "What will you do?"

"I shall take Julia home to the country. I am sorry, it appears I will miss your wedding. It's inexcusable, I know, but I cannot stay here another day. If this woman knows, then half the *ton* does. It's mortifying."

"The *ton* thrives on gossip. But their attention soon turns to the next scandal. This will be forgotten in less than a week. I do hope you can come to our wedding. As it's some time away, I shall not give up hope. But if you cannot, then you must not let it concern you. Charles will also understand." Nellie wished Eliza would stay and fight it out with Nat and ignore the gossips, but that wasn't in her nature.

"I can't bear telling your mother. I'm such a coward, Nellie." Eliza sniffed and dabbed her eyes. "Your parents will be angry."

"Leave that to Marian and me."

Eliza stood quickly, bringing Nellie to her feet. "I must go. I have a carriage waiting. Thank you for being so understanding."

Nellie kissed her cheek. "Nonsense. I am very sorry, Eliza."

When the door closed, Nellie stalked the room while Peter

watched her. "Nat is a brute! Why are men like this?" Peter yawned. Nellie sat down and stroked the dog's back. "Oh, poor Eliza!" Should she have it out with Nat? Somehow, she doubted it would make a scrap of difference. He already knew her feelings on the subject. If only Marian were here.

Nellie left the bed and tidied her hair before the mirror. She must tell her mother why Eliza left.

That evening, as the Dountry coach pulled up on the gravel before the front portico of Shewsbury Court, her mother turned to her. "Don't forget to smile, Nellie," she said as the door was opened and the steps put down.

"Yes, Mama."

She'd been in low spirits all day. Her mother had refused to talk about the situation between Eliza and Nat. She merely said to leave them to sort it out. Such things were so neatly brushed under the carpet! It left Nellie deeply sympathetic and apprehensive about her own future. Would Charles's mistress or another lady feature in it?

Eliza had left a note for Nathaniel. Not long afterward, he'd come to see Nellie, angry. And when he'd got no sympathy from her, he'd flung out of the room. An hour later, she heard he'd left the city.

In the lofty, black and white marble-tiled hall, they were greeted by the Shewsbury butler, Grove, who Nellie considered far less starchy than most. He ushered them upstairs and into a drawing room of breathtaking grandeur. Paintings and mirrors decorated the eggshell-blue walls, with chairs and sofas of gold damask. Swaths of the same gold fabric hung at the windows. High above them, the magnificent, coffered ceiling was painted with figures in gilt frames.

Charles and his brother rose from a matched pair of blue chairs near the Adams fireplace. Jason's wife, a petite brunette, smiled at them from the sofa.

In this sumptuous setting, it struck Nellie that Charles looked very much at ease and somehow unattainable. As he walked the length of the carpet to welcome them, his gaze caught and held Nellie's. She brought their kiss to mind, hugging it to her for reassurance, but then recalled Drusilla's malevolent presence. Nellie's face heated, and she ducked Charles's gaze as the worry hit her full force. Would he be unfaithful like her brother? He would only have to reach out his hand, and any number of women besides Drusilla would eagerly take it.

"We need to talk," he murmured as he escorted them over to Lord Jason and his wife.

Startled, Nellie tensed and glanced at him.

Charles's brother greeted her with a warm smile. He was a younger, lankier version of Charles, his coloring similar. She knew there was seven years difference between them. His wife, Lady Beverly, had a sweet face and beautiful brown eyes.

"I'm delighted to meet you," Nellie said. "Charles has told me so much about you both."

"Not all good concerning me, I fear," Lord Jason said with a rueful laugh. He took her hand, leaned forward, and kissed her cheek. "And it's Jason and Beverly, we stand on no ceremony here."

"Nellie, please." She smiled. "When we have a moment alone, Beverly, you must tell me who made that lovely lace gown."

Beverly placed a hand on the blue bodice. "It is pretty, isn't it? We shall have a nice coze when the men are drinking their port."

Jason's mouth quirked in a smile. "Men believe their time spent alone after dinner is to their advantage. But I believe it is an opportunity for the ladies to discuss intriguing matters they deem unfit for our ears."

They all laughed.

After they were seated and served wine, the conversation turned to the war and the hope that good news would soon reach them.

"Wellington has it well in hand," her father said. "I predict the end of war between England and France within the month."

Jason disagreed and offered him a wager.

Charles frowned at his brother. "I believe you may be close to the mark, Dountry." He turned to Nellie. "I should like to show you the house before dinner. Would you care to come, Lady Dountry?"

Nellie's mother began to rise, but her father stayed her with a hand on her arm and a subtle shake of his head. She subsided back into her chair.

"Forgive us, but this is soon to be Nellie's home. I feel she should familiarize herself with it." Charles escorted her from the room.

Stunned into silence, Nellie accompanied him upstairs. Surely it was bad manners to desert his guests, and it seemed most unlike him.

He threw open a pair of doors and led her inside. "The duchess's apartment."

Nellie's gaze went straight to the wide bed draped in deep red brocade. Her face hot, she was very much aware of Charles's proximity. Would he sleep with her there or just visit her? She found she didn't want to spend her nights alone.

"If the furnishings are not to your liking, you must change them," he said, breaking into her thoughts.

While certainly luxurious, the décor was too heavy for her taste, the walls papered in a magenta and gold silk, the windows draped with the dark red brocade. "It's beautiful, but I would prefer something lighter, floral, perhaps."

"Flowers?" He cocked an eyebrow, looking amused. "You expect me to sleep in a room filled with flowers?"

Pleased that he would sleep with her, she laughed. "I shall bear that in mind when choosing wallpaper."

Charles took her elbow and led her across the soft carpet. He gestured to a gilt and white paneled door. "Your boudoir."

He opened another door. The room beyond was both elegant and comfortable. A handsome mahogany desk and chair were placed near the window. "This is your sitting room." He gestured. "That door leads to my bedchamber, and beyond is my valet's room."

"I shall enjoy writing at that desk." She crossed the carpet to admire the fine piece of furniture. "Oh, there is a charming view of the garden."

"Nellie." He came to take her hands, clasping them in his big warm ones. "When you walked in earlier, I thought you seemed upset. Is it something to do with the wedding? I know it seems a little rushed. Becoming a duchess might be a little daunting, but you are the daughter of a marquess. You were brought up to make a marriage such as this." His intense eyes searched hers. "If there's something else, will you tell me about it?"

Drusilla seemed to stand between them, almost like a physical presence. Nellie had a moment of panic. "Eliza and Nathaniel have had a dreadful argument. She has left him and returned to the country with their daughter." She could not bring herself to talk to him about Nat's unfaithfulness. And nothing about her other concerns.

"Is it serious? Your expression suggests it is."

"Nat has left London to follow her. They may not return for our wedding. I hope you won't be offended should they fail to attend."

He raised his eyebrows. "Of course not. Married couples have disagreements. We will, too, I am sure."

Of course they would. But even so, his words disturbed her.

"It's upsetting to hear about them, but why this?" He lightly traced the faint line between her brows with a finger. "It seems a little excessive for a family quarrel. They will work out their differences. I hope when we're married, you will confide in me."

"I want no secrets between us, Charles." She gazed over his shoulder, unwilling to meet his eyes. She kept something from him, and he was astute enough to sense it. But didn't he have one or two of his own? Or was it a woman's role to turn a blind eye to them. Well, she would not. If she discovered Charles had a mistress, knowing herself, she would not run away as Eliza had done. She would confront him, despite her mother's advice to never question a man's fidelity. *"Some* men are unfaithful, Nellie," she'd said this afternoon. *"One must accept it. A lady never displays those concerns in public."*

"Nellie?"

"Yes, Charles?"

She turned away from examining a fine oil painting of some rustic scene on the paneled wall. She couldn't have described what was in it had he asked her.

Tilting her chin up, Charles forced her to look at him. "Why did you ask me to kiss you at the soiree?"

Her heart hammered. "It was merely an impulse. Did you mind?"

He gave a short laugh and dropped his hand. "Well, perhaps it's best not to examine the reason too closely, for that might spoil the mystery. It's not something I've done, stealing such a kiss when the *ton* was on the other side of the door."

"*Never*, Charles?" She was empowered by the thought that she might surprise him and get the better of Drusilla and other women like Amanda Forrester, who watched him like hawks watched their prey. Even the French mistress if she had to.

Charles moved closer. When his dark head bent toward her, she stilled, waiting for him to reach for her, wanting him to. The heated look in his eyes told her he desired her.

"Never," he murmured and traced a thumb over her bottom lip. For a moment, the only noise in the room was a clock clicking somewhere, and her heartbeat in her ears.

Charles broke eye contact and stepped away. "Everyone will wonder what happened to us. Perhaps we should remove ourselves from further temptation and return downstairs."

Absurdly disappointed, Nellie walked through the door he held open for her.

She took his arm to descend the stairs. Women didn't live by the same rules as men, and if she ever had to fight for him, well then, she would.

At the end of the evening, Nellie joined her parents in their town carriage. "I did warm to Jason and Beverly," she said.

Jason had been amusing company. He had imbued the occasion with gentle humor during dinner, and at one point, had them all laughing, including her father, who was not easily amused. She and Beverly were instantly at ease with each other, and she felt sure they would become good friends. Charles, on the other hand, had become rather thoughtful. He'd sat back and allowed Jason to entertain them.

Why hadn't Charles kissed her? Surely the temptation was difficult for him to resist? She saw the heated desire in his eyes. He was conscious of his position, she supposed. Nellie had no such concerns. She wanted him to kiss her, and more, and didn't much care what happened after that. Was she without shame? She suspected she might be where Charles was concerned. He stirred something within her that no man before had done.

Nellie had lost the thread of her mother's conversation. Something about the wedding, she merely nodded and returned to thoughts of Charles. She appreciated his expression of concern for her. He deserved her trust, as he'd done nothing to make her doubt him. He was not Nathanial. Not all men were cut from the same cloth.

"I shall place an order with Beverly's dressmaker, Madam Ambre, to make me a crimson ballgown, Mama."

Her mother looked shocked. "Crimson? Surely not."

"Lady Blake wore crimson the other evening. She looked wonderful."

"You are too young to wear such a color. Lady Blake has been married for years. She is a mother."

"Nevertheless, it would suit me better than the beige lace Madam Bonnet has suggested."

Seated opposite them, her father folded his arms. "You'll set tongues wagging, Nellie."

He looked quite sour. He was never a good traveler. She didn't know why he always insisted on riding with his back to the horses. In her opinion, gentlemen could be silly. He would certainly disapprove of the gown she had in mind. It would feature a low-scoop neckline and be made of crimson satin with an overdress of silver like fine gossamer. She was confident such a gown would make Drusilla envious, dressed in her blacks. The pleasant thought lifted her spirits. As a married lady, she might choose to wear whatever she wished.

She shrugged off the weight she'd carried since her first Season when she'd tried to be the daughter her parents wanted and failed when none of the suitors came up to the mark. Many had bored her. They had inflated opinions of themselves, talked too much of their wealth and their stables, and were either disinterested in her, or amused that she liked to read. She couldn't see herself spending the rest of her life with one of them.

She smiled to herself. Life as a married woman had begun to seem far more appealing.

<hr />

CHARLES AND JASON galloped their horses across the sun-warmed grass in Hyde Park toward the Serpentine. Thor was in an obliging mood, and Charles arrived ahead of his brother. As his horse lowered his head to feed on the grass, Charles stared into the blue-gray waters of the lake, reflecting on the previous evening. He had pulled back from kissing Nellie, although, dash it all, he'd wanted to.

He took her there because of her expression when she entered the room, for it alarmed him. She was unhappy, and he wanted to know what it was that had upset her. But once alone, the air fairly crackled between them. The bed, which they would share in a few short weeks, dominated the room and his thoughts. His questions died on his tongue as blood rushed through his veins. It didn't help when Nellie grew heavy-eyed as she watched him and licked her bottom lip, and he feared he would return downstairs in a state of arousal.

Although some things about her puzzled him, one thing he knew: Her passion matched his. If he'd kissed her, there was a good chance they would have been caught up in something inappropriate and forgotten all about the family downstairs. Charles grinned and shook his head. He could imagine their dinner growing cold on the table, her parents and his brother, fully aware of what detained them.

He admitted he hadn't been quite himself since Nellie came into his life. And while he wished to regain that sense of calm he'd relied on in the past, he still wished he'd kissed her.

As he gave his attention to Thor, Jason appeared and drew rein as he came up to Charles. He whistled. "That stallion you purchased from Dountry is a magnificent beast. But he has a devilish streak. He plans to unseat you."

"He'll get over it." Charles gave the horse's glossy black shoulder a pat as Thor sidled and fidgeted.

"I hope it's before he succeeds in his aim." Jason chuckled. "If I didn't know what a good rider you are, I'd be worried."

"We are getting to know each other. Let's walk them for a bit."

They dismounted and led the horses through the trees and onto the grass, heading for the park gates. "I must say, I like my future sister-in-law," Jason said. "A nice surprise. As I knew her to be part of the literary set last year, I was expecting a grim-faced bluestocking, quoting poetry at me. But she's good company."

"Yes, she is."

Nellie had been in fine fettle at dinner. He'd never seen her so animated. He'd always thought of her as pretty, but she grew lovelier as she became more familiar to him. He enjoyed seeing the humor dancing in her eyes. What had that earlier concern been about? Was it only her brother? He'd been distracted, too. That damn letter and the impending lawsuit. Would Nellie approve of a man who acted like a brute? He rather thought not.

"Nellie has a delightful laugh."

"She has." Charles recalled her husky tones with a smile.

Jason cast him a sidelong glance. "Another surprise is you."

"Me?" Charles cocked a brow. What was his brother getting at?

"The way you behave around Nellie."

Charles laughed uneasily. "I find her attractive if that is what you mean."

"Yes, indeed, but…"

"But?"

"Something Beverly said. You know women, they are far more aware of these things than we are. While we are busy striving to fix everything, women quietly observe. They sense many things which tend to go over our heads."

"That is true. What did Beverly say?"

"I'm not about to tell you, yet."

Charles raised his eyebrows. "How annoying, Jason." He suspected Beverly was romanticizing about him and Nellie. Imagining a passionate love match. And he wasn't about to pour cold water on Beverley's dreams. But Nellie certainly didn't love him—although she did want him, he thought with satisfaction.

Jason laughed. "I daresay. But I'd rather wait a while, at least until after you're married."

Charles gave him a stern look but decided not to pursue it. "Beverly has a steadying effect on you."

Jason sobered. "She makes me a better man."

Charles smiled, touched, and pleased at his brother's heartfelt declaration. He would not have believed it possible two years ago. "Marriage has certainly wrought a change for the better in you, Jas."

Jason chuckled. "Am I waxing too lyrical? Beverly's smart and very fair-minded. I'm a lucky fellow."

"You are indeed. See that you continue to deserve her."

"Still very much the head of the family," Jason said with a grin. "I am no longer in need of guidance."

"I gladly relinquish that duty. Now that Father's trust has been set aside, and you are comfortably settled. Besides, I have my own concerns."

"It was fortunate that the solicitors found a way around the trust. I shouldn't have wanted to wait until my twenty-fifth birthday. It's provided me with much-needed funds and our home." He frowned. "But I sensed you were troubled about something. Anything I can help with?"

"No, but thank you. I had an altercation with a journalist, Lord Ambrose, a month ago. He was writing lies about a friend of mine who is too ill to defend himself. I'm afraid my blood was up. I didn't handle the situation as well as I might have. The incident made *The Morning Post* and has been misinterpreted."

"Did you punch him? Break his jaw? You pack a wallop, Charles."

"No, just roughed him up a little."

Jason gave a whoop. "Shook him out of his shoes, I bet," he said approvingly. "Misinterpreted? It seems fairly clear-cut to me."

"An unprovoked attack, it's said. The newspaper is threatening to sue me."

"But was it unprovoked?"

"No. The fellow took a swing at me first."

He whistled through his teeth. "He dared to attack you?"

"He was on the defensive."

Jason grinned. "Scared, eh? You are very intimidating when you glower. Any witnesses?"

"Sure to be. The street outside Parliament is busy."

"If it doesn't blow over, you should tell the lawyers to ferret out those witnesses."

"It appears that I shall have to. Lord Ambrose is the Earl of Fairbrother's son, and Fairbrother has a hearty dislike of me. We have crossed swords in the Lords several times concerning a bill. The earl will welcome the chance to get at me, so it is likely to go before the magistrate. Messy business all around." Charles cursed. "And not the way a duke should behave."

"I would have gone further," Jason said. "Given the wretch a bloody nose. Might as well be hanged for a sheep as a lamb." He held up a hand in response to Charles's frown. "All right, perhaps not. But I was hoping you were becoming more like your old self."

"I'm sure I don't know what you mean by my *old self*," Charles said, suddenly nettled. "I prefer to move forward, not back."

"*Gah*." Jason refused to be fobbed off. "That's rubbish, and you know it. You threw yourself into life once, Charles. Before…"

Charles glared at him. "I advise you not to continue."

"I remain hopeful of Nellie's influence." Jason threw himself up onto his saddle. "I'm for breakfast." He nudged his mount's flanks. "Race you to the park gates."

"Trickster!" Charles yelled, already sorry for having snapped at his brother when he only expressed concern. He leaped onto his horse and took off after Jason. Thor, delighted to be given full rein, thundered over the ground. His lengthy stride gathered up Jason's mount within minutes. Charles laughed as he passed him.

"Call me a cheat," Jason yelled after him. "You gave me the slowest dashed gelding in the stable. Wait till we get to Shewsbury Park. I'll race you down the straight. And win!"

Charles slowed and allowed Jason to catch up. "When do you leave for Leicestershire?"

"Tomorrow."

"Then, we'll see you there. I have invited Nellie and her parents to visit next week."

"Excellent. We can play whist, which Mama despises."

"Nellie will be pleased. She and Beverly get on well. And Mother is a little distracted of late."

"Dear, Mama, she seems to be always caught up in some cause or other since Father died."

"I expect we'll see Aunt Frances, too," Charles said. "She spends more time at Shewsbury Park than at home with Uncle Ralph."

"No decent foxhunting in Kent. Aunt Frances was brought up to it. It's in her blood."

"Nellie tells me she won't ride to hounds."

Jason turned to him. "Really, why not?"

"Nellie's a fine horsewoman. But she's against the sport."

"Against it, is she?" Jason chuckled. "Wait until she meets Aunt Frances."

"That's what I fear."

Their strident aunt would attempt to change Nellie's mind, but, remembering the determination in Nellie's eyes when she expressed her strong feelings on the subject, he suspected his aunt might have met her match.

Chapter Ten

The horizon was a mass of gold-rimmed clouds as their coach reached the top of a hill. Along with her parents, Nellie glimpsed the Shewsbury estate for the first time, a patchwork of green fields stitched together by dark hedges and trees lending shelter and shade to the sheep. She could just make out the ruins of the old castle with its crumbling tower.

They traveled the road bordered by flowering hawthorn hedges. Ewes and spring lambs roamed the daisy-strewn meadows. The gatekeeper saluted as their coach entered the gates with Shewsbury Park emblazoned on them. He then waved on the carriage carrying Lilly, Nellie's mother's maid, Iris, and Burton, her father's valet.

In the park, she breathed in the pleasant smell of freshly scythed grass. From beyond a stone wall came the heady scent of bluebells and daffodils clustered around the trunks of majestic chestnuts and oaks. With a shiver of anticipation, she put a gloved hand to her mouth when they crossed a bridge and approached the mansion. It was less than a hundred years old, yet there was an aura of antiquity, emphasized by ancient stone terraces and dark yews planted before the first stone of this house was laid.

The coach pulled up on the raked gravel in front of the south-facing exterior of the house. A pair of tall, fair-haired footman appeared. Assisted out of the coach, Nellie paused in appreciation of the facade, the Grecian pediment and towering Doric columns.

At the door, the butler informed them that the duke was not home. "His Grace left his apologies," he said. "He has been called away to see to a matter concerning one of his tenant farmers." A footman in livery led them through the marble hall. "The duchess has been told you have arrived. At present, she is visiting the Dower house."

Dismayed, Nellie wondered why the duchess was not here to welcome them. She followed her parents up the curved staircase where enormous, gilt-framed paintings lined the walls. She would have liked to inspect them but hastened after the footman and her parents. A maid showed her into the bedchamber next door to her parents.

Nellie removed her hat and peeled off her gloves. She was tidying her hair when her trunk was brought in, and shortly afterward, Lilly entered with Peter on his leash. The maid released the dog, and Peter rushed over, tail wagging, to jump up at Nellie.

"Shall I unpack for you, my lady?" Lilly asked.

"No. Only my blue sarsnet with the beige spencer." Nellie gathered up her dog. "My goodness, Peter," she said as he licked her face. "Has it been so long since you last saw me?" Her mother had refused to allow the dog to travel with them in the coach.

As her maid busied herself, Nellie kneeled on the window seat and gazed out. Below her, gardeners slipped discreetly amongst the formal gardens, and beyond the garden wall, a wide meadow carpeted with a host of daffodils sloped down to a lake. She clutched the windowsill. This would soon be her home. Unable to contain her excitement, she turned to her maid. "Take out my Italian straw, Lilly. I'll go for a walk. Leave the rest of the unpacking. Go down to the servants' hall and have your tea. I shan't need you again until five o'clock."

"Very well, my lady."

"Introduce yourself to the servants," Nellie said with a smile.

Lilly's blue eyes twinkled. "Oh, my lady. The footmen are probably so uppity they won't even speak to me."

"Once you come here to live, that will change. A duchess's personal maid demands respect. Don't take any nonsense."

"I met a gentleman coming up the servants' stairs. He had such a nice smile. He fussed over Peter. Said he's the duke's valet. From County Cork. Been with His Grace for several years, but he misses Ireland."

"All that in passing?" A stab of warning gave Nellie pause. Her mother had questioned the wisdom of keeping Lilly on.

"You will require a more experienced lady's maid. Lilly is a young girl from the country. She will either leave or take liberties."

"We will learn together," she'd replied.

Mama had sighed. *"Lilly is likely to do something inappropriate and embarrass you. You never listen to advice, Nellie. I believe you will come to regret it."*

Outside, the breeze was fresh on Nellie's face as she led Peter along the path. It was a stately walk as he frequently stopped to sniff the tangy smells of plants. The gardens were impeccable, unlike Dountry Park, where her father's strict economies had been evident before the ball, with the hedges often in need of trimming and weeds left to multiply in the garden beds. Charles's visit brought great change. More staff hired, and the grounds and the house spruced up. She was gratified that her father now appeared less harassed.

Nellie entered a gate in the stone wall and emerged onto the drive leading to the stables. She was heading in that direction when the thud of hoofbeats came from somewhere behind her. She picked Peter up and swung around just as the horseman came into view, thundering down the drive, scattering gravel.

Charles riding Thor. The horse and rider seemed as one. Nellie, holding her wriggling dog in her arms, caught her breath as he reined in. He wore a dark blue riding coat, his thighs strong and muscular in the leather breeches. When he pulled off his hat, his black hair fell forward onto his forehead. He pushed it back, and his smile welcomed her. "Nellie! How good to see you." He dismounted and led Thor over to her. "I see you've brought Peter."

"Yes, he frets if I'm away too long."

"Walk with me to the stables. Did you have a good journey?"

"We did, thank you. I have been admiring your beautiful estate."

He chuckled. "I am pleased you approve, as it will soon be your home."

"My father will be impressed by how quickly you've settled Thor down." Charles had worked miracles with the fractious animal. She was sure she could not beat him now on any horse he offered her.

"Yes, but he still has his moments. Wishes to hang on to some level of independence, don't you, fellow?"

Nellie's attention was caught by his big hand in the leather glove as it stroked and patted the horse's glossy black neck. His actions were gentle but firm.

They entered the stable block, which was a hive of activity. Grooms and stable boys curried horses, polished saddles, and swept the cobbles. "I have a mare in mind for you," Charles said. "Come and meet her."

She followed him inside and drew in familiar smells of hay, leather, and horses. They walked along the stalls, the horses watching their progress. "Here she is. Her name is Belle."

The pretty chestnut had a heart-shaped, white patch on her forehead. She thrust her head against Nellie's hand and nickered. "I wish I'd brought an apple. My, but she's a beauty, Charles."

"She's frisky and will give you a good ride."

A groom came to take Thor from Charles and drew him into conversation.

"Excuse me for a moment, Nellie." Charles disappeared into the stable interior.

Tired of Peter wriggling in her arms, she wandered back out into the sunlight and put him down.

A woman strode into view from around the corner. Tall, and a little too thin, she was dressed in a severe habit of rifle-green cloth. She walked over to Nellie and offered her hand. "You must be Lady Cornelia. Lady Dickenson, Charles's Aunt Frances."

Nellie shook it. "How do you do?"

Lady Dickenson raised her eyebrows at Peter. The dog backed away behind Nellie, twisting the lead around her leg. "Charles told me you were pretty. Has he deserted you already?"

Nellie looked up from untangling Peter's lead, and smiled, very pleased Charles had described her thus. "He is inside speaking to a groom."

Lady Dickenson's observed Nellie closely. "Staying only a few days, Charles tells me. Pity. You'll miss the foxhunt at the Brathwaite's. Never mind. There will be more soon enough."

"I don't hunt," Nellie said, determined to make it clear from the outset.

Her ladyship stared at her. "You don't ride?"

"Yes, but I prefer not to hunt."

She raised her dark eyebrows. "But you must. Especially when Charles is the host, and the meet come to ride to hounds over your lands," she said brusquely. "The Duchess of Shewsbury not joining the hunt? Charles's mother only stopped riding last year. By the way, have you met Her Grace?"

"No, not yet." Nellie eased her tight shoulders.

Lady Dickenson shrugged. "No doubt, my sister is caught up in some cause or other."

Having no opinion to offer, Nellie was relieved to see Charles emerge from the stables. He frowned at her strained face and strode over to them. "I see you two have met."

"Nellie has informed me she won't take part in a foxhunt," his aunt said, her mouth forming a disapproving shape. "We shall have to convince her, eh, Charles? We can't have the duchess failing to attend."

"You should hurry if you plan to ride, Aunt," Charles said smoothly. He glanced at the sky and the threatening clouds rolling toward them. The breeze blew eddies of last year's fallen leaves over the cobbles. "You might manage an hour before the storm is upon us."

"A bit of rain doesn't bother me." She nodded at Nellie. "We shall talk again at dinner."

"My aunt can be a little forceful, but she has a good heart," Charles said when Frances disappeared into the stables. Nellie struggled to believe him, but she should not rush to judgment on first acquaintance. "Aunt Frances's home is in Kent, but she visits for the foxhunting."

"She seems determined to change my mind."

"This is Quorn country, Nellie," he said. "You will meet many enthusiasts of the sport."

As he was. Would he support her decision? She had no idea as to which position he would take. "I imagine I shall." She bit her lip.

"But that doesn't mean I want you to take part in it," he said, turning to her. "If you don't wish to hunt, then you will not."

Nellie turned to stare at him. "Oh! That is good of you, Charles."

"I don't want you to do anything just because it's expected, Nellie," he said. "I want you to be happy here."

They strolled back toward the house with Peter trotting beside them. "As you and your parents must return to London in a day or so, I want to show you over the estate tomorrow. We'll ride out in the morning. Take a picnic basket."

Still reeling from his surprising statement, she smiled up at him. "I do love eating alfresco. Shall Jason and Beverly join us?"

"No."

Nearby, a rabbit darted from the bushes, crossed the drive, and scampered out of sight. Peter, barking madly, pulled at the lead, catching Nellie by surprise. Charles's arm caught her as she stumbled. He took the lead from her. "Your dog thinks he's a wolf." He picked up the wriggling dog up and tucked him under one arm.

Her mind was still busy dealing with the knowledge that they would spend time alone tomorrow. "He isn't aware he's so small."

Peter quieted. Perhaps, like Thor, he knew he'd met his match. Charles held out his free arm to Nellie. She put her hand on it, and they continued down the path.

"Unfortunately, I will have to spend the rest of the afternoon with my steward and bailiff," he said. "A tenant farmer has a boundary issue."

"What does that entail?"

"A difference of opinion with a neighbor about water rights," he explained. "But I won't bore you with the details."

"I would not be bored," Nellie said. She resented the implication. Some men didn't believe women capable of solving problems. She'd hoped he wasn't one of them.

"No?" Charles turned to face her. "Then another time, perhaps."

At the front door, Charles addressed the footman. "Where is the duchess, Henry?"

Henry cleared his throat. "Your mother is at the dower house, consulting the architect concerning the alterations, Your Grace."

Charles sighed. "Where might Lord and Lady Dountry be?"

"They are taking tea in the blue salon, Your Grace."

He handed Henry the lead. "See that Lady Cornelia's dog is taken to her bedchamber, and escort my lady to her parents."

"At once, Your Grace,"

Charles turned to face her. "I look forward to spending time with you tomorrow." His eyes spoke of some half-promise. "Our neighbors are to dine with us this evening."

"I shall see you then at dinner," Nellie said, rattled by the look he'd cast her. Did he have seduction in mind? Some men believed it quite acceptable to anticipate their vows, a cousin had told her.

"Until this evening." With a slight bow, Charles left her.

She followed the footman up the stairs. She was a little exasperated with herself. One look from Charles could make her heart beat wildly. The prospect of facing his aunt again at dinner had a dampening effect. Nellie expected another attempt to be made to persuade her to embrace foxhunting, but warmed by Charles's support, she was confident she could handle the woman. Although she must not expect Charles to stand up for her against his relative.

In the salon, her parents were having tea with Jason and Beverly.

"There you are, Nellie," her mother said. "Where have you been?"

"I went for a walk, Mama. The spring gardens are simply glorious."

Beverly smiled. "The park is magnificent."

"I hope to see more of the estate tomorrow." Nellie sat beside her. "Charles tells me you are returning soon to Dorset?"

Beverly's warm smile settled on her husband. "I am eager to go home. We are very snug and happy there."

Jason gazed fondly at this wife. "It is considered the back of beyond by some."

"You were telling me about your home farm," her father prompted Jason.

"Pardon us for a moment, ladies," Jason said. "Yes, sir, I am adopting the new systems of cropping, with turnips and clover…"

The gentlemen were soon engaged in earnest conversation.

Beverly laughed. "I fear they are lost to us. Nellie, you asked about the dressmaker who made my gown with the Brussels lace? Should you have need of her, I can give you Madam Ambre's London address. She dresses the Countess of Lambert, who is always the first stare."

"How good of you to remember. I shall certainly consult her. I have a dress in mind for her to make for me." Nellie turned to her mother. "Mama? We have such a big order that we might need

Madam Ambre for my trousseau."

Her mother presided over the tea tray. She poured Nellie a cup of tea from the large silver teapot. "I should like to hear more about her."

As they discussed the current styles, Nellie became lost to her thoughts. She wondered if Beverly rode to hounds. She was relieved that Charles had chosen to support her. But the thought nagged at her that he might be disappointed in her. She still considered it a thorny problem to face in the first year of her marriage. His aunt would be one of a number of neighbors who were members of the hunt and would value tradition as she did.

Nellie took the cup and saucer from her mother and sipped her tea, still unsettled. Charles's Aunt Frances was a formidable lady, indeed.

That evening, the tall, dark-haired duchess entered the drawing room dressed in a deep violet, half-mourning gown. With a smile, Charles brought her to Nellie and introduced them.

Nellie curtsied low.

"Lady Cornelia, how very nice to meet you at last," she said, taking her hands. "We must have a quiet talk before you return to London. I want to hear all about you."

Charles's mother must have been lovely in her youth and still was with blue eyes and black hair only lightly threaded with silver. Pale and slender, there was something elusive about her. "I plan to move into the dower house after the wedding," she explained. "It has been empty for some years and needs extensive renovation." She patted Nellie's hand. "But I look forward to welcoming you to Shewsbury Park, my dear."

She was effortlessly charming, but Nellie had the impression her mind was elsewhere. Pleased that her future mama-in-law showed no antagonism toward her, Nellie began to wonder if the duchess was happy to leave this beautiful house. To relinquish all that one was accustomed to and held dear, to be relegated to the dowager set, must be hard, no matter how accustomed one was to its inevitability. Her sons doted on her, Charles bringing her a glass of madeira and Jason arranging a cushion at her back, but Nellie had the strangest feeling that in her mind, Charles's mother had already left.

AT THE DINNER table, Charles watched Nellie converse with Squire Harrowsmith's son, Blake. How natural was her manner. It pleased him to discover she was not a woman who looked down her nose at those on a lower rung of society and was keen to introduce her to his tenant farmers after they married.

Charles watched his mother, alarmed at the change in her, with purple shadows beneath her eyes. He met Jason's concerned look when she retired early, apologizing for being tired after a demanding day. In the short time since he'd last been here, she appeared to have grown thinner.

After dinner, Charles partnered Bullen for whist, while twenty-year-old Blake was Nellie's partner, having claimed the honor before anyone else could. Impudent young buck! At the table, Nellie charmed his neighbor's son, who watched her with undisguised admiration in his eyes. And while it pleased him, Charles felt a surprising sense of ownership and wished he could whisk her away to bed at the conclusion of the evening. But he must wait patiently until they married for that pleasure.

In the morning, he entered his mother's apartment. Jane, his mother's maid of some years, admitted him. She curtsied. "Your mother is still abed, Your Grace."

He crossed the crimson and blue carpet of her bedchamber. His mother appeared smaller in the massive carved, four-poster bed. Swathes of crimson bed curtains hung from the ducal coronet, falling from beneath the lofty ceiling, and held back with gold cords and tassels.

"Charles! Come and kiss me." She held out her arms.

He pressed a kiss to her soft cheek. "You were not here to welcome me when I came down from London last night," he half scolded, alarmed again at her pallor. "Have you been doing too much, Mama?"

"Heavens no. I enjoy being busy. You know that."

He sat beside her. "You don't get enough rest."

"I promise, I will today. Where are you and Nellie planning to ride?"

"I thought we might picnic by the river."

She smiled. "I like her, Charles. Lady Cornelia is a thoughtful girl. She reminds me a bit of myself when I was young."

"Does she? In what way?"

She shrugged her thin shoulders in the lacy wrap. "She espouses an interest in philosophical thought and poetry. She may wish to take up some cause or other beyond those required of her. You must respect that."

"Yes. I believe she will."

"And why does that make you frown?"

He wished he had some idea of what Nellie might do. Women were expected to obey their husbands, but he rather doubted his wife to be would follow that dictum too closely. "Providing it isn't riding naked through the streets of Coventry, or something similar, to make some political point."

She laughed. "You may not find marriage easy." She reached up to push back his hair from his forehead. "You have been too long pleasing yourself. And you have become set in your ways."

"Mama!" He raised his eyebrows. "You are finding fault with me?"

"I adore you, Charles. And your brother. But I'm not blind to the faults of either of my sons. Jason is too impulsive, while you are too reticent."

"Reticent? Are you suggesting I'm a dull dog?"

"No! It is not your nature, darling. Life has made you so."

"Life does tend to shape us." It wouldn't serve either his mother or himself to go into the reasons.

"Not irrevocably. Talk to your fiancée, try to understand her."

"I intend to." But he had no intention of revealing how difficult he found it.

"Good." She lay back on the pillows. "Now go and spend your day with her. Enjoy yourself. You work too hard. You have an efficient staff to take care of much of it. I don't know why you don't put them to work."

"I am constantly aware that I demand too much from them."

"Nonsense. They are extremely well paid."

"Perhaps I am like you and wish to remain in control."

She smiled. "Impudent boy! Go! I shall see you at dinner."

He tamped down his unease about his mother's health as he quit her room.

※

IN THE LATE morning, he and Nellie set out on horseback. The early mist had cleared away, promising a pleasant spring day. They rode their horses along a lane through woodland and meadows, while she asked him about his tenants.

He was pleased by her interest, interjecting at intervals with insightful questions. "I've chosen a nice spot for our picnic, which overlooks the river."

His footman waited on the wide patch of grass. An umbrella shaded a blanket and cushions, a large wicker hamper sat beside it.

"Well done, John."

"Oh, this is perfect, Charles," Nellie said.

"Then I have chosen well." He lifted her down from the sidesaddle, set her on her feet, and turned away to see to the horses.

A cacophony of noises rose up from water birds and ducks grubbing among the reeds. The breeze brought the smells of water and mud.

Nellie sat on a cushion and arranged her habit around her legs, while John poured them glasses of chilled champagne. Plates, napkins, and silverware were placed on a small table.

"You may leave us, John," Charles said. "We will serve ourselves."

"Picnics at home are usually sandwiches and a bottle of lemonade," Nellie said.

"Would you have preferred it?"

"To this magnificent feast? Heavens, no." She smiled at him. "And your company, of course."

He cocked an eyebrow. "And which is of greater import? My company or the food?"

She laughed. "Your company, of course. But I confess to being hungry after our ride."

"Then I must feed you."

"Thank you. This is very grand. It lacks nothing but music."

"An oversight," he said, coming to sit down. "I should have had a fiddler accompany us."

"Oh, yes. If music be the food of love, play on."

She lowered her head and busied herself rearranging the items on the table.

He had not missed the shadow in her eyes. What the devil? Had she come to accept the terms of their marriage? He was aware of her penchant for poetry and poets and was equally aware that he didn't particularly share it, preferring to read books, which offered clear, rational thought. But their union suited him, especially as he found Nellie extremely desirable. She might feel differently, however. Had there been another man in the picture before they met? The Irish poet, who he imagined would have shared her interest? It stood to reason a lovely woman like Nellie would have attracted many men. While he didn't expect or want her love, nor did he want his wife mooning over some other fellow from her past.

He held up his glass. "To our future together."

"Our future, Charles." She evaded his gaze as she leaned close to clink her glass against his. "Now, what have we here?" On her knees, she examined the array of dishes John had removed from the hamper. "Oh, my goodness. If I sample every dish, I shan't be able to get back on my horse. But I cannot resist game pie. Your chef makes superb pastry."

He watched as she busied herself with their plates. She'd been more relaxed with him yesterday. Couldn't be the foxhunting. He'd made that clear, hadn't he? But he'd attempted to discover what went on in Nellie's head before and failed miserably. He wouldn't ask again. She probably wouldn't tell him. Uncomplicated women tended to bore him in the past, but at this moment, he wished Nellie were a little easier to understand.

He decided to find a safe subject before he spoiled the day, trying again to dig into her thoughts. "Do you approve of Belle?"

"I do." She glanced at the mare tugging at the grass beside Thor. "She is quite spirited and light on her feet." Her lips twitched. "I would like a chance to beat you again, should we race."

He laughed.

"You doubt I could?" She gazed at him, eyelids half lowered. A slight smile played on her lips, and for a minute, he was privy to what she so often hid from him. That which he'd begun to look for and hope to see. So sensual, he caught his breath. "Shall I serve?"

"Please do." He watched as she busied herself, deftly filling their plates with deviled eggs, a slice of game pie still warm enough to spice the air, a leg of cold chicken, salmon, and salad. She placed a basket of warm bread and a selection of cheeses on the table.

"I shall resist your chef's elaborate dessert." She handed him a plate. "I have been measured for my wedding gown. It would be disastrous if it required altering."

The mention of their wedding brought a pause to the conversation. For several minutes, they ate in silence.

Charles nibbled the chicken leg as he half lay propped on one elbow on the rug. "You seemed to enjoy young Blake's company last night."

She looked up from cutting into a slice of pie. "He was most entertaining."

Charles felt a twinge of something indefinable. Blake was a good-looking young fellow, and attentive, and he'd made her laugh. "His father, the Squire, runs the foxhunting here. Keeps many hunters at his stable."

Her eyes met his. "I know." She pushed her half-full plate away. "Can we not speak of it now? I want to enjoy our lunch."

"Yes, there are important things we should discuss."

"Certainly." She'd become cool and unapproachable again as she forked up a piece of pie. "About the wedding?"

Charles tossed the chicken leg onto the plate and grabbed a napkin to wipe his fingers. He reached for champagne and drank half the glass. "Is it the wedding which worries you? Or something else?"

"There's nothing," she said coolly.

"Would you tell me if there was?"

"Of course, but you haven't told me what it concerns."

"That's because I don't know."

He leaned across and traced a finger down her cheek. "You have secrets, Nellie."

"Everyone does," she retorted, batting his hand away. "Including you."

"I accept that," he said dryly, unsure what she referred to. "I wouldn't care if it didn't affect us. But it does. You're like a will-o'-the-wisp. I want a wife I can count on. When I take her in my arms, I want to be sure she welcomes me." Maddened beyond thought, he moved over to her and took the glass from her. Putting it down, he eased her onto the rug and leaned over her. "I don't want a wife who goes somewhere else in her mind when she's with me."

"That's unfair!" She tried to pull away, but he held her lightly but firmly by the arms. "It wasn't like that at the soiree, was it?" Her voice grew husky with emotion. "When we kissed on the terrace?"

"No," he said softly. "It wasn't. Shall we make sure of it?"

She gasped. "Someone might be watching us."

"The ducks? My staff would not dare."

He took her mouth more savagely than he'd intended. She resisted for a moment, then with a sigh, her hands slid around his neck and her fingers coiled in his hair. With a longer sigh, her mouth softened under his. He cupped a breast, delighting in its fullness, wanting to touch more of her velvety skin securely barred from him by the high-necked habit. When she didn't try to move away, he kissed her again, slipping his tongue into her mouth, tasting champagne. And continued kissing her until she moaned.

"*Nellie…*" he murmured, breathing in her sweet scent. He longed to undress her, here in the warm sun, and make love to her, but dammit, he wasn't a complete oaf. Before things got out of control, he straightened up and sat with a hand resting on his knee.

They stared at each other for a long moment.

"At least you aren't repulsed by me," he said with a twist to his lips. "But you have not been the most eager of fiancée's, Nellie. Are you going to tell me why that is?"

"You are imagining it," she said, her voice tight. "There is nothing."

"Very well. I won't rush you." Charles swallowed hard and admitted he was doing a fine job of rushing her. He wondered why it mattered to him. He should be satisfied. He had wanted a marriage that did not claim his heart. But nor did he wish to play second fiddle to some other man.

He stood and held out his hand to her. "Shall we return to the house?"

She gazed up at him for a long moment, then gave him her hand.

Chapter Eleven

Nellie yawned. She was propped up in bed with a cup of chocolate, a pencil in hand, and a notebook beside her. The last few weeks, London had been in a fever of celebrations since peace was announced after the Battle of Waterloo. The metropolis was abuzz with those who'd come to witness the formal proclamation of peace and the Queen's official welcome reception for the Duke of Wellington. Then there was the visit from the restored French king, fetes, the opera, and grand balls.

She had accompanied her parents every evening to parties, routs, and endlessly dazzling balls where red-coated officers, aristocrats, and the elite of society mixed with royalty, visiting allied leaders and politicians, the feted Duke of Wellington taking center stage.

Charles accompanied them whenever he could, but apart from a few afternoons riding in the park, she seldom had him to herself. She missed him. His duties in the Lords, as well as being at the beck and call of the Prince of Wales at Carlton House, took up much of his time. And would continue, she expected, for some months to come, but at least she would be at his side as his duchess.

Tomorrow was her wedding day. Her stomach tightened whenever she thought of it. And that seemed to be every few minutes. She picked up the notebook and forced her mind back to the list of last-minute things to check. But really, there was little left to do. Mama had risen splendidly to the call. All the invitations sent out had been accepted. The reception, which was held here at their townhouse, organized down to the last detail. Nellie's trousseau was ready to be packed in the trunks. Her wedding gown and accessories laid out in readiness.

The end of the war with Napoleon had altered their plans. The demands made on Charles to be part of the reception for the important visitors to the city: the restored French king, the corpulent Louis XVIII, and the Tsar of Russia and his sister required him to remain in London for some time. When Charles was free of commitments, they hoped to spend a few weeks at Shewsbury Park before embarking on their honeymoon.

Nellie put down her cup. She and Marian were shopping this afternoon. As Nellie's matron of honor, her sister had decided she needed a new hat.

The door opened, and Alice flounced in. "I am ready," she announced.

"Are you, poppet? What for?" Nellie bit her pencil. Should she pack the red velvet bonnet with the long curling feather? Or was it not summery enough? It did go well with her pelisse. But her mother didn't like the color. Nellie paused. She made a tick on her list. She would take it.

"To be your bridesmaid, of course," Alice said with emphasis as if Nellie had suddenly turned deaf.

"No bride could ask for a prettier bridesmaid."

"Charles gave Marian a diamond brooch and me a bracelet of seed pearls set in gold." She held out her wrist to display the dainty bracelet.

"It's perfect, but you should not wear it now. Wait until my wedding, poppet."

Alice sighed and fiddled with the catch. "I suppose I should take it off then."

Alice was not at all nervous. Nellie was all admiration for her little sister. She was sure her knees would knock, and she would trip walking down the aisle. She huffed out a breath. And afterward, she and Charles would…

"You don't listen to a word I say, Nellie."

"I'm sorry, Alice. You'll have to forgive me. *Tomorrow is my wedding day!*" She fell back onto the pillows.

Alice grinned. "I forgive you. It's just like a storybook wedding. And Charles is the handsome prince." She went to look again at Nellie's white satin wedding gown, embellished with extravagant lace and embroidery, and the short wedding veil, light as a cobweb. "It's *so* beautiful." Alice groaned. "Mama insisted I wear blossom pink, which is not my color!"

Nellie nodded sympathetically, glad her years of wearing what pleased her mother were almost behind her.

That afternoon, Nellie and Marian visited Rundell and Bridge, the fashionable jewelers at Ludgate Hill where Nellie bought a wedding gift for Charles, a diamond cravat pin. In Bond Street, Marian purchased a flattering bronze-green, high-crowned bonnet, and Nellie a pair of lavender kid gloves.

Arm in arm, they strolled along the street, glancing in shop windows. Marian wandered over to examine an evening cloak she admired made on some gold material, which was featured in a shop window, when a carriage pulled up. The groom assisted a lady and her son down onto the pavement. The elegant woman straightened her Prussian blue skirts whilst the child, in leading-strings, was held by the groom and set on his sturdy short legs. In a heavy accent, the Frenchwoman ordered the servant to mind the boy, while she purchased an article in the store.

"Yes, Mademoiselle Girard." The groom took the boy's hand.

"*Maman.*" The boy's face crumpled, and he reached out his arms to his mother.

With a sharp rebuke in French, she crossed the pavement to where

Nellie stood. Her green eyes widened in recognition when they settled on Nellie. "You are Lady Cornelia Dountry?"

"Yes. I'm sorry, I don't believe we've been introduced…" Nellie began.

The Frenchwoman murmured to her in her language as she brushed past Nellie. Leaving behind an expensive fragrance, she entered the shop.

Marian hurried over. "She spoke to you? What did she say?" she asked as Nellie stood shocked, staring after the woman.

"She said I won't hold onto him." Nellie swiveled to face her sister. "She meant Charles!"

"Well, of all the nerve. I've a good mind to go in there and confront her."

"No, don't, Marian. Charles might hear of it."

Nellie tamped down a shiver. The Frenchwoman wouldn't blink at causing trouble. She took Marian's arm, and they walked on. "Her son has black hair and blue eyes."

Marian scoffed. "You surely don't think…"

Nellie shook her head. "Why not? She is blonde and has green eyes. The boy's father must be dark-haired. And those eyes are the same color as Charles's."

"Many people have blue eyes."

"Not that deep, intense shade of blue."

"You are obsessed and losing your mind," Marian said with feigned dispassion, which didn't fool Nellie. "I look forward to you becoming a married lady and gaining it back."

"She was Charles's mistress. The boy would be about three or four. It is possible."

"May we go home?" Marian asked. "My feet have begun to hurt in these shoes."

"I did advise you not to buy them." Nellie hailed their carriage, which waited down the street. Would Charles tell her if he had an illegitimate child? Her chest squeezed painfully. "It's just as well Charles and I are not in love," she said in an undertone.

Marian linked arms with her and drew her along the street.

※

ON CHARLES'S LAST night of freedom, Lawrence hosted a bachelor party in the smoky air at White's club. He enjoyed the conviviality of four of his friends who dined with him. Phillips attempted to ply him with liquor, no doubt with something insidious in mind for Charles later on in the evening. Having heard the blood-curdling tales of bridegrooms being tied naked to lamp posts, and worst, Charles resisted, determined to pace himself. "I have no intention of being married with a bad headache."

Lawrence Frobisher grinned. "The headaches usually come after the honeymoon."

"I planned to invite several ladies to entertain us, but Charles refused." Brandon, Viscount Phillips, blew out a cloud of smoke. "I am disappointed in you, Shewsbury. Is it so long ago that we got up to hijinks at Oxford?"

"Yes, it must be. I don't recall any hijinks," Charles said with a chuckle.

"It was that Scot, Montgomery. He taught us the drinking game," Julian Pennycuik, Earl of Stowe, recalled. "We'd each roll dice to determine who would drain the cup. And the loser would have to perform some task, which proved difficult when senseless."

"Let's not revive our memories of those pranks," Charles said in mock horror. "They hardly relate to who we are now."

"You had your moments," Lawrence said. "I remember you and a small dark woman, the barmaid, wasn't she? From the local tavern…"

"Enough." Charles motioned sharply with a hand, as the waiter, pouring the wine, struggled to keep a straight face. "My thoughts are firmly fixed on my betrothed tonight."

"Good Lord! How very uncivilized," Brandon said, disgusted. "What has happened to your spirit of adventure?"

"I don't believe I ever had an excessive desire for adventure," Charles said, annoyed that his words echoed Jason's. "My desire is to spend as much time in the country as I am allowed. No adventures or surprises, beyond those one might hope for. I'm sure my duchess will be in complete agreement."

"I hope you're right about Nellie," Lawrence said. "She sounded very enthusiastic about setting up a literary salon in London."

Charles tightened his shoulders, annoyed that Lawrence was privy to information Nellie had thus far failed to discuss with him. And why the devil was he on a first-name basis with his fiancée?

"You need another glass of wine." Brandon signaled the hovering waiter. "This is an excellent vintage. And I must say, the trout was very good tonight."

"I was a few years behind you three at university and confess to being somewhat lacking in hijinks," Nicholas, Marquess Penning, said. "But I must agree with Charles. A quiet country life is to be wished for."

Charles rested a hand on his friend's shoulder. "If you can bear the solitude after years in the army." He raised his glass. "Congratulations, Nicholas, lauded for your bravery in battle by our estimable Regent."

With a resounding cheer, they raised their glasses.

Nicholas bowed his head, a slight smile in his gray eyes.

"How about a game of billiards then," Lawrence said, sounding disgruntled. "Seeing as we are too old for hijinks of any kind."

"Please don't include me in that assessment," Brandon said as he followed them from the dining room.

"Nor me." Stowe slung an arm around Brandon's shoulders. "We've still got some life in us."

In the billiard room, Charles rubbed chalk on his cue. While his friends laughed around him, he was thinking of Nellie. Tomorrow could not come too soon. She would make a beautiful bride. Would a contented married life lie ahead for them? Or would he spend it trying to understand his wife? While he was pleased Nellie planned to have an interest beyond those required of her, he wondered why it unsettled him. This marriage had begun to appear more difficult to negotiate than a love match. He thought back over his earlier observations on the married state. How fatuous he'd been!

Chapter Twelve

The carriage bearing Nellie, Marian, and Alice arrived at St. Paul's. A clamor rose from the crowd gathered around the entrance to the huge domed cathedral to watch the guests arriving for the wedding, and most particularly, Wellington and the Prince of Wales.

Her knees trembling, Nellie placed an anxious hand on the wreath of white roses on her head, then took her father's arm to climb the stairs. With an encouraging squeeze of her hand resting on his arm, Papa escorted her through the massive great west door.

Marian, in cream and rose pink, and Alice, in the despised blossom-pink dress, which really did look pretty, followed behind. The organist began to play, and the music swelled in the perfect acoustic space. With measured steps, she and her father proceeded down the long nave between the great Norman pillars hung with tapestries. Murmurs swirled around her from the guests dressed in their finery. Her heart pounding in her ears, she spied the Prince of Wales resplendent in oyster satin, his brother, the Duke of York, at his side, along with wives and dignitaries.

Charles stood with the reverend before the altar. Dressed in midnight blue, with fawn pantaloons and a white waistcoat, he turned to smile at her, his groomsmen, Sir Lawrence Frobisher, and Nicholas, Marquess of Pennington, beside him.

Reaching them, Marian took Nellie's bouquet of white roses and silver ribbon from her nervous fingers. Nellie smiled up at her handsome bridegroom. Charles leaned down, his blue eyes soft. "You are beautiful, Nellie."

The reverend, in his black and white robes, began. "We are gathered here…" When he came to "Who giveth this woman…" her father slipped away to be seated beside her mother. Nellie turned to look fondly at her parents, suddenly aware that this was the end of her girlhood, her years spent at Dountry Park, and the beginning of a new life as a married lady.

Earlier, Nellie had firmly banished Charles's French mistress from her thoughts. She would not be able to blight her marriage, because Nellie intended to embrace it with all of her heart.

She floated through the ceremony and was sure she would remember little of it later, while focused on the man beside her, his deep voice stating he would love and cherish her. And then her voice, at first barely audible before she raised it.

Charles slipped the sapphire and diamond ring on her finger. They smiled at each other. They were wed.

She and Charles emerged from signing the marriage lines in the vestry and stepped into a perfect summer day. They descended the steps to the dark blue carriage bearing the ducal crest on its door panel, the footmen in livery standing by.

As Charles took her elbow to assist her inside, a scarlet rose landed at his feet. Nellie glanced around. The Frenchwoman stood near one of the constables controlling the crowd. She held the hand of her tiny son beside her. Did she throw the rose?

Nellie couldn't tell if Charles saw the flower or who tossed it, for he ushered her inside. She arranged the skirts of her wedding gown as he joined her in the carriage. He settled beside her and took her gloved hand in his.

The footman put up the steps and shut the door.

"Nellie, my lovely bride." Charles leaned forward and kissed her lightly on the lips.

Loud cheering erupted through the coach window from the crowd of onlookers. The coachman's whip sounded, and the team of matched grays darted forward, the carriage rolling on toward Ludgate Hill.

The reception was held in the ballroom of her parents' Grosvenor Square home.

Nellie curtsied low before the Prince of Wales. His amused blue eyes studied her bosom displayed by the scooped neckline. "I approve of your bride, Shewsbury," he commented before strolling away.

Nellie thought him unattractive and licentious as Charles took her to meet other distinguished personages.

Charles's mother hugged her and then Charles. "A lovely ceremony. I look forward to spending time with you when you come to Shewsbury Park, Nellie."

"I hope you'll forgive me when I ask you a hundred questions," Nellie said. "I have so much to learn."

"You shall do very well," the dowager said. "But please don't hesitate to ask me anything. I approve of both my sons' brides. I am hopeful at last of gaining at least one grandchild."

"Just one, Mama?" Jason asked, coming to join them.

She smiled at him fondly. "I'll leave it in the Lord's hands."

Nellie saw the glance which passed between Jason and Charles. They worried about their mother. Although she was elegant and poised and had cast off her blacks to wear lavender, she seemed fragile, and Nellie noticed again that slightly distant air, as if she wasn't wholeheartedly there with them.

In the supper room, Marie-Antoine Carême's wedding cake took center stage on the long buffet table. The English plum cake was a tall affair with stiff white icing, lavishly decorated with French flair. An array of delectable dishes and desserts to tempt the guests' appetites covered the snowy white linen tablecloths.

When the orchestra stuck up the waltz, Charles led her onto the floor and took her in his arms. "And how are you bearing up, my beautiful bride?"

"I feel as if I have one foot in my old life and one in my new," Nellie confessed.

He gave a wry smile. "It's my hope that you will feel more like my duchess in the morning."

"Your Grace!" she murmured, her cheeks heating. Some guests were now joining them on the floor. Sir Lawrence was within earshot and chuckled.

"You are incorrigible, Your Grace." Nellie couldn't help smiling. She was happy. She had not tripped or committed some terrible faux pas. At last, she could begin to breathe. Soon, they would depart for Shewsbury Court, leaving the guests to continue to enjoy the party.

Her first night with Charles. She would try to remember what Marian had told her but feared her anxiety would turn her brain to mush. "Surely I must take Charles's lead and try not to resemble either a startled fawn or a poker," Nellie had told her sister earlier.

Marian laughed. "As long as you forget *everything* Mama has told you," she said.

Nellie finally had a chance to talk to Marian. "The wedding will be talked about until Christmastide," her sister said with an approving smile. "You looked beautiful, and you didn't stumble or choke on the words as you feared you might."

Nellie smiled with relief. "Where is Alice? I wanted to congratulate her on her poise. She really is extraordinary for someone of her age."

"Indeed. She was most indignant when Mama had Miss Dale take her upstairs."

"I must go and see her before we leave."

Her visit with Alice over, she left with Charles.

He gave her hand a squeeze in the carriage. "Nellie, you're trembling."

She huffed out a breath. "It's been quite a day, hasn't it? A perfectly lovely day," she amended, resting against his arm.

His smile sent her pulse racing. "Yes, my sweet. And it's not over yet."

"No." She cleared her throat. "I must speak to my maid. Lilly is from the country and has much to learn."

"Why not replace her?"

"Because I like her." Would he expect his duchess to engage a superior lady's maid?

His answer reassured her. "My valet is a rascally fellow. Although competent at his job, having made it his business to charm John Weston, who makes my coats, Hobby my boots, and Lock and Co, the hatters, he is not what you'd expect. Perhaps because he is not at all toplofty, I enjoy his company."

"Yes," she said, smiling with relief. "When one must spend so much time with a person in such proximity, one must like them. I never wished for a French lady's maid like those my friends choose, although they say the French are *tres chic…*" At the sudden thought of his mistress, her voice petered away. *You won't hold him*, the woman had said. Nellie drew in a sharp breath. "Lilly has much to learn, it's true, but she is intelligent and very keen."

"Jane, my mother's dresser, might be of help."

"Oh, yes. I'm sure she would be, that's an excellent idea."

"You worry too much." Charles smiled and folded his long fingers over hers in her kid glove.

⸻

As they traveled the short distance to Shewsbury Court, Charles observed his nervous bride. In the blue and cream striped dress, a stylish bonnet covering her hair, Nellie sat tensely beside him. She always looked beautifully turned out, so it appeared her maid from the country had already learned her craft well. Charles completely approved of her intention to improve the girl's lot in life. It was a sign that Nellie's view of the world matched his.

When they entered the house, his staff, from the butler, housekeeper, and footmen, down to the maids and the boot boy, stood on the black-and-white marble floor of the hall waiting to be introduced to their new mistress.

Nellie greeted each one in a friendly, natural manner, which was sure to warm them toward her. Charles approved. A happy staff was an efficient one.

When they entered the duchess's apartment, her maid was busy in the adjoining dressing room unpacking the trunk. All thoughts of spending a few moments alone with Nellie fled.

"I have some work to do in my study," Charles said. "I'll leave you to organize your unpacking. We'll dine at seven here in the ducal suite."

With a nod, he left her, noting the panicked expression she cast him. He was aware he'd have to be careful. While they were physically drawn to each other, Nellie was an innocent, while the women he'd known were experienced. He wanted their first time together to be perfect for her. It would surely be special in a woman's life and something to remember.

Charles sat at his desk and took out his estate books. They usually held his interest, but he found it impossible to focus. He moved uneasily in his chair. His lovely wife was upstairs, but she needed time, and rest, after such a taxing day. He sighed. "Bring me an ale, will you, John?" he asked when the footman answered the bell.

Charles forced his attention onto his books and took up his pen.

Chapter Thirteen

In her dressing room, Nellie luxuriated in a perfumed bath, allowing the warm water to ease the tension from her limbs. Lilly then assisted her into a gown of russet silk and dressed her long hair in a loose bun.

The sitting room was cast in soft twilight when Charles entered through his bedchamber door.

A table laid for supper was placed before the brocade sofa.

When Charles joined her, she smelled his spicy soap, and the familiar heavy sensation settled low in her stomach. He had come from his bath and was dressed dishabille, in a royal blue silk banyan over his open-necked shirt, snug fawn pantaloons, and backless shoes. He arranged his long legs in the space, so big and masculine; he reminded her of a large jungle cat. A lion, perhaps. So sure of his control over his pride. She almost giggled as nerves made her tremble.

A pair of footmen entered, carrying trays of aromatic dishes. "Leave the bottle of wine. We will serve ourselves," Charles said.

They bowed and left the room.

Charles poured them both a glass of wine as she served the meal. He leaned back to watch her. "Tell me something about your childhood."

Nellie placed a portion of roast beef, potatoes, and peas on each plate. "I preferred to be outdoors rather than sewing or painting.

"I can picture you, a little hoyden, I suspect," he said, as she placed the plate in front of him.

Nellie laughed. "I had a favorite old oak tree in the garden. I used to climb it with a book and an apple. I fell out of it once and skinned my knee. I still have the scar."

"May I see?" he inquired politely.

She laughed and shook her head. "Mama despaired of me. I wouldn't keep a hat on outdoors and freckled every summer."

"Any freckles now?" He leaned over, his blue eyes roaming her face.

"Copious applications of lemon juice," Nellie said with a grin.

"Ah. But not so effective. I've spied two tiny golden freckles on your nose." He reached over and touched them lightly with a finger. "I've discovered I approve of freckles."

She smiled wryly and handed him a napkin. "I am to believe that?"

He chuckled. "I wonder if there's any more? I shall have to do a thorough search for them."

She blushed furiously. "I don't believe I have."

He raised his eyebrows. "But you're not sure?"

She caught her lip in her teeth, trying not to smile. "No."

"Then, I see it as my task. I am an earnest fellow. Most thorough."

Was it possible to giggle and shiver at the same time? "Your meal is getting cold," she said reprovingly.

He laughed and took up his cutlery.

For a while, they ate in silence.

Nellie drank from her wine glass. She could visualize the small boy in this large man beside her. All lanky limbs and tousled black hair. "What were you like as a lad? I have revealed my failings, so it's only fair that you tell me."

"Foolishly adventurous," he admitted, cutting a piece of meat.

"In what way?"

"I liked to swim in the lake. I almost didn't make it back to shore once. I was smart enough not to go in during the winter." He grinned. "Cramp."

Nellie ate some potato, finding this side of Charles completely irresistible. "Were you rescued?"

"My dog, Samson, swam out to me. I was afraid he'd go under, so I simply had to make it back then."

She smiled approvingly at him.

"I liked to ski in winter."

"Where?"

"At Shewsbury when it snowed. I fashioned skis from wood and tied them on with twine. Skied down the steepest hill."

Nellie laughed. "How enterprising." She could visualize him skiing down that hill the horses had struggled up when they'd visited his estate.

"I was what is called a *neck or nothing rider*. Fell off one of Father's hunters and broke my leg when I was eight."

"Your father didn't scold you? Try to rein you in?"

"Certainly not. We were put on a horse as soon as we were out of swaddling clothes. Taught to jump soon after."

"Well, I don't believe I shall let my son…" Flustered, she pushed away the vision of that small boy holding his French mother's hand. She bit her lip, annoyed with herself.

He reached for the bottle and poured her another half glass. "You were saying?"

She avoided his caressing blue eyes. "A family tragedy. My cousin, William, died after a fall from a horse when he was twelve."

Charles gave a sharp intake of breath. "It happens. But death can claim a person's life in many ways. One might become ill."

Nellie watched the expression play over his face, a deep sadness, he quickly shrugged away. She placed a hand on his arm. "Oh, Charles. Your brother, Michael. I am clumsy."

"No, sweetheart. That's one thing you're not."

"I was saddened to hear of his death. He was far too young."

"Thank you. But Michael would disapprove of me talking about him on my wedding night."

Her gaze moved from the heated expression in his eyes to his mouth. Recalling their passionate kiss on the terrace, a throb settled low in her stomach. She put down her knife and fork, suddenly unable to take another bite. She picked up the wine glass and took a good swallow.

Charles leaned forward and took her glass from her hand. He put it down. "Nellie? Shall we retire?"

Her pulse skittered. "Yes, Charles."

He opened the door to a bedchamber and took her hand to lead her inside. She was barely aware of where she was when he lowered his head and covered her mouth with his own. His kisses became insistent, deliberate. Nellie trembled as need and longing filled her. How she had wanted this.

"Charles," she murmured, holding onto his shoulders, her voice wavered, sounding husky and low.

"Let's take this slow, Nellie."

She felt the tension in his hands as they slid down her arms to grasp her wrists, but how in control he was.

Nellie nodded, swallowing as desire and nerves pulled at her. She wished she could be cool like him. But he was experienced, he must have had many women, apart from…her. She pushed the thought away hurriedly. She was hanging on by a thread as it was, her knees threatening to give way.

⊱⊰

"Hold still, sweetheart." Charles struggled to undo the row of tiny buttons down the back of her gown. "Was this dress a wise choice?"

"I didn't think…" Nellie gave a breathy giggle. "You are teasing me."

"*Never.*" He drew in a breath and slipped a hand inside the silk fabric to stroke the velvety-soft skin of her shoulder and the delicate bones of her spine. Her tender nape revealed to him, he had to press a kiss there, and below her ear, as he breathed in her perfume and the underlying scent of her skin, while his passion raged hot through his veins. *Take it slow.*

"Mm." She leaned back against him.

Charles eased the dress down over the curve of her hips. The silk puddled on the floor, and Nellie stepped out of it. She untied the strings of her petticoat, and when that, too, went the way of the gown, she turned to face him. In her thin chemise and corset, with blue garters gracing the silk stockings on her lissome legs, he lost his ability to breathe.

Aware of an already burgeoning erection, he turned his attention to her corset laces.

"Charles?"

"Yes, Nellie?"

"I have been advised about what happens between men and women, but it wasn't particularly helpful."

"It wasn't?" Intrigued, a smile played on his lips.

"No. What Mama and Marian told me differed greatly. But I don't want to be boring in bed. You must teach me."

"Oh, sweetheart, that is my heartfelt intention." Her corset fell away to reveal the thrusting curve of her lush breasts through the thin chemise. He paused to thumb and kiss each firm nipple jutting through the fabric as she clutched onto him and moaned.

He hefted her up into his arms. With his free hand, Charles pulled the latch on his bedroom door, then kicked it open and strode over to the bed. He deposited her gently and stepped back to divest himself of his clothes. Once stripped, he tossed them onto a chair and turned.

But for her stockings and the blue garters, Nellie was naked, having removed the last of her clothing.

"*Nellie.*" He suspected his wife might prove to have the same instincts for seduction as the best courtesans in London.

Her sultry, blue-gray eyes wandered over his body as he crossed to the bed.

At the shrill bark somewhere nearby, Charles halted mid-stride.

Her eyes widened, and her hands flew to her cheeks. "Peter. Lilly put his bed in my dressing room. He's used to sleeping in here."

"How very sensible Lilly is." He eased her back onto the bed. "I can see why you have kept the maid on."

He leaned over her, resting his hands on either side of her.

"Poor, Peter," Nellie murmured, curling her fingers around Charles's neck and drawing him down.

"But happy me," he said as his mouth covered hers.

He lay beside her, delighting in every inch of her. The pulse at the base of her throat, the luscious feel of her heavy breasts in his hands, her rosy nipples hardening as he drew them into his mouth. He traced the delicate bones of her ribs, the soft swell of her belly, and down. Her skin was the color of clotted cream, a triangle of golden hair at the apex of her thighs, deeper pink at her moist center.

Nellie moaned and wriggled and clutched his head. After a brief flicker of concern for the risk to his hair clutched in her fingers, Charles lost himself in the wonder of her.

Chapter Fourteen

Nellie woke. Sunlight streamed through the break in the curtains. She smiled and turned over, but the bed beside her was empty. It was not her bedchamber but his, filled with solid furniture and damask bed hangings. A swathe of the same silvery-blue damask decorated the row of windows.

Where was Charles? With a heavy sigh, she stretched and curled her toes, recalling every moment of their night of passion. It thrilled her and made her warm and wish he were here. He was an exciting yet tender lover. Her body felt slightly sore. She lay still, enjoying the wonderful, languid sensation which still lingered. It was as if her bones had melted.

She roused herself and threw back the blankets, stepping down from the high bed. Her dressing gown lay over a chair along with her slippers. She shrugged into it and tied the belt, then wandered into their sitting room. A pile of congratulatory letters, invitations to balls and parties, awaited her reply on the desk. Nellie turned away, and with a sigh, studied her messy hair in the gilt-edged mirror above the marble-topped bureau. Below it, on its polished surface, sat a vase of red roses, the exact shade of the rose thrown at Charles's feet when they left the cathedral after the wedding. Who had thrown that rose? She had seen the Frenchwoman. It must have been her.

Disturbed, Nellie rang for Lilly. She shivered and rubbed her arms, suddenly cold. They were just flowers, possibly ordered by the housekeeper. Was she foolish?

But the worry still tugged at her. She couldn't bear to think that Charles had done his duty as a husband, then left her with his heart and mind filled with thoughts of another woman. Might his mistress have sent these roses to remind him of her?

Their strong perfume made Nellie sick. She plucked a rose from the vase as the maid came in. "Who brought these, Lilly? Do you know?"

"No, Your Grace."

Nellie opened the door to her bedchamber. With a welcome woof, Peter scampered over to her. She put the rose on the dresser and picked him up. "My poor boy. Were you lonely?"

A little while later, as Nellie sat brushing her hair before the mirror, Lilly carried in a tray and placed a cup of chocolate, a basket of hot rolls, and a pot of jam on a table. "Peter has had his walk and his breakfast, Your Grace." She went to inspect the rose. "How pretty. Shall I put it in water?"

"No. I might press it in a book." *Or crush it underfoot.*

"What shall you wear this morning, Your Grace?"

"The primrose, Lilly." Nellie sat on the chintz armchair, holding the cup in both her hands, with the hope it would warm the cold, uneasy knot in her chest.

"I saw His Grace's valet in the kitchen when I was making your chocolate," Lilly said. "Mr. Feeley said the duke is in the library with his secretary."

"Yes, he's very busy." Nellie lowered her head over the cup.

Charles must have dressed quietly in his dressing room so as not to wake her. Did he enjoy the night as much as she did? They had barely spoken, for she'd fallen asleep. She had never imagined men and women could give each other such pleasure. Her first night with Charles was very special to her. Whatever happened between them, it would always be so. But perhaps it was not that way for him, for he hadn't felt the need to be there when she woke.

She would dress and take the rose down to Charles and ask him who sent them. The prospect filled her with purpose, which warmed her far better than the chocolate.

***

"Either you or your legal representative must appear before the magistrate at Bow Street at ten o'clock this morning, Your Grace. Your solicitors, Crambery and Challener, have received sworn testimonies from two witnesses who saw Lord Ambrose swing a punch at you first. But Ambrose wishes to pursue it, nonetheless. The solicitors need to know if you will allow them to appear on your behalf. Or will you go yourself?"

"I'll attend. I need to have this out with the plaintiff and his father, the Earl of Fairbrother, should he appear. The duchess is not to hear of this, Barlow."

His secretary nodded. "Very well, Your Grace."

"I'll see to the mail before I leave."

When it was put before him, Charles flicked through them. He frowned at a perfumed letter and slipped it into a drawer without opening it. Then turned to the rest. Invitations to routs, parties, and balls every night for a month.

His plan to whisk Nellie off to Shewsbury Park, where their honeymoon could begin without these distractions, must be delayed. He separated out a few. "Accept these, Barlow. Decline the rest."

"Yes, Your Grace."

Charles settled his hat on his head, pulled on his gloves, and left the house. He needed to see Nellie. They had not had much of a chance to talk. But first, he must deal with this business. He would hate her to hear about it. He'd prefer it never to reach her ears, in fact, for whatever the outcome, he considered it presented him in a poor light.

When he'd inherited the dukedom, it was his intention never to behave in a manner that was beneath his station. He considered himself honorable and even-tempered, not a thug. The slightly built Ambrose was no match for him in a fight. Charles had easily ducked the man's wild punch. But Charles's anger had taken hold of him, and he'd shaken the fellow so hard, he'd fallen to his knees in the street.

He should not have lost his temper, merely reasoned with the man, or failing that, walked away. His days of scrapping were long over. Even though his good friend, Ogelsby, was lying on his deathbed at the time with his family at his side, and should not have had to deal with blatant lies written about him which questioned his character. Charles sighed and hailed a hackney. Although now, with Ogelsby below ground, what followed mattered less, but he intended to bring it to an end today.

Chapter Fifteen

Nellie, having changed into a morning gown of sprigged muslin trimmed with peach satin ribbon, found her way to Charles's study. The room was empty. Nellie was caught by its neatness. Papers and files were stacked with precision. Not so much as a pencil out of place, an unmarked blotter on the desk. Nellie thought guiltily of the state of her own desk at her parents' home, the half-written poem, the inkblots on the blotter, and scattering of pen nibs. She left the room and crossed to the library.

Charles's secretary, a stocky, sandy-haired man named Samuel Barlow, sat engaged in writing in a ledger. He downed his quill and rose quickly to introduce himself. "I'm afraid the duke has been called away, Your Grace," he said with an eye on the rose she held. "He expects to return at midday." He nodded at the flower. "They are lovely, aren't they? Delivered fresh from Covent Garden."

"Who sent them, Barlow?"

"I'm afraid I couldn't say. There is never a name on the card."

"Then it has happened before?"

He blinked. "Yes, Your Grace."

"How often?"

"Every morning this past sennight."

Nellie's stomach churned. "Are they always sent upstairs?"

"Yes, Your Grace. The note states they are meant for the ducal suite." He frowned. "Shall I order a maid to remove them?"

"No need, Barlow. Should more red roses arrive, please continue to send them to me."

His shoulders sagged. "Certainly, Your Grace."

Unable to dismiss these bouquets as a casual gesture on someone's part, Nellie struggled to remain calm. "The duke is attending the House of Lords today?"

"No, Your Grace. Another matter has claimed his attention."

"Which would that be? He mentioned several matters."

Barlow tugged at his cravat and cleared his throat. "I'm afraid I cannot say, Your Grace."

Nellie stared at him. "His Grace didn't tell you?"

"I…I cannot say, Your Grace," he repeated, his face reddening.

He looked so miserable, Nellie relented. "I shall just have to await his return to assuage my curiosity." She forced a smile. "Thank you, Barlow."

He bowed low.

The rose stabbed her fingers as she left the study and returned to her bedchamber. What reason could Charles have not to leave word for her of his whereabouts? She tossed the flower onto the dressing table and, sucking the sore finger, stalked the carpet, turning with a swish of her skirts. Peter trailed behind her, his big eyes on her, but then yawned and returned to his pillow.

There would be a logical explanation. She wanted to think the best of Charles. She *did* think well of him. But who sent the roses? The Frenchwoman? It could hardly be anyone else.

At luncheon, when Charles failed to return, Nellie dined alone. She barely ate a bite of food, her stomach tied in knots.

Charles arrived home late in the afternoon. He strode into her sitting room where she lay on the sofa, attempting to read a book, and stooped to kiss her. "I'm sorry, sweetheart, I was called away on business this morning." He walked over to her desk and moved her pens and tidied her papers. "I thought it best not to wake you."

Nellie sat up, her hand on her hair. "Barlow told me. Did the matter end satisfactorily?"

He frowned. "What did Barlow say?"

"Very little." She waited for him to elaborate.

He avoided meeting her eyes. "There was endless discussion in the House." He bent over and picked up the book from the sofa beside her and flicked through it. "*Emma*? It's popular. I wonder who the author is." He handed it back to her.

"It has definitely been written by a woman," Nellie said. *Ask him about the roses*, she urged herself. She had moved the flowers onto an occasional table.

Charles's gaze flickered over them, but he made no comment. "You think so?"

"Absolutely."

"We are invited to dine with the Hammonds and attend their Victory Ball. These affairs tend to end close to dawn. You must rest."

"Yes, I shall lie down." Nellie turned to the door.

He stopped her with a hand on her arm, gazing down with affection. "I believe I shall join you."

She wanted him to, so much that she almost agreed. But she couldn't. She just couldn't. "Would you mind very much if I went in alone?" she asked. "I am rather tired."

"Of course," he said, disappointment deepening his voice. "Rest well, darling. I shall see you at eight."

Nellie was relieved when he entered his own apartment before he could see the tears in her eyes. He had lied to her! Barlow had been evasive and uncomfortable, but he'd clearly said that Charles was not in parliament. The only reason must be because he'd been with some woman. Or perhaps he had gone to see his son? She put her hands to her wet cheeks and moaned.

How absurd she was, she didn't understand herself. She expected too much from this arranged marriage. And she needed to stop. She must make a life for herself within it. The huge bed looked unwelcoming. With a heavy sigh, she lay down in her wrapper and pulled up the covers. Sleep eluded her as she studied the swag of heavy fabric above her. She began to take stock of the room, the wallpaper, curtains, the selection of art hanging on the walls. Even the furniture. She would change it all. Make it hers. Then she might feel a little less forlorn.

She drifted off.

A knock on the door brought her out of a deep sleep. She blinked. Her hopeful thought that it was Charles who could not stay away was shattered when Lilly entered with the tea tray. "I thought it best to wake you, Your Grace."

Nellie plumped the pillows behind her and sat up. She felt much better; she had been tired. She took the cup and saucer from the maid and sipped the reviving hot brew. She didn't know what had got into her this morning. Her thoughts had been nonsensical. Selecting a strawberry tartlet, she bit into it. "I hope the duke didn't ask for me. You should always wake me if he does."

"I haven't seen him, Your Grace."

Charles had said eight o'clock. She glanced at the mantel clock. It wasn't yet six.

"I've laid out your apricot beaded gown, as you requested, and the matching slippers," Lilly said." Shall you wear your pearls?"

"No." Nellie finished her tea and left the bed. "I'll wear the red tonight."

As the clock chimed seven, Nellie stood before the mirror, somewhat satisfied with her choice. Her mother would not approve of her new gown. It was exquisitely made, the low neckline quite revealing; the slender crimson satin slip featured a border of white satin and was ornamented at the hem with clusters of flowers. The three-quarter length overdress of silver-striped French gauze flowed about her when she walked.

Nellie chose silver kid slippers, and Lilly had braided her hair very cleverly with pearls in the style *a la chinoise*.

At the dressing table, Nellie pulled on French kid gloves, then clasped the sparkling diamond bracelet onto her wrist. It was Charles's bridal gift. Her gaze settled on the hated rose Lilly had placed in a bud vase. The color almost matched the crimson of her dress. Drawing it out of the vase, she was about to throw it away but changed her mind. She pinned it to her silver beaded reticule.

While putting on diamond earrings, Charles entered. She watched his face in the mirror, fearing he might disapprove of the color or the low cut of her gown.

He came over to her chair with a large velvet box in his hand. "That's a beautiful ballgown. You look stunning, Nellie."

The black and crisp white evening clothes suited him. How handsome he was. She tried to ignore the tug at her heart. A desperate need to rise and step into his embrace caused her heart to pound. She pushed back her chair, wanting his arms around her, but he'd bent his dark head over the box. Opening it with a thumb, he laid it before her on the dressing table.

Diamonds flashed from the velvet bed. Two necklaces, one intricate like a spider's web, featured a large diamond at its center, the other a dainty diamond choker.

Charles selected the choker. "I had in mind for you to wear the Shewsbury necklace, but you need little adornment with that gown."

His fingers were light on her nape as he did up the clasp. He bent and kissed her shoulder, sending tingles over her skin. "Did you have a good rest?"

"I did, thank you. I slept quite deeply. I was tired, Charles." Nellie picked up her shawl and the black-beaded reticule.

Charles eyed the reticule. "Where did you get the rose?"

"From the vase in the sitting room."

"I don't care for it."

"Do you wish me to remove it?"

"I do." He didn't wait for her and instead, plucked the rose from her reticule, scattering petals and tossed it, sadly crushed, onto the dressing table.

"We must leave, or we'll be late." He offered her his arm. "Shall we set London on its ear?"

He seemed annoyed. Was it with her for refusing him earlier or the sender of the roses? She forced a laugh. "I believe Wellington has that pleasure."

They descended the stairs to the entry.

Grove waited, holding Nellie's evening cape in his hands. Charles took it from the butler and placed it around her shoulders. And they walked out, to where the coach waited on the gravel drive.

Charles gave the coachman his direction as the steps were put down.

"Shall we try to leave the ball at a reasonable hour?" Charles asked as they took their seats. "I have seen too little of you."

His blue eyes offered an invitation she knew she could not resist. She brushed away her confusion and concern. If a battle for his affection was to be fought with another woman, let the terms be to Nellie's advantage. She had his nights.

⸻

CHARLES HAD INSTRUCTED Feeley to send any further bunches of roses to the housekeeper. He must tackle the even more thorny problem of his former mistress before Nellie became aware of where these flowers came from.

In the Hammond's ballroom, decorated with enough exotic blooms to suggest they'd robbed all the hothouses in England, Nellie quickly became surrounded. He thought her graceful and self-assured, and in that gown, she stood out among the more soberly dressed ladies, and the debutantes in their white dresses. He'd anticipated some disapproval, for the satin clung to her curves, and there were a few sour faces, but many more clearly admired her. It pleased him how Nellie set her own style and was already putting her stamp on society. He had married a spirited woman, it seemed. Although one he wished he could know better.

With a regretful sigh, he thought of the passion they'd shared. Had her wish to rest alone been merely physical? He might have pursued her, offered just to lie down with her without asking anything more, but the way she'd looked at him, as if she distrusted him, gave him pause. There was that wall between them again. She could not know who sent the roses or the details of the court case, for Barlow had assured him nothing had been said.

He and Nellie barely knew each other. But it still bothered him more than it should have. A cold, indifferent marriage was never in his plans. He could demand she tell him what had happened to change her from the warm, passionate woman of last night, but better perhaps to ignore it and hope it passed. And he'd had a devil of a day and was a little bruised by the battle with Fairbrother after they'd carried their disagreement into the House of Lords. Although at least his problem was at an end now, the earl finally realized that using his son as a pawn to strike at Charles would not work.

Nellie laughed and employed her fan while chatting to Lawrence. By God, Charles wanted to see that sparkle in her eyes when she looked at him. He wanted to drag her home like a caveman and demand she tell him what troubled her. To kiss her, make love to her, hold her until she confessed. He feared that even then he wouldn't get the full story. He shook his head and went in search of male company. Men at least could be relied upon to be relatively uncomplicated and fairly rational.

When Charles saw Nellie again, she talked to the poet, Walsh, who had returned from Ireland. He watched the way the Irishman looked at his wife and decided it displeased him. It clearly wasn't poetry that drew him to her. He suspected the man was after a means to better himself socially. But no sense in warning Nellie. He'd look like a jealous fool.

Charles spent the evening in conversation with friends. He danced with their wives, spying Nellie on the dance floor with one partner or other.

The night grew late when a footman brought a note to Charles. He excused himself from those he was with and moved to a branch of candles to read it. It was an appeal from Drusilla to meet him in the antechamber off the hall. Charles had caught sight of her earlier. He searched the room for a black gown and saw her exiting the ballroom. *Damn it!* What the devil did she want with him? This must be dealt with swiftly before it caused a scandal. And before Nellie got wind of it. Charles strolled out after her.

Seated on a satin chair in the curtained alcove closed-off from the hall, Drusilla smiled a welcome, her black skirts arranged around her, her gloved hands resting in her lap. With a cautious look down the corridor leading back to the ballroom, he pulled the curtain to and faced her.

"What is it, Drusilla? Your note sounded urgent." He searched her face for signs of distress, but her brown eyes danced.

"Thank you for coming. Please sit down, Charles," she said, gesturing to the seat placed beside her with her fan.

"I prefer to stand. We should not be found together like this. It will only cause gossip."

She lowered her eyes and fiddled with her fan. "We have never been able to talk about what happened when Father ended our engagement. I did try to speak of it at the Brocklehurst's soiree…but you…" She shrugged.

"I don't see any necessity to talk of it," he said gently. "It's in the past, surely."

She leaned forward. "You've no idea how miserable I've been. The marquess was a monster. A savage hunter and vicious…" she lowered her eyes, "…. in the bedroom. He would not allow me to leave our country estate. He threatened to lock me in my bedroom if I tried. And it was the same when we came to London."

"I'm sorry, Drusilla," he said quietly. "But should you be telling me this? What possible good does it do now?"

She sighed, a hand on her bosom, drawing his attention there. He had once wanted desperately to kiss that delectable part of her anatomy, but now he could only think of Nellie.

"You were such a gentleman, Charles, such a perfect suitor. I wanted so much to marry you."

"Did you? Then could you not have done so? Didn't your father tell you to choose?" he couldn't help asking. The pain of rejection was not quite finished with him, perhaps. But he didn't really care anymore. Drusilla was just as lovely, but his passion for her had gone.

"Father lied. I had no choice. The truth was, Thorburn's situation was much more appealing to him. It was expected that Michael would live long enough to produce an heir…"

"I'd rather we did not discuss my brother," he said, cutting her short. He eyed the curtain, which closed them off from the ballroom. It wouldn't do for someone to pass and overhear their conversation. "This is pointless, Drusilla. I am married." He turned to leave her, but Drusilla had begun to cry.

Alarmed, he pulled his handkerchief from his pocket and handed it to her.

She dabbed her eyes. "I just want someone to care about me. You used to, didn't you? You loved me? It's no secret your marriage to Cornelia was due to a family obligation. You married into the family because poor Michael could not." Her eyes implored him. "You and I could give each other such pleasure. You must know that. Many married men take a mistress."

"You refer to my wife, Her Grace of Shewsbury," he said abruptly. "I don't intend to discuss my marriage with you." He shook his head. "You are a beautiful woman, Drusilla. Your husband left you more than comfortably placed. You will be free to marry when your mourning period is over. You can then cast around for a husband, better surely than a lover. It won't be difficult. Many men are interested." He'd heard the talk and knew there were wagers in White's betting book as to which successful man would claim Drusilla.

She pursed her lips. A small mouth, he noticed, not generous like Nellie's. "But I always wanted you, Charles. Am I never to have you?"

"No, Marchioness. Our time together ended years ago." He bowed and swept the curtain back.

"You will change your mind and come to me," she called after him. "I know how much you loved me."

Charles let the curtain drop behind him and walked swiftly back to the ballroom. Had he loved her? At the time, he'd thought losing her made his life not worth living. But he wondered if he'd been mad with lust, for at this moment, he couldn't rustle up enough emotion to even like Drusilla. He had been too young to see past her mesmerizing beauty, he supposed, to examine too closely what sort of person she was. Like many beauties, spoiled and vain. But if she spoke the truth about her marriage, he did feel sorry for her.

Damn it, Drusilla had kept hold of his handkerchief. It annoyed him how she'd disrespected Nellie. Deeply thankful for the turn his life had taken, he went in search of his wife.

He located her among the dancers on the floor, Nellie looked animated as she conversed with Walsh while they danced. Had they been close once?

Charles turned swiftly away. Jealousy was beneath him.

Chapter Sixteen

NELLIE HAD SEEN Charles leave the ballroom as she danced with Walsh. She had struggled to assume an expression of interest in what Walsh was saying. Had she never realized how loquacious the poet could be? And he talked mostly about himself.

When Charles walked through the door again, she wanted to leave the dance floor and go to him. But the set had not finished.

She plastered a bright smile on her face. "Why do we find you in London again, Mr. Walsh?"

"Society is more entertaining here than in Dublin at present." His eyes twinkled. "And the ladies more charming."

Nellie felt her smile slip. She had accepted his invitation to stir some jealousy in Charles. It had failed, for Charles had left the ballroom without a backward glance.

Walsh seized the opportunity as the steps brought them together to tell her more about his latest poem. "I do hope you still intend to set up your literary salon, Your Grace."

Distracted, Nellie nodded. "I do, Mr. Walsh."

He beamed. "And shall I be invited to read one of my poems?"

"Of course." Nellie wondered why she'd ever found the man attractive. Her thoughts scattered when Drusilla came in through the same door as Charles had minutes before. Had they been together?

She struggled to hide her distress as Walsh elaborated on how he'd adopted the Petrarchan sonnet, much in the same manner as Wordsworth. "We can talk further when we're alone. It's too noisy here in the ballroom," he added after she'd failed to comment while watching Drusilla move through the crowd.

"It will be discussed when you visit the salon," Nellie said crisply, in no mood to be flirted with. "An invitation will be sent to advise you of the day."

He blinked, and his mouth turned down at the corners. "Certainly, Your Grace."

She was relieved when he made no attempt to talk again for the rest of the dance. Leaving him as soon as she could, Nellie moved through the crowd in search of Charles. She found him with Gerald Belfries.

"Did you enjoy the dance, Nellie?" Charles asked as she joined them.

"Yes, such an amusing man, Mr. Walsh. And so knowledgeable about verse, I was surprised when the set ended." Nellie was in no mood to admit how tedious she'd found the poet.

"I'm pleased for you, and Mr. Walsh," Charles said crisply.

Gratified to have annoyed Charles, she turned to Belfries. "Do you know where Marian can be found?"

Gerald turned to look around. "She danced the last set with Blanchard." He motioned to the far end of the room. "She will be talking to his wife. They are good friends."

Charles smiled down at her. "My dance next, I believe."

Belfries chuckled. "Waltzing with your wife? The old dowagers will be appalled."

"Let them be," Charles said, his eyes remaining on Nellie. "We should be on our honeymoon. And would be, were it possible to leave London."

"I'll join you once the waltz is announced," Nellie said. "I must find Marian while the orchestra takes a break." She left the men and made her way to the row of seats near the French doors. Charles always made her feel special and desired. Was he like that with other women? With the Marchioness of Thorburn, for instance?

She moved her fan before her face.

"Dreadfully warm, is it not," A lady Nellie walked past murmured sympathetically.

"These affairs always are," Nellie said with a smile. But while her face was hot, her stomach seemed oddly chilled.

"How tired I am of suspecting him," she confessed to Marian. She'd explained about the roses and Charles's absence from the ballroom after they'd found a sofa in a quiet alcove. "Am I being unfair?"

"I don't know," Marian admitted. "But it might be nothing, Nellie. I would wait for more proof. And in the meantime, eclipse her."

"Eclipse the beauty? How shall I do that?"

Marian smiled. "I'm sure you'll think of a way."

Lady Moncrief entered the alcove and sat on the spare chair. "The ball is such a crush. I hope I receive no more invitations to dance. These shoes pinch my feet most dreadfully," she sighed. "And they cost me fifty pounds."

Marian smiled in sympathy. "How very annoying." She rose. "I have promised the next set to Lord Lacombe. Meet me tomorrow for luncheon at Grillon's hotel. At one o'clock."

When the orchestra struck up for a waltz, Nellie stepped into her husband's arms.

He settled her more closely.

"You will have everyone talking." She enjoyed being in his strong arms, despite her misgivings.

"We are known to be recently wed. Many here attended our wedding."

"Men can get away with behavior that a woman cannot," she said, hating how petulant she sounded.

He moved back a little with a perplexed frown. "What's the matter, Nellie?"

"I have a slight headache," she confessed. It was true, her head had begun to throb. "It's very smoky and hot beneath the chandeliers."

"Then we shall leave directly after this dance."

"Thank you." Nellie smiled up at him, a little shamefaced. She was dancing with the handsomest man in the ballroom, and he expressed concern for her. Was it merely a coincidence that he and Drusilla were absent from the ballroom at the same time? She almost managed to believe it. She must get control of her emotions and think clearly. Marian had said to fight for him, and she was right. Nellie would not go into a decline. "I am still enjoying myself. You dance divinely," she said as he guided her into a series of turns.

Charles raised an eyebrow. "I do?"

"Yes. I have had my toes trodden on twice tonight by others."

He grinned. "Such praise might turn my head." His blue eyes gazed into hers. "Is there something you might want from me?"

She met his gaze boldly. "Possibly."

"Shall I have to wait to find out what it is?"

"I believe it would be prudent."

He chuckled. "Dare I suggest it might be the result of Marian's advice?"

She shook her head with a smile. "I'm sure I don't know what you mean, Your Grace."

His long fingers tightened around hers. "I'm sure you do, Nellie. And if you continue to look at me like that, I might drag you off in the middle of this dance. That will give the gossips something to talk about."

Nellie stifled a nervous giggle. Could she bury her concerns and just enjoy what she and Charles had? She wanted to, so much.

The streets were dark on their way home in the coach, the streetlamps having been extinguished. The ball was held a fair distance from

Mayfair. She was very aware of the man beside her. She wanted to draw him to her, to have him make love to her, while thoughts of his warm smooth skin beneath her hands, his mouth on hers, him inside her, made her restless. At home, in that bed all her concerns would come rushing back.

He tucked her hand into his. "Tired?"

"No." She leaned close, and with a hand on his shoulder, whispered in his ear.

He laughed, then closed the blinds. Turning to her, his mouth found hers in a passionate kiss.

NELLIE. CHARLES HAD long suspected she would be unpredictable. And she had been keeping him constantly on his toes. But he had not anticipated her request to make love in the coach. He found himself smiling as his pen hovered over the letter. His earlier concerns about Walsh, evaporating. In the dim light of the coach lamps, he and Nellie had made urgent and passionate love. His bold and beguiling wife had climbed onto his lap and rode him until he groaned. He would have difficulty meeting the smug gazes of his coachman and groom this morning.

His thoughts drifted. Nellie's soft body beneath his hands, her sweet breath on his neck, her mews of pleasure. She would be awake now, and perhaps… A desire to go to her had him half out of his chair.

"Your Grace?"

Charles sank back down, reluctant to let go of the memory. "Yes, Barlow?"

"You asked me to tell you if more roses were delivered."

Charles glared at his secretary. "And were they?"

"I believe so, Your Grace."

"The housekeeper has them?"

"They were sent to the duchess's suite, Your Grace."

"The deuce!" Charles stared at him. "Why were my instructions not carried out?"

Barlow gulped audibly. "Her Grace requested roses to be sent to her. It appears she is fond of the flower."

Was this coincidental? Nellie could not possibly know who sent them. But it could not continue. He removed the still unopened perfumed letter from the drawer of his desk and shoved it into his pocket. He would have this out with Angelique today. He left the letter he was writing, his train of thought lost, and nodding at the pile of correspondence, climbed to his feet. "This can wait, Barlow."

"There are several more to be signed, Your Grace and that matter from…"

"I am aware of it. We'll attend to them later."

Barlow bowed. "Very well, Your Grace."

"Have a cup of tea, Barlow." Charles had been harsh with the man. "I'll return at eleven."

He took his hat, gloves, and cane from Grove, who after a glance at Charles's expression, knew better than to offer him a cheery good morning, then he strode off down the street.

CHAPTER SEVENTEEN

NELLIE YAWNED AND stretched her arms in the wide bed. Peter barked from his position on the end, pleased to see a sign of life. She leaned over and rang the bell for Lilly, hoping she was within earshot.

It was close to noon, but she was still drowsy, her limbs deliciously heavy. She buried her nose in Charles's pillow and breathed deeply of his male smell. There was the musky aroma of sex. They'd made love again before he rose, this time more leisurely, which had left her melting and mindless, before she drifted back to sleep.

She put her hands to her hot cheeks, recalling their rowdy lovemaking in the carriage. After she had saucily suggested it, Charles had closed the blinds and, kneeling before her, eased up her gown and made her breathless, drawing ripples, waves, and shudders before he pulled her onto his lap, and anchored her upon him. How good it could be in a cramped space. She'd arched over him, loving the sense of power the position afforded her, until he'd wrestled it from her and holding her hips, drove hard into her with a loud groan. Nellie had fallen against him, half giggling, half gasping.

"My reputation will be in shreds when you've finished with me, my lady wife," he'd said with a laugh.

"You might have to carry me to bed," she'd confessed when the coach drew up outside the house. "My knees are weak."

Laughing, Charles had carried her inside, causing the porter to drop into a low bow and avert his gaze. Charles put her down. They were disgracefully disheveled. His cravat was untied, his hair tousled, and her attempts to restore her hair to its former elegance had been in vain. When they'd entered her bedchamber, he tossed her onto the bed and made love to her again.

All her earlier fears seemed banished in the afterglow of pleasure. *And love.* She gasped. "I must not fall in love with him," she said sternly.

Peter wagged his tail.

"I'm a fool, aren't I?" she asked the dog. She planned never to chance her heart again. Was it possible to love someone so much you forgave them anything? She frowned. Charles had not spoken of love. Even in the throes of passion, the declaration had not passed his lips.

She ran her hands through her tangled locks. If only she could overcome the distressing fact that he had not married her for love. Had she forgotten that during the evening, the woman he wanted, Drusilla, Marchioness of Thorburn, had been absent from the ballroom at the same time as he had?

Nellie sat up in bed and clasped her knees. She would not allow the marchioness to hurt her. She would not think of her now.

Lilly entered with her tray. "Good morning, Your Grace. I hope you and the duke had a lovely evening."

"It was very enjoyable, thank you, Lilly." Nellie took the cup of chocolate and sipped the flavorsome drink while her maid drew back the curtains.

"It is going to be a nice day."

"How do you plan to spend your afternoon, Lilly?"

The maid twisted her fingers in the folds of her apron. "I thought I'd walk in the park, Your Grace."

"An excellent idea, with so many celebrations in London, there's always something to see. But you mustn't go alone."

"One of the servants will go with me, Your Grace."

"Good." Nellie put down the sweet roll she'd taken a bite out of, her mind on her wardrobe. "I'll get up. I'm lunching with Lady Belfries this afternoon." She felt guilty that she had worried Marian. She would put her sister's mind at rest.

Lilly disappeared into the boudoir.

Nellie was in the act of donning her dressing gown when a downstairs maid entered. She bobbed. "Your Grace."

Dismayed, Nellie stared at the vase of red roses she carried. "Who sent those, Maude?"

"Mrs. Knox, the under-housekeeper, said there wasn't a card, Your Grace. I was told you asked for any roses to be brought up...."

"Yes, I did. Thank you. You may go."

Nellie threw off the covers. She walked the length of the carpet. On her way back, she narrowed her eyes at the hated roses in their crystal vase, while she fought the urge to take them to Charles's bedchamber and dump them, water and all, onto his bed. She turned away. The servants would only have to clean it up.

"Lilly?"

Her maid emerged from the dressing room with one of Nellie's hats in her hand. "I've sent for the hot water, Your Grace."

"Take the roses down to the housekeeper. They displease me. The color clashes with the walls."

Lilly looked mystified. "Yes, Your Grace."

Charles was absent from his study again. She was a little relieved. It was not her intention to fight with him, not with Marian's advice ringing in her ears. She resisted asking Barlow of his whereabouts and left the house. When she entered the hotel dining room, Marian waved from a table.

Nellie sat down.

"That is a very fetching bonnet," Marian observed. "I love the green ribbons and the dyed feathers. Which milliner made it?"

"This green isn't my color, so I shall gift it to you." Nellie eyed her sister as she pulled off her gloves. She told her about the roses.

Marian sighed and patted Nellie's hand. She picked up the menu. "We'd best order. The waiter is hovering."

Nellie peered at the list of dishes, but the words swam before her teary eyes. "So you think I'm overreacting?"

"I don't know. But if there is something between Charles and another woman, you are not one to run away like Eliza did. Talk to Charles, Nellie. Decide what it is you want from this marriage. Demand it of him. And if he doesn't agree, well, make your own life. Women do it quite successfully."

"But it sounds so hollow," she said, realizing it was precisely what she had intended her marriage to be. "Without love in their life."

"Some are. They raise their children or take up some cause or other."

Her literary salon had been her dream. It meant everything to her before she met Charles. But if a woman came between them, it would be the end for her. She would endure the marriage without the intimacy they had thus enjoyed. But without his humor, tenderness, and generosity, it seemed too bleak to endure. She gazed around the busy hotel dining room, fearing people would stare and gulped back a tear.

"YOU SHOULD MARRY, Angelique. Your boy needs a father." Charles sat on his former mistress's sofa, in her new apartment, her dashed parrot cursing at him from its cage. The bird seemed to remember his and Angelique's prior argument and took umbrage.

"I cannot marry Luis's father. You know he is married," she said with a toss of her head. "And I was quite happy with you."

"But we had an understanding. Our association was to end before I married," he said. "You are not without funds? Do you still receive an income from your family in France?"

"Oh, *oui*. And you have been most generous." She held up her wrist and admired the bright flash from the diamond bracelet. She came to perch on the arm of his chair. "You miss me, no? These English virgins, *pah*! She will not know how to please you."

"I am most pleased, I assure you." He removed her letter from his pocket unopened and tossed it down. "Any letters you send me will go unread into the wastepaper basket. Any flowers sent will be given to the poor to sell on the streets." He stood. "Understand this, Angelique. Our relationship is over. I wish you well, but this is an emphatic goodbye. And as for you," Charles said, turning to catch the beady black eyes of the parrot. "You'd best be careful, or one day someone will turn you into a pie."

A deafening squawk followed him down the stairs.

Charles headed straight for Jackson's Boxing Salon. He would vent his spleen on someone willing to take him on and hopefully return home in a calmer mood.

Later, when he entered his suite and stripped off his shirt, Feeley clucked his tongue. "That's a fine bruise you have on your chest, Your Grace. How is the other fella?"

Charles grinned. "Has a sore jaw, I imagine."

In the evening, when Charles passed through the sitting room, vases of delphiniums were the only floral arrangements on display. And when he knocked and entered Nellie's bedchamber, there was a pleasing lack of red roses.

In her wrapper, Nellie emerged from her boudoir to greet him, her hair a silky waterfall swinging almost to her waist. "How was your day?" She threaded her fingers through the hair at his nape and kissed him.

"Annoying. I missed you." Charles held her close, his hands sliding over her hips to bring her closer. "What did you do?"

"Marian and I lunched at Grillon's."

"How is your sister? Any more helpful advice?"

Nellie raised her eyebrows, a smile lifting her lips. "I'm sure I don't know what you mean."

"I have resisted thanking her on several occasions."

Nellie laughed. "Stop talking nonsense and go. Lilly is about to do my hair."

His hands moved up into her hair. "Why mess with perfection?" He lowered his head to her locks, breathing in the scent of lavender. His lips traced a path down her neck and made her shiver.

Nellie sighed and wriggled away. "Don't distract me, Charles."

He looked amused. "Was I?"

She shook her head at him with a wry smile. "I must dress. We are to dine with Mr. Constable, are we not? He might have a new painting to display."

"If he does, it will be magnificent. You wish me to buy it?" Charles pulled his pocket watch from his waistcoat. "We dine at eight o'clock. And it is almost seven," he said pointedly.

Nellie gave him a push. "Then go!"

She undid the ribbons on her wrapper, distracting him with a view of her luscious creamy breasts rising above her corset. Was there time for even a quick moment or two…he hovered considering it, then the urgent correspondence he had to deal with for the mail tomorrow entered his head. Better to do it now rather than later.

"I'll be in my study." He pressed his lips onto the soft, perfumed skin of her shoulder, then reluctantly left her.

Had something occurred at this luncheon? There was a playfulness, a lightness of spirit about Nellie tonight that was utterly captivating. *Deuce it*, he didn't want to go to dinner. There were too many distractions in London. The sooner he took her away to Shewsbury Park, the better.

Chapter Eighteen

After she returned from breakfast, Nellie sorted through the pile of beads, silk flowers, feathers, bits of net to trim hats, and gloves in her dressing room. She planned to send a note around to invite her mother to shop with her this morning. She wanted to purchase a toy for Marian and Gerald's son, Frederick, who was turning three. And she needed a new pair of riding gloves. Charles had suggested riding in the park later in the afternoon.

As she settled her hat in place before the mirror, Lilly entered, carrying a package. "This just arrived for you, Your Grace."

There was no name on the brown-paper package. Curious as to who sent it, Nellie placed it on her desk and cut the string with her scissors. Inside was a folded square of exquisitely hemmed linen and a note with the ducal monogram. It belonged to Charles. Nellie's chest squeezed, and she reached for the note.

Your Grace, please return the duke's handkerchief to him with my heartfelt thanks. He was such a comfort. Yours sincerely, Lady Drusilla, Marchioness of Thorburn.

She could smell the woman's perfume, and it almost choked her. The words on the page seemed to blur before Nellie's eyes.

She dragged in a breath.

"Listen to what Charles has to say," Marian had instructed her.

"Don't leap to conclusions."

But this was too much! Nellie clenched her fists and stalked the carpet. Arabella Forrester had fawned over Charles at dinner last evening, while Nellie attempted to remind herself that harmless flirting went on amongst the *ton*. But she was tired. The constant upset was a weight on her chest that pulled her down.

Snatching up the handkerchief, she descended the stairs to Charles's study. A footman in the corridor hastily stepped forward to open the door for her.

She unceremoniously entered.

Alone, seated at his desk, Charles looked at her in surprise. "What is it, Nellie?"

She crossed the carpet into his orderly world. He had said something only yesterday about the untidy state of her desk, an innocuous comment, but for some obscure reason, outrage now bubbled up inside her like a torrent. "This!" She tossed the handkerchief down onto the leather desktop.

Charles eyed her, then picked it up. "It's my handkerchief, so?"

"It was sent to me. Here is the letter." She thrust it at him.

He pushed back his chair and took the note from her, scanned it, then tossed it aside. "I lent my handkerchief to the marchioness at the ball. Is that an offense? What are you accusing me of, Nellie?"

Did he look a little discomforted? "You left the ballroom to meet her. I saw you!"

He sighed. "Drusilla asked to speak to me on an urgent matter. I thought she was in trouble. She was upset, and I offered her my handkerchief. As there was nothing I could do to assist her, I left." He frowned. "Is it necessary for me to account for everything I do?"

Nellie snorted. "I am tired of these mistresses of yours. You should keep better control over them."

He eyed her coolly. "And just what mistresses would they be?"

She hated that he sounded so cold. He seemed like a stranger. Did she know him at all? She curled her hands at her sides. "I won't be treated like a fool."

"I don't believe I do."

"Arabella Forrester flirted shamelessly with you at dinner last night."

He threw up his hands and gazed at her with disbelief. "And did I flirt back?"

Nelly feared she was losing the argument. "You laughed at something she said."

"So laughing is no longer acceptable?" He smiled and rested a hip against the desk. "I can see you're angry. I'm sorry this note has upset you, Nellie, but you are making a fuss over nothing."

"*Nothing!*" she said through her teeth. Now she'd begun, she couldn't hold back. The blood began to pound in her temples. "What about your French mistress, Mademoiselle Girard? She approached me in Bond Street."

"What!" He slipped off the desk. "She spoke to you?"

Nellie nodded. "She said I could not hold on to you. A small dark-haired boy was with her. He has blue eyes. Is he your son, Charles?"

He scowled. "No, he isn't."

"I thought that he might be after she threw a red rose at your feet at the cathedral right after our wedding. And then the bunches of red roses have arrived every morning."

Charles muttered under his breath. He turned, and with a sweep of his arm, sent everything on his desk flying: inkwell, pens, ledgers, a stack of files. Ink spilled over the carpet, the pounce pot spilled its contents, and the quills rolled about on the floor.

Shocked, Nellie stood stock still. She trembled. The controlled, calm man she had married made no attempt to pick them up again. He leaned forward and placed his palms flat on his desktop, not looking at her. "He is not my son," he said in a cold voice. "And my association with Mademoiselle Girard ended months before I married you."

"I saw the article in the gossip column of a newspaper."

Charles straightened and faced her. "What article? It mentioned my name?"

"Of course the journalist didn't mention your name. But it could only have been you. He described how he witnessed you leaving a burning building with the Frenchwoman in your arms."

"This is not something I wish to discuss with my wife." He frowned. "I see I shall have to, however. I visited the lady to end our association long before we met. Mademoiselle threw a lantern at me. Started a fire." He sighed. "The child isn't mine, Nellie. I can't give you proof. You'll have to take me at my word."

"Perhaps you ask too much." Nellie swiveled and left the room.

She heard him call her name as she ran down the corridor to the staircase. *The rake! Two women!* Might there be a third? Too many for him to claim to be innocent. Take him at his word? *Ha!* Surely, he didn't expect her to believe him? Relieved to find the hall empty, she sniffed and gripped the banister. Her heart beat unsteadily, tears spilling down her cheeks, and she stumbled upstairs with the hope no servant would make an appearance.

She didn't want Charles to see how much he could affect her. But she needn't have worried, for he made no attempt to come after her. She supposed he didn't care enough. In her bedchamber, she took out a handkerchief and blew her nose.

Thank God Marian was in London. Nellie needed her calm, wise sister. Snatching up her reticule and bonnet, she flew down the stairs. Grove raised his eyebrows but said nothing when she called for her pelisse. He assisted her into it and opened the door for her to exit the house. She half ran to the corner in search of a hackney.

Farther down the square, she found a carriage had just deposited a neighbor onto the footpath. Nellie gave him Marian's address and climbed inside. Her shoulders heaving, she dragged a handkerchief out of her reticule and dried her tears, then made a hasty effort to tidy herself.

"Nellie. What on earth has happened? Come upstairs." Marian ordered a footman to bring wine and took Nellie to her sitting room, where she made her sit on the sofa.

"I've just come from Charles," Nellie gasped, dabbing her eyes.

Nellie accepted a glass of Madeira, which was quickly brought. She drank down half a glass. The wine calmed her a little as she described Drusilla's note.

"That conniving woman!" Marian exclaimed. "She wishes to cause trouble. Are you going to let her?"

"I can't help it, Marian." Nellie hiccoughed. She'd drunk the wine too fast. "Am I supposed to ignore it?"

"No, but Charles could be innocent. Powerful, attractive men like him are besieged by women."

"I know that." Nellie waved her hand as if to dismiss Charles's obvious attractions and drank more of the Madeira. "I told him how his French mistress accosted me in Bond Street." She finished the glass and coughed.

Marian removed the decanter and returned it to the tray on the bureau. She pulled the bell cord. "We need coffee."

She came back to sit on the sofa beside Nellie and took her hand. "What had Charles to say in his defense?"

"He denies the child is his. He was furious, Marian. I've never expected him to be like that, although there was that article, you know, the one about him attacking the reporter. He has always been so composed. Except when..." Nellie blew out a breath. "Well, he is a very good lover. I suppose that's why these women keep after him." She rubbed her eyes. "I refuse to share him! I would rather not have him in my life."

"Oh, dearest. How very upsetting." Marian put her arm around her.

"You should have seen it! Charles swept everything off his desk.

Papers and pens scattered over the floor, everywhere. Ink spilled on the carpet. And he made no attempt to clean it up!"

"Mm. Not like Charles, is it?"

"Of course, he flatly denied meeting Drusilla with the intention of pursuing an affair. He said she asked to see him on some urgent matter, but he left soon afterward." She put her hands to her head, which was fuzzy. "I saw him leave the ballroom, casual as you please. And then return sometime later. Drusilla came directly after him. Brazen woman didn't even attempt to hide it."

"How long were they away?"

"I don't know, I was dancing with Walsh. It couldn't have been much more than ten minutes."

"Hardly long enough for a tête-à-tête. Perhaps he is telling the truth."

Nellie shrugged. "But time enough to arrange one." She sighed. "I knew this would happen. Drusilla was his first choice. He didn't want to marry me, Marian. He has never told me he loves me. I suppose he never will." She covered her eyes with her hands. "Trouble is, I admired him. I liked him, Marian."

Marian sighed. "Dearest. You love him."

Nellie shook her head. "No, I don't. I can't. He has a horrible temper. Who would have believed it?" Nellie nodded sagely. "Well, I witnessed it today."

"Did he frighten you?"

"His anger wasn't directed at me. I know Charles would never hurt a woman. That he would attack a helpless journalist is inexplicable."

"What did Papa say about that?"

"He didn't believe it. Said there was another side to the story."

"Well, maybe there was. Don't give up on him, dearest. Married couples have these quarrels. Making up is half the fun."

Nellie scowled. "Two, and possibly three women in as many

weeks? It is intolerable."

The footman entered with the tray. Marian gestured to the small table. "Put it down, William, and leave us."

"This will help." She filled Nellie's cup with the hot brew from the coffee pot. "You must think about what next to do."

"I've already decided." Nellie straightened her shoulders. "I shall become very busy. I'll set up my literary salon and invite Walsh to participate."

"The salon is an excellent idea, but I'm not sure about the Irishman." Marian eyed her anxiously. "Charles might not like it."

"Well, of course, he won't, *stupid!*" Nellie said with an affectionate smile.

Marian nodded in approval. "I knew you wouldn't stay down in the doldrums for long."

CHARLES WAS LEFT with the image of Nellie, her chest rising and falling with rapid, harsh breaths. With intense disgust, he studied the mess on his study floor his temper had created and cursed. He'd acted like a bad-tempered oaf. And he prided himself on being a rational man not given to acts of violence.

He might have been a young fool at university and behaved in a manner he'd rather forget when he'd beaten up a bully who was all mouth and little muscle, while the men cheered him on. And again when he'd given Fairbrother's son a good shake. Unforgiveable losses of self-control. And now he'd lost it in front of Nellie, the most unpardonable of sins.

He should have taken her in his arms and reassured her, insisted that what she feared wasn't true. But he'd been shocked to the core by the distrust and accusation in her eyes. The lack of affection. As if she just didn't know him. It crippled him, stopped him from reaching out to her. He heard her flee along the corridor, then her feet on the stairs, but struggled to compose himself. What could he say in his defense when she was clearly determined not to believe him?

The deuce! All he wanted was a peaceful life. Might that be impossible? Would Nellie now go off half-cocked every time he looked at another woman? Angelique's behavior was, and he hoped he'd impressed on her that it must stop. He'd grown to depend on Nellie's affection. He had no wish to take another mistress. He and Nellie must work out their differences, for he did not intend to live like a monk.

But she'd eyed him as if he was the worst kind of rake. *Damn Drusilla!* That note had been nothing short of combustible. As she had intended. A woman spurned? Might he have handled it more tactfully? He seemed to be failing on all counts.

Charles straightened his study. He refused to leave the mess to Barlow. On his knees, he ordered the sheets of paper, then dabbed ineffectually at the rug with the despised handkerchief. Then tossed it into the bin. His housekeeper would take care of the carpet stain. While he worked, he questioned why Nellie had not trusted him enough to come to him when all this began. He'd sensed an element of distrust in him almost from the moment they met, in fact. Unfathomable. And then he thought of the article she'd mentioned describing that business with Angelique. When had Nellie first seen it? Was it before they met?

He groaned as he regained his chair and clasped his head in his hands. He and Nellie had been together such a short time. He'd been content with his marriage, admiring Nellie, falling under her spell. Delighting in the passion they shared. How could he ever get that back? Convince her that he wasn't guilty of adultery? He racked his brain for ways to put his case to her.

Finally calmer, he went upstairs with the hope she might at least listen to him.

"The duchess isn't here, Your Grace," Lilly told him when he entered her bedchamber.

As he made his way to his suite, his gaze settled on the mantel clock. They were to ride this afternoon. That was out. Nellie would be with Marian. It was a wonder his ears weren't burning. No sense going there. But Marian was a wise soul. He could only hope she would present an alternate view, and not damn him to hell. Maybe she should for his blinkered short-sightedness. He had seen Angelique toss that rose at his feet outside the cathedral and chose to ignore it. He should have gone straight to her. Had it out with her. But he didn't want to think of her while his head was filled with Nellie.

He entered his suite, where his valet brushed his riding coat. He sighed deeply. "I shan't ride this afternoon, Feeley. My plans appear to have changed."

"Right ye are, Your Grace." Feeley put down the brush with that familiar expression, the one which matched his opinion of all women—more trouble than a barrel full of monkeys but worth every bit of it. It usually annoyed Charles, who thought the Irishman brought trouble on himself, but he didn't have the energy to reprove him, not when he found himself in agreement.

"I'll visit Jackson's. I will return in two hours and require a bath."

Leaving Feeley surprisingly silent, Charles, a tick in his jaw, stalked out of the house.

Chapter Nineteen

Nellie stayed some hours with Marian before she summoned the courage to go home. She finally entered the house with a fluttery feeling in her chest. "Is His Grace at home, Grove?"

"He returned an hour ago, Your Grace."

Where had Charles been? Visiting his rose-loving mistress, or was it Drusilla? Nellie climbed the stairs slowly, trying to think what best to say to him. Marian cautioned her to be calm and reasonable, but she feared it was beyond her capabilities.

In her bedchamber, as she removed her bonnet and tidied her hair, Charles knocked and entered. She glanced at him with what she hoped was a cool expression. "I have been visiting Marian, in case you wondered."

"I guessed as much." He leaned against the bedpost, his legs crossed in a casual pose, which didn't fool her. There was a troubling light in his eyes, the atmosphere in the room laden with tension. Her pulse beating fast, she put down her hairbrush.

He straightened and moved away from the bed.

She was relieved. Charles and beds brought too many memories to mind. And she would never win an argument there. *The closeness and tenderness they had shared, could it be that way again?*

"I don't expect there's much I can say to alter your low opinion of me, Nellie," he said in a low voice. "You are determined to think the worst."

Nellie longed for him to come and put his arms around her, but he kept his distance. She put a hand to her aching head and bit her lip. "The mistress, I might have been able to understand, Charles, if you swore she *was* in your past. But the marchioness, too? Or was Arabella Forrester about to be added to the list?"

He folded his arms with a frown. "That's not worthy of an answer."

Her throat was horribly tight. "Isn't it? Then let's not discuss it. It will get us nowhere."

"I see that." He bowed his head. "If you'll excuse me, madame, I will be tied up until dinner." He opened the door and strode out, shutting it quietly behind him.

Madame? He had never referred to her in that manner. Nellie gulped. Trembling, she sank onto the bed. Her world seemed to have fallen apart. She huffed out a gasp of annoyance. And really, why should she feel guilty?

After several minutes, she stood, and after dredging up a renewed sense of purpose from somewhere deep inside, she rang for Lilly.

"I'll wear the red satin to the opera ball tonight, Lilly."

It was not done to be seen in the same gown again so soon, but she needed that dress to give her courage and the confidence to get through the evening. She would add a silver lace shawl and lace gloves and wear the rubies.

She and Charles were unfailingly polite at dinner. They barely talked, and when they did, it was with excruciating politeness on inconsequential matters: the excellence of the roast beef and the freshness of the oysters, plus a newsworthy item in *The Times*. Nellie felt sick and didn't want to eat. She pushed her food around the plate and tried not to look at Charles, the tension strung as tight as a fiddler's bow.

In their box at Covent Garden, their cool treatment of each other went unnoticed as friends and acquaintances crowded in at intervals to talk to them. To Nellie's disappointment, the opera was rather dull as the aria sung by the stout, but handsome Elizabeth Billington was not quite as good a performance as usual, and she was almost drowned out by the noisy patrons.

At the following opera ball, she and Charles parted at the door, seeking their own group of acquaintances. As this was the usual way of things, most saw nothing unusual in it, although Nellie did overhear a comment from an aged dowager she passed. The woman spoke loudly behind her fan to a lady beside her. "The honeymoon is over."

"Of short duration, wasn't it?" her companion replied, not quite managing to hide a smirk.

When a waltz was called, Nellie accepted Walsh's invitation with the intention of pursuing her plan. She only hoped he had more sense than to dredge up the past or try to flirt with her.

Walsh did not dance as well as Charles. But what man did? She hid the contempt she had for the Irishman. She could only be relieved and thankful her father had been far wiser than she was at eighteen. Was Marian right? Had the poet been hopeful of the marriage merely to better himself? If he had been tempted to use her to raise himself up in the world, she felt justified in putting him to good use now.

They paused after a series of steps. "I am to hold my first literary salon next week," she said, offering him a sweet smile, more for the benefit of Charles, whom she suspected was watching them, than Walsh.

"Am I to be invited?" Walsh's eyes brightened. "I thought perhaps because of our, shall we say, unfortunate past, I thought perhaps—"

"Nonsense. We shall not speak of it again. I should like you to be our first poet. Would you entertain us with a reading of your latest poem, Mr. Walsh?"

"Delighted, Your Grace. I have two that might suit. Perhaps the…"

Nellie suffered a stab of remorse as he elaborated at length about his poetry. This was not like her. She detested conniving and underhanded behavior. But it was not enough to change her mind. She offered him another warm smile. "That will be perfect. The salon is to be held on Wednesday in the music room at Shewsbury Court."

While Walsh enthused in his lilting Irish tenor voice, which lent an air to his poems, Nellie searched for Charles. She found him with Jason. As they talked, Charles watched her with a stony expression. Her pulse thudded, and she turned another brilliant smile on the poet.

"I have sorely missed our exhilarating discussions, Your Grace." Walsh's hand tightened around hers. She should rebuke him but secretly hoped Charles would be jealous. After all, what was good for the gander…

"I hope to fill the room with devotees of the literary arts, Mr. Walsh," she said, wishing the dance would end. "And entice Wordsworth to come. And hopefully, Byron."

He smiled thinly. "How agreeable."

>>><<<

JASON FROWNED. "Is something wrong, Charles? You look like you've lost a shilling and found a sixpence."

Charles drew his gaze away from Nellie. "I grow tired of these celebratory affairs."

"Don't we all? I shall be glad to leave London tomorrow."

"You are to return to Dorset?"

"We go first to Shewsbury Park." Jason smiled. "Beverly is with child."

"I say!" Charles slapped his brother on the back. "That is excellent news. I trust Beverly is in good health. She didn't wish to come tonight?"

"No, she was a little tired from preparing for our departure."

"Mother will be pleased to see you both."

"We'll spend a month or so with her before returning home. Shall we see you there?"

"Matters in the House and royal demands keep me in the city," Charles said. "I've been too long away from the estate. I dislike depending on staff. Without overseeing the work they do, things can go amiss. I'm keen to see my additions to the flock, and the bailiff has a thorny matter to deal with."

Jason smiled wryly. "You worry too much, Chas."

The Prince of Wales beckoned to Charles from where he sat with his lackeys and fawning acolytes among the visiting dignitaries.

"I must go. Have a safe journey, Jas. I hope we will see you at Shewsbury Park very soon."

"And I, my poor fellow," Jason said. "I will tell Nellie the news before I leave." He cocked an eyebrow. "You two seem to be avoiding each other."

"Not at all. Such is the way of these affairs," Charles said casually. Jason was too astute; it was just as well that he was leaving London.

The waltz ended, and as Charles crossed the floor to the prince, Nellie promenaded from the dance floor on Walsh's arm. Her throaty laugh at some aside from the Irishman reached Charles's ears as if he was especially attuned to her voice. He clamped his jaw, doubting the poet deserved such a response.

The Irish were born with a heavy sense of tragedy, which in Walsh's case, infused his poetry with gloom. Charles had taken the time only recently to glance through Walsh's latest published work. His poems lacked the passion of Byron or the intellect of Wordsworth, or the heartfelt tug of emotion Keats inspired. He was damned if he knew what Nellie saw in the fellow.

Nellie was often in the Irishman's company. Might she care for him? Could they have been in love once, and her father sent him packing? Charles scowled. He disliked the direction of his thoughts. He gazed their way again. Nellie did look wonderful tonight. He approved of that crimson gown. It was cleverly designed, one could not criticize it for being indecorous, yet he found it quite sensual the way the material moved and clung to Nellie's curves beneath the sheer silvery overdress. He glanced around the ballroom. Several ladies wore a similar design tonight, and red was popular among the married ladies. Pride in her warmed him, but despair quickly followed. How he missed her smiles, her affection, her sense of humor, and especially their lovemaking.

How long would they continue to behave like strangers? Would she listen to reason? After all, Angelique had finally accepted their affair was at an end, and Drusilla, although present tonight, had not even smiled at him, he noted with relief.

CHAPTER TWENTY

WHEN JASON RELATED their news to Nellie, she felt so happy for them. She would write to Beverly at Shewsbury Park. It also made her a little sad, for the chance for her and Charles to have a baby seemed to diminish every day unless things could change between them. If she couldn't find a way to mend the hurt between them, would she send him into another woman's arms? But how could she when he seemed so distant and unfriendly?

On the carriage ride home, Charles sat opposite her. His gaze rested on her, his brows drawn together in a frown. "Your flirting with that undistinguished poet must be viewed by the *ton* with some considerable mirth."

His harsh criticism made her gasp, and she opened her mouth to rebuke him. But then she recognized a note of jealousy in his bitter tone and smiled to herself. A spark of hope for their future together warmed her. Where there was jealousy, there was caring and need. She glanced down at her hands so that he might not see the smile in her eyes. "I don't intend to quarrel with you over Walsh. He has no claim on my heart."

"Oh?" Charles's voice sounded indifferent, but she wasn't fooled by it. "I applaud you. Better to pick on one of the better poets."

"I shall keep that in mind. Who would you recommend? Not poor Keats? He is not robust. Byron, perhaps?"

"He would be willing."

"Perhaps he might be. But I am not attracted to poetical gentlemen in that manner, Charles. You must know that, for I married you, remember?"

Charles chuckled. *"Touché,* Nellie." Charles's smile faded. "Beverly is enceinte. Did Jason tell you?"

"Yes, and I couldn't be more pleased for them. Your mother will be thrilled."

Nellie glanced up at him, but in the dim light of the carriage lamps, couldn't read anything into his expression. She thought again of the little boy she'd seen in Bond Street with his mistress. That he might have a son no longer seemed to have the power to hurt her. If he was Charles's son, did Charles love him? And support him? She suspected Charles guessed what she was thinking, for he fell silent.

When they reached home, Nellie said goodnight and retired alone.

It was several days before Beverly's reply to her letter came. She wrote that she was in good health, but Jason fussed over her too much. The dowager duchess, however, was ill, and a physician had been called up from London.

"My former governess, Mrs. Perlew, has written to me," Beverly added. *"She wishes an introduction to you. Mrs. Perlew is in the process of setting up a home for orphaned children in London and hopes you might agree to be their patroness. I said I would recommend her to you as she is a determined woman committed to her cause. I have included her address here, should the orphanage appeal."*

But of course she would. Nellie set about replying immediately. She would invite Mrs. Perlew to come and see her.

Nellie asked Charles about his mother that evening when they dined alone before attending the theatre to see the famous actor, Edmund Kean, perform in *Richard III.*

He pushed his plate away and rubbed a hand over his jaw, his blue eyes darkening, making Nellie regret she'd raised the subject. "I am worried about her," he said heavily. "Jas will keep me up to date."

She reached out and touched his hand. "We must go soon to see her."

Charles nodded abstractly. She was aware of the long hours he spent at the beck and call of the government since the war had ended.

"You look tired, Charles," she said with a throb of concern for him in her heart.

"I am a little tired of London, I must say. It was expected that the end of the war would bring good fortune, but we are facing an economic slump and much unrest. The agriculturalists with Fairbrother's backing have secured a new Corn Law."

"What does that mean?"

"It places a heavy duty on foreign wheat. Its intention is to aid the English farmer by keeping out cheap foreign grain."

"Isn't that a good thing?" she asked.

"Taxing imported grain will keep up grain prices and rents and raise, rather than lower, the cost of bread."

"So more hardship for the people."

He nodded, and she was gratified to find respect for her in his eyes.

"You are a good man, Charles,' she couldn't help saying.

He smiled. "An imperfect man, perhaps, Nellie."

"No." She shook her head as she put down her napkin and rose from the table. "But some of us are a little less than perfect, I grant you."

He rose from his seat and approached her. She waited, hoping he would enfold her in his arms, but he merely raised her hand and pressed a kiss to it. "I must change for the theatre." He bowed his head and left her.

Nellie bit her lip as she hurried to her bedchamber to change. Had irrevocable damage been done to their marriage? Would he ever allow her to get close to him? To love him?

THE FOLLOWING TUESDAY, Mrs. Perlew, a stiffly upright woman with a strong chin, dressed severely in brown, came to see Nellie. Her face gentled when she spoke of the children and her orphanage. She and Mr. Perlew had not been blessed, but there was a son from her husband's previous marriage.

Nellie was quickly caught up in the lady's plans, for her enthusiasm was infectious. And the cause a heartwarming one. "I shall visit tomorrow," Nellie told her. She was seized with the desire to make a difference. To help the poor and make Charles proud of her. She had always wanted to have this opportunity and seemed to have lost sight of those dreams of late.

The next afternoon, Nellie came home from visiting the orphanage sobered by the experience. The waifs were so vulnerable. She would do what she could to ensure that they received good food and warm clothing and began to consider what else she might do to assist Mrs. Perlew in her endeavors.

She told Charles about it that night at dinner. It certainly made a change from their dry discussions of the daily news.

He nodded, and the usually cool expression in his eyes faded. "Well done, Nellie. That is a good cause, indeed."

"So many poor children without a parent to care for them. Some are fatherless, and the mothers cannot keep them and must give them up." Sipping her wine, the blue-eyed boy she'd seen on Bond Street came to mind. She wanted to talk to Charles about him but feared his reaction. She sighed and remained silent.

Nothing more was said, and the evening continued with the usual civility at the Montford's soiree. Nellie felt terribly tired when they reached home.

Charles said goodnight and retired to his bedchamber.

She settled into her cold bed and curled up in a tight ball. Charles didn't seem to want her anymore. She could have handled things better. Listened to her mother's advice and remained silent, but that wasn't her. She had to be true to herself.

Nellie received dozens of letters requesting attendance at her salon. It was more successful than she'd dreamed and proved a wonderful distraction. Three salons had been held in the music room and were always well attended. The affair had become fashionable and was talked about at dinners and parties. Nellie was questioned at balls as to who would grace her salon next.

Another week passed as she sat at her desk, opening her mail with Peter lying at her feet. Somehow the salons had not thrilled her quite as much as she'd anticipated. With Marian enceinte again and gone to the Belfries estate in Kent, Nellie filled the lonely hours corresponding with poets and writers.

She considered Byron, who consented to read his latest poem, her crowning achievement. Nellie was as eager to hear him as the rest.

A knock at the door drew her to her feet, in hope that it might be Charles. He would never knock on her sitting room door. He would stride right in with that air of authority she grudgingly admired.

The footman bowed. "His Grace requests your presence in his study, Your Grace."

"I have a few matters to deal with first, James. Tell him I shall come in a moment."

James cleared his throat. "The duke said he wishes you to come immediately, Your Grace."

Nellie felt a stab of anxiety. She put down her quill, "Very well. Thank you, James." She'd been replying to the Countess of Avonley, a woman involved in the arts, who wrote that she had heard excellent things about her literary salon and wished to attend.

Descending the stairs, Nellie wondered why Charles should wish to speak to her so urgently.

When she entered his study, he glanced up at her. "Nellie."

Picking up a journal from his desk, he pushed back his chair and stood.

Recognizing the publication, her heart sank.

"A friend of mine at Whites has given me this fascinating article to read. A diatribe against foxhunting, written by someone called Clarence Downs."

Her mind raced. "Oh? Did you find it interesting?"

"Don't toy with me, Nellie."

"I'm not I…" She desperately sought the right words to explain. There had never been a good time to raise it with him.

He crossed his arms. "You wrote it. Are you going to deny it?"

"No." She wondered how he knew it was she. "Charles, I intended to tell you…"

"When the time was right?" His brows snapped together. "And when might that have been? It would have been prudent, one might think, to do so before several of my associates and friends at my club registered my surprise and found my ignorance amusing."

"They can't have known I wrote it, Charles. Not under a male pseudonym."

His angry blue eyes searched hers. "Alexander Pendle happens to be a friend of your favorite poet, Kealan Walsh. At Brook's club, the Irishman was in his cups and bragged that you and he wrote it together."

"Oh! The wretch!" Nellie cried, outraged at Walsh's treachery. "Yes, it's true," she said miserably. "We did write it, Charles."

He nodded. "I forbid you to see him again. You might be tempted to write another. I can just see you two putting your heads together."

"I have no intention of seeing him again." She hated that she had embarrassed Charles. Naturally, she would cut off her association with Walsh. But Charles's emphatic order infuriated her. "Can you not trust me to make my own decisions? I dislike being told what I can and cannot do as if I can't think for myself."

"A lack of thought went into writing this outrageous piece. You would have offended many great families. But fortunately, none would be likely to read this publication." He tossed down the journal. "Is it an unreasonable request? Or do you and Walsh plan more?" He pushed back from the desk to stand in front of her.

Was he jealous? She had tried to make him so, but to have succeeded and distressed him brought her no joy. "After he has betrayed me? Of course not." She searched his eyes, finding hurt and anger there. "You should trust me to do what is right."

"You've given me little reason to trust you," he said slowly, as if the suggestion was absurd.

Her heart constricted. "I don't believe it is outrageous. I thought Walsh and I made a good argument against the sport. As you can see by the date, it was written before you and I met. I certainly would not have written it afterward." She sighed. "I hate to think I've embarrassed you."

He waved a dismissive hand. "You and Walsh were often together, then? Just how close were you?"

"You have no reason to be jealous of Walsh."

"Jealous? The Irishman doesn't warrant thinking about. I should hope you had better taste."

He stepped close enough for her to breathe deep of his skin, his soap, and the starch of his cravat. Something sparked in his eyes. Her untrustworthy body responded with heat and a rush of warmth.

"I forbid it, Nellie," he said, his eyes dark with emotion.

"You forbid it?" Charles's overbearing manner threatened to strip her of her fragile confidence, and the small amount of independence she could claim for herself in this marriage.

They were both breathing heavily. The charged atmosphere in the quiet room deepened. His gaze roamed her face, settling on her mouth. She should step away, but her knees trembled, and she moistened her lips. She was such a weak fool, one look from him could bring her undone.

"*Nellie.*" He reached out and brushed his fingers over her cheek, and her lips parted. She finally found her resolve from somewhere deep inside and stepped away from him until her bottom rested against the desk. He intended to seduce her. And heaven help her, she wanted him to.

"Be reasonable," he said, following her, his voice husky.

"*Reasonable?*" It was like a dash of cold water. Be sensible, be a good girl, Nellie. Never complain. Never do anything to ruffle anyone's feathers. She wanted to scream at him. Instead, she firmed her trembling lips.

Charles's heated gaze drifted over her body.

They both were startled by the knock on the door.

"Come," Charles called with a muffled curse and turned away from her.

Barlow entered the room and smiled at Nellie. "Good morning, Your Grace." He turned to Charles. "Mr. Chance is here for his appointment, Your Grace."

"Ask him to wait," Charles said through his teeth.

Her heart thudding, Nellie fought to gain control of herself. "No, please don't let me keep you." She nodded to Barlow and walked out the door.

Nellie mounted the stairs so fast she was breathless when she reached the landing. Another minute, and Charles would have made love to her right there on his desk. And while she'd longed for him, it would have solved nothing, because it arose from anger and disappointment and betrayal. He was confident he could, and she feared she would have succumbed, which only made her madder. She would have lost too much when he persuaded her to give up any notion of independence.

When she reached her sitting room, Nellie cooled down a little. She had no intention of writing anymore articles on foxhunting. If she wanted some measure of independence, she must choose her subjects wisely. She had vented her spleen and made no impact on the foxhunting world whatsoever. It wasn't written to spite him or anyone else who took part in the sport. Merely to point out the cruelty of it. But right now, she seethed with anger at Walsh's treachery. He had taken umbrage when she grew tired of him behaving in an overly familiar manner and had not offered him another invitation to the salon.

Nellie sat down at her desk, selected a piece of bond, and took up her pen. She would couch her letter to Walsh in terms which made him understand he would not be welcome to any further literary discussions in the future and was not to approach her again.

Charles made no further attempt to see her until the evening. They dined out with friends and might have been casual acquaintances when alone in the carriage. He was a proud man, and she had hurt him. That the gulf had widened between them tore at her heart. Feeling helpless, she wished she knew what best to do about it.

The following week, Byron visited her salon, drawing a huge crowd to the music room. Extra chairs had to been brought in to fill every space. In a black suit, his white cravat carelessly tied, his hair tousled, Byron stood by the fireplace, a graceful hand on the mantel, and, as a collective sigh rose from the women guests, he began to recite his recent and already famous poem in his attractive voice.

> *She walks in beauty, like the night*
> *Of cloudless climes and starry skies*
> *And all that's best of dark and bright*
> *Meet in her aspect and her eyes;*
> *Thus mellowed to that tender light*
> *Which heaven to gaudy day denies.*

It was a moving and beautiful poem. Nellie glanced around. But for the occasional gasp or sigh, one might hear a pin drop.

Much to the ladies' disappointment, he did not linger long afterward. He greeted each lady in turn, then departed, leaving breathless conversations in his wake.

The poet was handsome in a dark, broodingly sensual fashion, Nellie had to admit. His lyrical poem was written in praise of a lovely woman's inner beauty. His cousin, Mrs. Wilmot, inspired it, it was said, when she wore a black mourning gown decorated with glittering sequins.

After it was over, Nellie returned to her apartment. She felt decidedly flat, as if she'd reached the apex of her achievements, and really had little to show for it. While she was constantly written about in the newspapers—the Duchess said this, the Duchess wore that, it did little to warm her. She had failed in her marriage.

While nothing more was said about the journal, she and Charles still had not shared a bed since that dreadful day Drusilla sent his handkerchief. He was either busy in his study or absent from the house during the day. She realized his presence was called upon by many, but the knowledge didn't help to make her feel any less lonely. Was this to be the way of things? She feared it was.

Might he and the Frenchwoman have continued their relationship? It seemed unlikely as he was here in his study often and in her company at night. Nellie tried to convince herself she didn't care and pushed away the throb of pain in the region of her heart. She'd heard gossip about Drusilla and a certain earl, and Arabella Forrester had become engaged to Viscount Blathely.

Her next guest was John Clare, whose rural poetry had made him a celebrity in London. He read two of his poems and was politely dismissive of the applause afterward. When the modest gentleman had departed, Nellie discussed his poetry with Caroline Faulds.

"His poem, *First Love*, is my favorite," Caroline said. "First love can be wonderful, but painful. A study of a loss of innocence."

Nellie wondered whether Caroline had experienced such emotion, as it sounded so heartfelt when the door opened, and Charles walked in.

There was a rattle of teacups. The women rose and dropped into curtsies.

"It seems I have missed the poetry," Charles said, offering them a smile and a bow.

Nellie thought he'd timed it perfectly. Charles had little time for poetry. She poured him a cup of tea, which he took standing, while the ladies crowded around him.

"Are you a devotee of the arts, Your Grace?" Mrs. Milson asked him, twin spots of color on her cheeks. "Who is your favorite poet?"

Nellie sighed as frustration battled with admiration. Charles managed to slay hearts wherever he went.

"Byron," Charles declared. "I was sorry to miss his reading."

Her guests murmured assent and employed their fans.

"Very good, but not quite up to *Childe Harold's Pilgrimage*," Caroline said stoutly.

"Oh, no. *When We Two Parted*," another woman said. "So romantic."

A fierce discussion ensured.

Charles placed his cup and saucer down on the table. "If you'll excuse Her Grace for a moment, ladies, I must speak to her."

In the corridor, Nellie smiled at him. "I doubt you have read even one of Byron's poems." She had seen his reading material, farm periodicals, sporting journals, and much-thumbed classics.

A brief glimmer of a smile crossed his face. "One really can't avoid it. Byron's poetry and his manner of living are on everyone's lips these days."

His expression appeared so grave, she was startled into placing a hand on his sleeve. "Why, what is it, Charles?"

His large hand covered hers and squeezed it, surprising her. "Jason has written to say that he and Beverly have delayed their return to Dorset. Mother's health has worsened, and he feels we should come soon to see her." His eyes, shadowed with worry, might have undone her, and caused her to wrap her arms around him, had she not been aware of the ladies in the music room gathering up their things, ready to depart. "You shall have to forgo your literary salons for a while," he said.

"Oh, but what of that! Of course we must go. I shall have Lilly pack. When do you wish to leave?"

"Tomorrow. Thank you, Nellie. I shan't keep you from your guests."

"As if that matters," she said, but he was already striding away.

Nellie tactfully brought the affair to a close. When the last of the guests left, she hurried to her bedchamber.

It had been Lilly's afternoon off. The maid came in some minutes later. "The butler told me you rang for me, Your Grace," she said with a bob. "I'm most dreadfully sorry. I didn't expect you'd need me 'til this evening."

Nellie explained about their departure in the morning as two footmen carried in the trunk. "Did you have a pleasant afternoon?" she asked in her dressing room as she considered what should be taken. Had the laundry woman sent back her gray morning gown?

Lilly flushed bright pink. "I did, yes. I…we went to see the troop reviews in Hyde Park. It was ever so exciting."

Nellie was only half-listening, but she noticed Lilly's flush, and it gave her a moment's worry. "Fanny went with you?"

"Oh, no, Your Grace." Lilly bent her head over a hatbox. "No sense in asking Fanny. She wouldn't come."

"Mm?" Nellie concentrated on the last-minute things which must be done. She acknowledged Charles's suggestion to engage a secretary to be a sensible one. She would look for a suitable person on her return to London. There were several letters to be sent concerning the salon. And she must call on her mother. How long did Charles intend to stay? She would send a footman with a note of apology to Mrs. Perlew at the children's orphanage she planned to visit tomorrow.

James could pick up the boxes of food and clothing promised in the carriage and deliver them.

On the trip to Leicestershire, Feeley and Lilly accompanied them in the coach. The fourgon, piled high with their luggage, had been sent on ahead. Their conversation was desultory, focusing on the clement weather, the state of the roads, the quality of the food at the posting inns where she and Charles had separate chambers.

The warm breeze blew in, ruffling Nellie's hat, as Peter, seated in Nellie's lap, put his head out the window to sniff the country smells.

When it was necessary for the coach to stop for the dog, Nellie expected Charles to be annoyed, but he didn't seem to mind the dog. He even offered to take Peter for a short walk. She admired his patience when the dog dallied too long. For the last few miles, the conversation turned to pets from their pasts, Charles's beloved dog, and Jason's boyhood faithful friend.

They were not far from Shewsbury Park when forced to stop again. Nellie climbed out with Charles and Peter to stretch her legs. It was cramped in the coach. She wished she could rest her head on Charles's shoulder, but even if things were better between them, it would not be seemly in front of their servants.

Returning to the coach, Nellie was aware of a furtive movement as she settled back inside. She glanced at Lilly, who clutched her hands in her lap. Feeley stared intently out the window. Nellie dismissed it as nothing, turning her mind to what awaited them at Shewsbury Park.

>>><<<

CHARLES FOLDED HIS arms and eyed Feeley with some disfavor. What was he up to? The Irishman couldn't help himself around a pretty girl. His valet's bright blue eyes returned his warning glance with a questioning lift of his brows. Charles shrugged inwardly and turned instead to Nellie, a veritable picture in her violet-gray pelisse and high-poke bonnet, the dog in her arms.

He allowed his imagination to create a new picture. Replacing the dog with a baby. His son or daughter. He allowed himself to dwell on that very pleasant outcome and began to think of ways to bring it about. It made for rather distracting daydreaming, and daydreaming it was, for Nellie looked as untouchable as usual. He admitted his pride had made things worse, but Nellie's failure to take him at his word had brought him low. His feelings were too raw to put into words.

Disgruntled by the state of affairs, he watched the passing landscape for familiar landmarks. He wouldn't beg his wife if she didn't want him. Ah, the coach began to climb the steep hill. The one he'd skied down in winter and rode dangerously fast down on his first horse. From the top, it offered an excellent view of his estate.

Aware he was remiss, he offered Nellie a warm smile. "Almost home."

Her lips trembled into a smile. Was she uneasy about what awaited them? *Mother!* Fear struck at him again like a knife. *Dear Lord!* She must not be desperately ill. Jason was inclined to exaggerate.

As soon as they arrived, Charles went straight up to see his mother in the bedchamber she now occupied, after she was moved back from the dower house. He fought to hide his reaction to finding her considerably changed. *So thin!* She barely lifted her head from the pillow. His heart thumped, and he swallowed the lump in his throat as he took the chair beside her bed. "How are you, Mama?" he asked, using his childhood name for her he now considered himself too old to employ.

"I cannot look well if you call me Mama," she said with a faint smile.

"Nonsense. You look far too well to be languishing in bed. What does the physician say?"

She clutched the sheet. "He wishes to bleed me again."

Charles reached for her hand. He felt the tension as he pressed a kiss to the pale skin threaded with blue veins. "I shall consult the doctor. And speak to Jason."

"They have gone to church," she said reprovingly.

"So the butler tells me. I am remiss, but I was eager to see you."

She nodded. "You are forgiven, dear boy. How are you? You look tired."

"Just the trip, Mother, I am fine."

She gazed at him shrewdly. He could almost see the questions ticking over in her mind. "How is Nellie?"

It pleased him that his mother called her Nellie. "She is extremely well. Concerned about you, naturally."

"Tell her to come and see me. But not for a few hours. I slept badly last night and need to rest." She closed her eyes.

His tread heavy with despair, Charles left the room.

Nellie hovered in the corridor. Her lovely eyes were clouded with worry. "How is she?"

He opened his mouth, but to his distress, only a slight groan emerged. "Not well," he managed to utter. Tears flooded his eyes. Afraid he looked like a weakling, he attempted to push past her.

Nellie put out a hand to stop him. She took his arm. "Come to my bedchamber. We can talk there."

Chapter Twenty-One

In Nellie's bedchamber, Charles fell into a chair and passed a hand over his eyes. The surge of love and compassion she felt for him tightened Nellie's throat and rendered her silent. She had come to recognize the rigid control he kept over himself at such times. Her vision blurred with tears, which she quickly dashed away. She wanted to be strong for him. And she would not allow him to shut her out. The past didn't matter. Not even her fear that he didn't love her.

"Darling, what is it?" Finding her voice, she kneeled beside his chair and rested her head against his thigh. She refused to withhold her love from him.

His hand smoothed over her hair, his eyes dark and miserable. "Nellie," he said softly. "I've missed you. *So much.*"

"I've missed you, too," she murmured, a catch in her voice.

She climbed to her feet and held out her hand to him. "Come and lie down with me."

"On the Sabbath?" A sensual smile lit his eyes. There was the man she'd fallen in love with. With one look, he could make her weak with wanting, but she wished now only to hold him in her arms.

She managed a tremulous smile. "I don't recall it worrying you in the past. But I mean only to offer you comfort."

His eyes held a gleam. "And while that is a most appealing offer, it's best I don't risk it." He reached for her hand and drew her down onto his lap, wrapping his arms around her, his warm breath feathering her cheek. "Nellie," he said softly. "Just let me hold you." She leaned into him, listening to the beat of his heart, comforted by his familiar smell and strong arms. "I want things back to the way they were when it was good between us."

"I want that too, Charles."

He stirred on the chair, and she could sense the tension flowing through him. "I must speak to Jason and find out about this doctor. His treatment doesn't seem to be helping my mother."

A knock on the door brought Nellie and Charles to their feet.

The footman carried in her dog. "Lilly wishes to know if you require her services, Your Grace."

"Yes, tell her to come, James."

Peter scampered across the carpet and made several unsuccessful attempts to leap onto the high bed.

"Into your basket, you rascal," Charles ordered, half-amused by the dog's antics. Peter merely wagged his tail.

Charles stood with a hand on the door latch. "We must talk, sweetheart. But I'll see Jason now. They have returned from church. I heard the crunch of carriage wheels on the gravel." He shook his head. "I give it two minutes before that dog is on your bed. He is not to be there when I am."

"I'll explain your feelings to Peter."

A faint smile flickered over his lips. "We shall continue this at a later time. When you've changed your clothes, join us in the drawing room."

After the door closed, Nellie curled up on the bed with her dog. "You shall have to sleep in your basket when your master is here." She buried her face in his soft fur. "Oh, he is so worried, my heart aches for him. She must be so dreadfully ill."

Peter whined and licked her cheek.

Nellie was sitting at her dressing table, sorting through her jewelry box, when Lilly entered.

"There was a bible reading in the servants' hall after the meal," Lilly called through the open dressing room door, where she was taking Nellie's clothes out of the trunk. "Mr. Feeley read it beautifully. He has such a pleasant voice."

Nellie paused with a gold chain necklace in her hand. "There is nothing between you and Mr. Feeley, is there, Lilly?"

Lilly appeared at the door. "I do like him, Your Grace." Nellie turned and took note of the maid's wide eyes and flushed cheeks. She replaced the necklace and rose from the stool. "He has a bad reputation with women. Please, please be careful, Lilly."

"Yes, Your Grace." Lilly cast her eyes down and became intent of smoothing out the rumpled shawl she held in her hands.

Exasperated, Nellie let the matter go. She had little time for it but would have to remain vigilant. After all, she was responsible for the girl's welfare. It would be a lapse of her care if Lilly succumbed to Feeley's advances. The result of such romances could result in an unwanted pregnancy and dismissal. And while no servant would be dismissed from this house, it would ruin Lilly's life to give birth to a child without the father's support.

⇢⇾⇾⇽⇽⇠

AS HE CROSSED the gallery, Charles spied Jason and Beverly below in the great hall where Grove relieved them of their outerwear. He leaned on the balustrade and hailed his brother.

Jason ran up the stairs and enveloped Charles in a brief hug. He pulled away to search his face, his eyes anxious. "I gather you've seen Mother?"

"Yes." Charles grimaced. "She doesn't look at all well. Thank you for writing and alerting me."

"I'm glad you're here," Jason confessed. "It was getting too much for me to handle alone."

"Charles, I am so pleased to see you." Beverly reached them, her pregnancy obvious as she moved ponderously up the stairs.

Charles kissed her cheek. "You appear to be in rosy good health, Beverly. I trust it is so?"

"I am, thank you, Charles."

"Nellie is anxious to see you both. I want to know about Mother's treatment, Jas. I have little confidence in this surgeon."

After Beverly left them, they settled in the drawing room with glasses of claret. "Who is this new physician?" Charles asked.

"Wells is from London," Jason said. "Came well recommended."

Charles waved that aside. "Some of these medical men support each other. Where is Dr. Chapman residing these days?"

"He retired to Loughborough. He's a good age now, Charles. Tended my ills and yours before me, remember."

Charles nodded. "A competent surgeon. Set my broken leg, which another doctor had said would cripple me, and he saved Michael's life more than once. What do you think of this, Wells?"

"He is keen on bleeding his patients."

Charles scowled. "Mother looks too pale. She's very weak."

Jason rubbed the back of his neck. "I agree. What should be done?"

"Is Wells still here? Or do we have to go to London to fetch him?"

"He is putting up with his sister, who lives near Oakham. We expect him to visi Mother this afternoon."

Charles tossed back his drink. "Good. I will have words with him."

Jason frowned. "Should you anger him, Charles, she will be without a doctor for some time."

"I'll deal with it. If it means driving to Loughborough to bring Chapman back, then I'm happy to do so."

Chapter Twenty-Two

"I'M TOLD CHARLES disagreed with the surgeon's treatment," Beverly said while she and Nellie took tea in the small south parlor. "Jason is unsure it was wise."

"I don't believe things could have been left as they were. When Charles advised the surgeon that he intended to get a second opinion, Mr. Wells took exception to it. Charles invited him to leave. I believe the surgeon has gone back to London."

"What will happen to our mama-in-law now?" Beverly asked with a catch in her voice.

Nellie, aware of her sister-in-law's delicate condition, reached across and patted her hand. "Charles has driven the curricle to Loughborough. He intends to bring Dr. Chapman back with him. He has great confidence in the doctor."

She stared out at the heavy dark clouds beyond the tall windows, which made the room dim. "I pray they return before nightfall. If it rains heavily, the roads will become impassable."

An hour later, while drenching rain continued to fall, Nellie watched the carriage drive for a sign that Charles had returned. He was an excellent driver. She had observed his skill with the reins, and Jason, in an attempt to reassure her, spoke of a curricle race Charles had won some years ago. But if the rain continued, the roads would soon become mud-filled ditches, which could bog down a curricle, or upturn it.

She was summoned at last to the dowager's bedchamber. When she entered, Nellie fought to hide her shock. There was the odor of sickness in the room. The dowager looked frail. She lay back against the pillows as if her neck weren't strong enough to hold up her head covered in its lacy cap.

Nellie sat by the bed and took her cool hand in hers.

"How anxious you look, Nellie. Is there something wrong?"

"Only concern for you, Mother."

"Oh, do call me, Catherine, Nellie, please. You have a mother, and I rather hope we might be friends. Life is too short for formality."

Nellie smiled. Catherine was such a pretty name. If she ever had a daughter… "Is there something I can do for you?"

"No, thank you, my dear. I know I don't look well, but I have no intention of departing this earth until I see my grandchild."

"Jason and Beverly are keen to oblige you."

"I had hoped you and Charles might bring happy news."

"I'm afraid we have not yet been blessed."

"You haven't been married long. Don't lose heart." She squeezed Nellie's hand.

Nellie felt a nervous fluttering in her belly as she cast her mind back over the past weeks. Could she possibly have missed her monthly menses? With the wedding and all that had happened since, she'd failed to notice. Ordinarily, she was as regular as clockwork. She felt her face grow warm and lowered her gaze to her hands, not wanting to give Catherine false hope.

After a moment's silence, Nellie glanced up. Catherine might be ill, but she hadn't missed Nellie's reaction. Her blue eyes, so like Charles's, met hers. "Perhaps there might soon be an added incentive for me to remain on God's earth."

"I do hope so. I want a baby very much." Overwhelmed by the possibility of a baby, Nellie fought not to place a hand on her stomach.

Could it be? She and Charles had not made love for weeks.

"Forgive me, my dear." Catherine's head sank back onto the pillows. "I am weary. I'll sleep a little. Send Charles to me after my nap, will you please?"

Charles had not told his mother of his intention to fetch Dr. Chapman. "Of course. But have a good rest." Nellie kissed her cheek.

With a fervent prayer, Charles would soon return. Nellie slipped from the room.

Catherine's personal maid, Jane, hovered outside the door, fidgeting with her handkerchief. "Her Grace has decided to sleep awhile," Nellie said gently, aware of the maid's distress.

In the gallery, Nellie paused at the long window. She stared out at the incessant downpour. It was growing late, and dusk would soon be upon them. Was Charles on his way home? She could not tell him about the baby until she was sure. She would hate to give him false hope, not now when he was so upset about his mother.

She descended the stairs to the library in search of a book to distract herself. The lofty room smelled of polish, leather, and the musty odor of old tomes. Gilt-edged books filled the shelves around the walls. A leather sofa faced the marble fireplace with a pair of comfortable armchairs on each side of it. Above the mantel hung a framed portrait of the old duke, a big man with solid shoulders and a square jaw. She could see some resemblance to his sons in his features, but his gray-streaked hair was light brown, and his green eyes looked weary and sad, as if life had defeated him.

Nellie crossed the exotic carpet and stood before Charles's carved oak desk. His correspondence was stacked neatly on its polished surface. She ran an admiring finger over the wood and examined the walnut letter opener, the handle carved with putto amongst acanthus. A pounce pot and his silver wax seal were lined up along the top next to standish. A black feather quill perched in the inkpot.

With a brief smile, she moved the inkwell farther to the left, confident that Charles would move it back. She turned and picked up the newspaper left on a small table, finding the edition was several weeks old. Charles's name featured. It wasn't unusual, he often appeared with the Prince of Wales or the prime minister or some mention of a bill. She sank down onto the leather sofa and began to read it.

Jason strolled through the door. "No sign of Charles?"

"No."

He sat beside her. "What have you there?"

"I was looking for something to read. Charles is mentioned."

"May I see?" Jason took *The Morning Post* from her and began to read it. "Ah, yes, I knew about this. The altercation outside Parliament. Charles defended Lord Ogelsby against scurrilous lies written by Lord Montrose. His friend was desperately ill at the time and has since passed away. This is the retraction. A feeble effort, it is, too." Jason read it out: *"This newspaper wishes to apologize for a misinterpretation of the incident between the Duke of Shewsbury and said journalist outside parliament. Lord Montrose admitted in court that he had thrown the first punch, and the duke then responded. He regrets publishing what has since been proven to be less than the truth concerning Lord Ogelsby, now deceased, and apologizes to the Duke of Shewsbury and Lord Ogelsby's family for the upset he has caused them."*

"Charles would have been upset for his friend." Nellie sighed. Marian had shown her Montrose's article before Nellie and Charles met. She had worried that he might be a bully. How wrong she'd been.

"I would have knocked the journalist's head off." Jason tossed the newspaper onto the table. "My brother is a stickler for correctness. Which makes it hard for lesser mortals such as I to measure up."

"And I," Nellie admitted. She climbed to her feet and hurried to the window. Frustrated, she found that rainwater obscured the view. "Oh, if only he would come."

"He will, Nellie. Charles is a very able fellow. Have faith."

Jason ambled over to pour a glass of brandy from the drink's tray. He held up the decanter of madeira, but Nellie declined with a shake of her head. She couldn't wait in the house a moment longer. "I think I'll go for a walk."

He swiveled the crystal stopper in his hand. "A walk?"

"I like to walk in the rain."

"Please forgive me if I don't join you." With a chuckle, he turned back to the table. "Where's Beverly? Have you seen her?"

"She's in the south parlor."

In the great hall, Nellie shrugged into her pelisse and put on her hat. She thanked Grove for the umbrella and went out into the easing rain, cutting across the soggy lawns to the turn in the carriage drive. From there, she might be able to see the curricle approaching from some distance away.

Breathing in the wet scent of old leaves, she crossed the gravel. She had only gone a short distance when the sound of horses' hooves thudded over the ground.

She stepped onto the grass verge. A few minutes later, the curricle appeared, traveling fast. Charles was driving a pair of grays. An older man sat beside him, clutching his bag in his lap. Charles nodded to her as they passed, and the man raised his hat.

Relieved, Nellie hurried back to the house.

Charles and the doctor came in. He introduced him as they discarded their dripping oilskins. "I have Dr. Chapman to thank for my leg mending as good as new when I was a stripling." Charles frowned down at her. "What were you doing out in the rain? We don't want you to fall ill, too."

"A little rain won't hurt me," Nellie said, a little indignant, but so pleased to see him.

"Where is Jason, Nellie?"

"He was in the library. He will be with Beverly. The south parlor."

The doctor's bright eyes beneath craggy gray eyebrows settled on Nellie. "I shall be here overnight, should you wish to consult me, Your Grace."

Before Nellie could register surprise, Charles, impatient to see his mother, ushered him upstairs.

Did he mean...? *What presumption,* she thought, her cheeks hot. But she paused, a hand on the banister. Surely a doctor couldn't make a diagnosis so early?

The urge to tell Charles of her suspicions tightened her chest. What if she were wrong, what if there was another reason? Worry, perhaps. She just couldn't risk disappointing him.

>>>><<<<

AN HOUR LATER, the doctor was shown into the drawing room where the four of them tensely waited. Nellie had ordered a large tea, with plates piled high with the chef's cakes and pastries, and ham and cress sandwiches. Her mother believed food was calming when one was worried. Nellie wasn't in agreement today. Her stomach churned at the sight, and she could only sip the tea.

The doctor accepted a cup and saucer from her, drank, then sat back to observe them. "I found the dowager duchess very weak."

"She is," Jason agreed with a savage twist of his lips. "That surgeon was a fool."

Charles cautioned him with a hand. "What is your opinion, Dr. Chapman?"

"I am not an advocate of phlebotomy. The removal of blood from a patient can have serious adverse effects if overdone. I would not recommend any more be taken in your mother's case."

"Can a cure be found?" Charles asked.

There was sympathy in Dr. Chapman's eyes. "Your mother is very ill, Your Grace. I believe we can lengthen her life for some months. A year if we are lucky."

"Oh, no," Beverly murmured and took out her handkerchief.

Looking grave, Jason put his arm around her.

Nellie sagged in her seat beside Charles, who sat upright and grimly silent.

"Your mother needs to build up her blood. She must rest, eat red meat, preferably liver, and drink several glasses of burgundy every day. I have some medicine which will help her to feel better. Laudanum can be administered for sleep, but be careful with the dose. Then we shall see. It is not a cure, however. Your mother has cancer." He shook his head. "I believe she has been aware of it for some time."

"Cancer! Good God! And kept it to herself?" Jason sounded outraged.

"She would not want to worry you," Nellie said, finding her voice.

Charles nodded. "Mother would hate that."

Nellie rose. "A bedchamber has been prepared for you, Dr. Chapman. If you'll excuse me, I must discuss the menu for dinner with our chef."

She left the room. In the corridor, her steps faltered as tears blinded her. She fumbled for her handkerchief. How pleased she had been to have a mama-in-law like Catherine, and now it seemed they would lose her. Nellie hoped she would live long enough to see at least one of her sons' babies come into the world. She placed a hand on her stomach, and then with a moan of distress, went down to the kitchen.

⇶⇷

WHEN CHARLES ENTERED his mother's bedchamber, he gently chided her. "You should have told us, Mama."

"What good would that do, Charles? You are so busy in London and don't need to worry about me."

He shook his head. "Of course we will worry. But we still wanted to know. To make sure you're getting the best of care. You should have family around you at a time like this. I have sent word to your sister."

"Frances is coming?" She sighed. "I do hope she doesn't nag at me to take up riding again. She will keep reminding me of how I rode whilst I was carrying you and Jason."

He smiled. "Not for a while, perhaps, but Frances is a determined person, is she not?"

"Too forceful at times. She's always been so strong. So sure of herself."

"I shan't let her bully you into getting back on your feet."

"Thank you, my dear boy. She will busy herself organizing the foxhunt. We are hosting it if you haven't forgotten with all this fuss."

"I remember."

He kissed his mother and left her. He wished he could cancel it. He had no taste for it. The thought that he could lose his mother devastated him so much his throat hurt. He needed Nellie.

He found her seated in her bedchamber. She clutched her handkerchief, her eyes red, her smile encouraging. "Your mother might surprise you and be with us for far longer than the doctor says. There is much to keep her here."

"Jason and Beverly's baby?"

"Yes." She turned the crumpled handkerchief in her hands. "Beverly promised to return here with the baby as soon as they are able to travel."

He bent and drew her up into his arms. Nuzzling her neck, he breathed in her flowery scent, which he'd missed so much. "And if we should be blessed, that would please Mother even more, would it not?"

"I'm sure it would," Nellie murmured. She cradled his face in her hands. "But our baby might be a girl."

"I shall be delighted to have a daughter. I don't think we should wait any longer, though, do you?"

Nellie shook her head.

He took her hand and led her over to the bed.

Chapter Twenty-Three

There was a tender light in Charles's eyes. He cradled Nellie's face in his hands and pressed kisses to her cheeks, her forehead, chin, and nose. He took her mouth, and his kisses grew more demanding and passionate. She had denied her feelings for him for months, and starved of him, made love to him with wild abandon, until they both fell back, hot and panting.

She watched the worry lines ease on his forehead as he lay beside her, his wide chest rising and falling in slumber, then she curled up beside him, heavy and sated. It would be difficult to keep her suspicions from him. Next week she would be sure. But for now, she didn't want him to become too concerned about her. Marian had reassured her that making love would not harm the baby. She closed her eyes and slept.

The next morning, when Charles reached for her again, she wanted so much to tell him she loved him. He needed her, but she didn't know if it was love he felt. What if he felt compelled to respond? Or worse, said nothing?

The following week was spent quietly as they watched for signs of improvement in his mother. Nellie spent some time with Catherine every afternoon. She seemed brighter. They chatted, and Catherine expressed an interest in Nellie's literary salon. "I wish I could have seen Byron," she said with a wistful sigh. "I met him once, a splendid poet."

"The ladies all enjoyed it. I might see if he'll visit us again when you are able to be present." Nellie smiled, feeling that such enthusiasm from Catherine must be a good sign.

Nellie told her about the orphanage. She had received a letter from Mrs. Perlew, thanking her for the food and clothing and advising her of the improvements to the building and the benefits to the children brought about by Nellie's patronage.

The children were all comfortably fed and clothed, and with the injection of funds from Nellie, were being taught to read to enable them to find work when they left the orphanage. But she despaired that so many homeless roamed the streets of London, prey to danger and starvation. She took in more every day. She would soon need to find bigger premises and had an eye on a building in Cheapside. Nellie immediately wrote back with the promise to do more when she returned to London.

Going to her bedchamber, Nellie heard Lilly crying in the dressing room. She found her maid seated on a chair, her head bowed over the sewing basket in her lap, one of Nellie's shifts in her hands.

Nellie placed a hand on the girl's heaving shoulder. "Lilly, whatever is the matter?"

"I am a bit troubled, Your Grace."

She was usually such a contented soul, Nellie grew alarmed. "Why? What on earth has happened to upset you?"

"I didn't want to worry you, Your Grace, not with the dowager duchess so ill."

Nellie took her by the elbow. "Come into the sitting room. We can have a nice talk. There's always a means of dealing with troubles." Dreading what the girl had to tell her, Nellie joined her on the sofa. *That valet of Charles's*, she thought with a rush of anger. She never trusted the fellow. She should have been more observant. Why had Charles kept him on?

"It's Mr. Feeley."

Nellie stiffened and nodded. "What has he done?"

"He is going back to County Cork."

"I see. And is there something you'd like to tell me?" she asked, expecting the worst.

"Feeley refuses to take me with him."

"Does he indeed!" So he was escaping and leaving her maid pregnant! "Has he taken liberties with you, Lilly?"

Lilly nodded.

Furious, Nellie tried to stay calm. "Are you with child?"

Lilly's eyes widened. "Oh no, Your Grace."

Nellie put a hand over hers. "Can you be sure?"

"I am perfectly sure I'm not, Your Grace." Lilly blushed. "He never did the deed, that is, he wouldn't... I wouldn't have said no, though. I love him."

"I see." Although she didn't see at all. Had she accused the man unfairly? "It's just as well then."

"But if he had, and I was with child, then he would've had to take me with him, wouldn't he?"

Nellie sighed. "I'm not sure that's necessarily so. Is this what upsets you? That he won't marry you?"

"He says it is better for me to remain in your employ. His family is poor, and he must find work, which could part us from each other."

Nellie nodded. Had he been dallying with her maid? Didn't he care about her? "Has he taken any liberties at all?"

"We kissed, and..." Her blush deepened. "But not that. I do know. I am a country girl, Your Grace."

Nellie nodded, relieved. She must speak to Charles. "Leave it to me. I shall see what can be done."

"Feeley won't get into trouble with the duke? He will need a good reference."

"Why is he going back to Ireland? Has he told you?"

"His mother is alone now that his father has died."

"I am sure the duke would not let Feeley go without a good reference."

"Oh, Your Grace. If you could talk to him, I should be so grateful."

"But should Feeley decide to take you with him after all, are you sure you want to leave England? Especially now, when you have become a skilled lady's maid? You may not find such work in Cork."

"You've been so very good to me, Your Grace. I know I wasn't up to snuff when you first employed me. But a servant's life isn't a rich life. I want a home, a man's love, and his children."

Nellie silently agreed. But how long would the romance last once they were faced with poverty? "Of course you do. I shall speak to His Grace when he comes home."

As Charles returned from a ride with Jason, Nellie met him on the path.

Jason waved and continued on, while Nellie explained about Lilly.

"I know Feeley is returning to Ireland, and I've provided him with a reference. I'll talk to him, sweetheart, but I can't make my valet take your maid with him if he doesn't wish to." He gave a wry grin, which she was pleased to see, as he'd been so dreadfully subdued of late. "I must say I'm surprised he hasn't had his way with her, seeing as she's willing. Not Feeley's style."

"Maybe he loves her?"

Charles wrapped an arm around her. "Well, maybe he does. And maybe he's being sensible about it."

"You'll talk to him?"

"Yes. I'm not sure what good it will do, though. Jas tells me as Mother's improved a little, they are to return home in a couple of days. He can't leave matters to his staff indefinitely."

"No, of course, not. I will miss them."

Nellie would have liked to confide in Beverly about the baby. But Dr. Chapman had left without her consulting him. She wanted this baby so much, she almost feared she was conjuring him up. She must tell someone. Marian was increasing and would be her usual supportive self, offering great advice. Nellie would write to her this afternoon.

Charles spent each night with her. It was wonderful to lie in his arms again. The distance from London made her worries ease, but not vanish completely. She tried not to think of the little boy and his mother, the Frenchwoman who had been so determined to hang onto Charles.

Did Charles love her? He was passionate and caring with Nellie, but she still waited for the words she longed to hear. If and when he said those words, it would complete her.

THE SUN BEAT down on Charles and Jason as they sweated and toiled together, digging a ditch at the Jameson's farm. Charles took a moment to wipe his brow with his handkerchief. His tenant farmer, Mr. Jameson, had fallen ill a month ago, and as he was not quite up to scratch yet, Charles preferred not to have him undertaking such heavy work. If he became ill again, his wife and family would be in trouble.

Jason stopped to stretch his back. "Do you think Mother appeared better this morning?"

"Certainly brighter," Charles said, resting on his shovel. "But we must accept that it will not last."

Jason shoved his hat back on and took up his spade, savagely attacking the irrigation ditch.

"It's not alive, Jas," Charles said with a sympathetic smile. "You don't need to kill it."

Jameson carried over two tankards of draft. "Me missus can't believe her eyes. A duke and a lord diggin' ditches for us. She's plannin' a feast for ye."

"Tell her not to go to any trouble, Jameson," Charles said.

He'd hoped to have luncheon with Nellie. He constantly thought about her when she wasn't with him and cherished their nights together. He had never intended his marriage to be more than convivial, nor expected to feel so deeply about another person. It seemed that where Nellie was concerned, he was helpless. If he was setting himself up for heartbreak again, so be it. He would screw his courage to the sticking place, as Shakespeare had written. He had never considered himself a coward, but he admitted he had been in matters of the heart. The air seemed to lighten around him with a sense of new purpose.

Jason took the tankard with a nod of thanks and raised it to his lips. "I could certainly eat a plowman's lunch."

"Aye. Cheese, fresh from the dairy, milord, sausage, and bread."

"Pickles?" Jason asked, downing the rest of the beer.

"Aye, and pickles." Jameson chuckled and walked back to the house.

When Charles arrived home several hours later, Feeley waited to assist him with a much-needed bath and a change of clothing. "I have ordered hot water, Your Grace. I expected you'd want a bath."

"You anticipated correctly, Feeley." His valet always did. He would miss him.

As Feeley filled the bath, Charles stripped off his dirt and sweat-stained clothing. He stepped into the water, sat, and took up the soap, while Feeley waited with the jug to pour more water over him.

Charles chose this moment to speak to him. "I am told that the duchess's maid, Lilly, wishes to go to Ireland with you," he said as he lathered the soap over his hair.

Feely cleared his throat. "You know about that then, Your Grace?"

"I do."

"I never tumbled the girl, Your Grace. I hope you believe me."

"That did give me pause, Feeley. But yes, Lilly has said as much."

Feeley poured the water over Charles's head.

"Knew I'd be off some time. Didn't want to leave a decent lass like

Lilly in some kind of bother."

Charles brushed the water from his hair with his hands. "I am deeply impressed with the nobility of that sentiment. But it appears that she loves you. You don't feel the same?"

"She's a grand girl, Your Grace. That she is."

"Would it make a difference if I wrote to a friend of mine? I could recommend you both for a position on his staff at his castle at Kinsale in Cork?"

Feeley's eyes brightened. "The castle at Kinsale, Your Grace?"

"Yes. Would that suit you?"

Feeley's voice had been unusually subdued but rose along with his grin. "It would, indeed, Your Grace."

"You would marry the girl?"

"Yes. If I must." He chuckled. "That I would, indeed."

"Then, you shall marry her before you leave."

"Sweet Lilly. 'Twill be my pleasure to become her husband."

Having finished washing, Charles rose from the bath and took the towel handed to him. He wouldn't place a wager on Feeley remaining faithful. But he supposed stranger things had happened.

CHAPTER TWENTY-FOUR

Nellie stood beside Charles as the carriage bearing Jason and Beverly away to Dorset rattled down the drive.

"They will be missed." Charles put his arm around her as they walked back inside.

"I do hope the birth goes well," Nellie said.

"Indeed." Charles kissed her cheek and left her to go to the stables, planning to ride out with his gamekeeper.

Nellie went to see how his mother fared. She would read to Catherine if she felt well enough. They were almost finished *Pride and Prejudice* and would soon begin on *Sense and Sensibility*.

In the evening, Charles, Catherine, and Nellie played three-handed whist. It was the first evening Catherine had left her bedchamber.

"We must invite our neighbors for dinner when you feel up to it, Mother," Charles said, reaching for his wineglass.

"There's absolutely no reason why you can't entertain them now. I shall return to the dower house in a day or so."

Charles frowned. "I'd rather you didn't."

"*Tut, tut*, Charles, how you do fuss." She placed down a card. "I am a great deal better. And the dower house is only two miles away."

He glanced at Nellie in appeal.

"But we will miss you," Nellie complained.

His mother reached across and patted Nellie's cheek. "I suspect I am being coerced. But I consider myself very lucky indeed. I will stay a little longer."

The next day, Marian's reply to Nellie's letter arrived in the post. Nellie curled up on the sofa in her sitting room to read it.

"Oh, my goodness, Nellie, are you with child?" Marian wrote. "Let me know <u>as soon as you are sure</u>. (Heavily underlined.) The most splendid news, if so! Are you well, dearest? Because by now, you would have missed two of your monthly menses, I feel quite confident you are pregnant! You must tell Charles. Even if you are wrong, he will wish to comfort you in your disappointment.

I am only in my fifth month, and nothing fits me! This baby will be enormous! Belfries is so delighted to have another child, he has agreed to me purchasing a new wardrobe. I shan't, however, not yet. I'll have some of my gowns altered. After the baby is born, I'll splurge on some new dresses. I am sure I shall require something more than a new hat to cheer me. I fear my figure will never return to its original shape. But for the moment, there's no sense in spending money when one is an unattractive lump who must hide from Society!

But I digress! I am eager to tell you my news! As I left the dressmaker's rooms in Camberwell, I walked past a small church where a wedding took place. A few guests emerged, and I paused, because so many of them were French. And I love a wedding. Well! The bride shall surprise you, Nellie. It was the (former) Mademoiselle Girard. The woman who accosted you in Bond Street, Charles's ex-mistress. She is now Countess Lafontain. I chatted for a few minutes with one of the guests. An excellent opportunity to try out my rusty French. A garrulous woman, she was quite happy to reveal their history. Apparently, Angelique ran away from Paris carrying the count's baby almost five years ago. He was married, apparently. But his wife has since died, and as soon as the war ended, he came to England to claim her. The boy, such a handsome child, was with her, and I must say he is the image of his father. I wonder if the count knows about Charles? And if Charles knows about him? How intriguing but best left to the past, dearest.

I found some beautiful fabric for an evening gown in Pall Mall at Harding Howell, silk velvet in a deep, deep green. You know how I adore green, so I *will keep it until the next Season...."*

Nellie lowered the page and stared into space. She had come to believe Charles when he'd assured her the boy was not his. He was not a man to lie. But how relieved she was that the Frenchwoman would not be in London eager for his return. Marian was right, however. She would not mention it. It was best left to the past.

She took up the letter again, the two pages crammed front and back in her sister's small hand. *Nat and Eliza have returned to Town, finally. Eliza says they have reconciled. She appears happier than she has been for a long time. And Nellie, they are expecting another child! This is a fecund period for our family, I must say. Mama is beside herself. Wait until she has your news...*

"Oh, that is so good to hear," Nellie said as Charles entered the room.

He came to sit on the arm of her chair. "What is, sweetheart?"

"Marian writes that Eliza and Nathaniel are expecting another baby."

Charles stroked the back of her neck. "Good news indeed. It might be a late spring. Lambs are cavorting in the meadows."

Could she detect a hint of disappointment in his voice? Nellie gazed up at him, and her lips trembled into a smile. "I think I might be with child, too, Charles."

Rising to his feet, he stared down at her, hope in his eyes. "Nellie? Are you sure?"

"I've been waiting to tell you. But I am quite sure now, darling."

"Oh, Nellie, my love!" Charles sank onto the chair and drew her into a fierce hug. She had expected him to be pleased but found his eyes dark with concern. "I must send for Dr. Chapman."

"Don't be silly. I'm in perfect health. Women give birth all the time. And it's months away."

"Nevertheless, I shall advise him of it. And alert him to the fact that we might call upon him at any time."

"If you must, darling." Nellie sighed and leaned her head against his chest, breathing in his comforting smell.

As the sun peeped through a crack in the curtains the next morning, they lay in bed discussing how Feeley had asked Lilly to marry him. There had been a small celebration in the servants' hall.

"How clever of you to find them employment together," Nellie said. A letter had reached them from London where Baron Lynch was staying. He was only too pleased to engage a married couple at his home in County Cork. "Now Feeley will have to marry her," she said. "There will be no backing out."

Charles chuckled. "You don't trust the fellow."

"Not much, but I may be unfair." She sighed. "And now, I shall have to replace Lilly. I will miss her."

Charles murmured agreement. "And I, an excellent valet. Barlow will have a pile of applicants' letters arriving in the mail in a day or so, which I must vet. But I will never find a valet quite as entertaining as Feeley."

"Of that, I am sure." She traced a finger over his jaw, enjoying the rasp of his heavy beard. "I should get up. I promised your mother I would take her out into the garden after breakfast in the bath chair."

"It's still early." Charles's hands stroked over her body. His kisses on her neck prickled and made her shiver with delight. "We have plenty of time. Aunt Frances won't arrive until this afternoon."

Nellie stiffened. She had not seen his Aunt Frances since the wedding. "I must make sure everything is in readiness for her visit."

"And there's the foxhunt planned, weather permitting," Charles said in a casual tone, which didn't fool her.

Nellie sat up. "How can I forget," she said stiffly. "It is the main subject of conversation among the staff, Lilly tells me. I daresay, there is much to be done to prepare for it."

"Nellie." He frowned. "I thought we were done with this. What's the matter?"

"I just hope your aunt doesn't upset your mother."

"Why should she? Aunt Frances will be engaged with the hunt. Only thing that concerns me is that even though the younger dogs have been trained, there are some as yet untested because we haven't had a fox hunt here for some time." He rested his head on his hand and surveyed her, drawing a wisp of her hair back behind her ear. "You needn't fear my aunt will ask you to take part. I don't anticipate it, but if she does, you must refuse. You have ample reason for it now, and even if you didn't, I would never expect you to."

Charles threw back the blankets and stalked naked to where his dressing gown was thrown over the chair. Nellie studied his splendid body regretfully. The mood was spoiled. Aunt Frances was sure to cause some kind of fuss. It was in the woman's nature. She did not know Nellie was pregnant, but that would make little difference to her even if she did.

"I must write to my mother about the baby. Shall we tell your mother together?"

"Yes, I should like that."

As she moved to leave the bed, a wave of nausea rolled over her. Nellie fell back and moaned.

ALARMED, CHARLES SWIVELED. Shrugging on his dressing gown, he strode over to the bed. "Nellie, what is it?"

Nellie was pale and distressed on the pillows.

"Marian told me to expect this. It's something we suffer in the mornings. It will pass shortly. Send a footman for Lilly and ask her to bring me a weak cup of tea and a biscuit, please, Charles."

"I'll ring. I don't want to leave you."

She reached for his hand and squeezed it. "You men. Jason is just as bad. You must not treat me like delicate bone china, Charles. I won't have it. It's a natural state, and I'm a healthy woman. I intend to live a normal life."

He had wanted children. A son and heir, and a daughter or two, but now the danger facing Nellie came home to him with force. Women died in childbirth.

When Lilly brought the tea, Charles arranged the pillows behind her.

The tea brought some color back to her face. "I feel much better, darling. I won't have you fussing over me. After breakfast, shall we go and see your mother? Then you must do what you planned to do today. And I shall take your mother outside into the garden. It looks like a beautiful day."

Charles took a deep breath. "Very well, sweetheart, I'll spend a couple of hours with Barlow, then visit one of my tenants who could use a hand fixing his leaking roof. I'll be back around two."

"Come back before your aunt arrives, please?"

He laughed. "You will manage my aunt. Better than I can, I suspect."

It was hard to remain too worried while riding Thor across the green paddocks, the sun warming his back. Especially finding his mother so pleased with their news. Charles pushed back his hat and grinned. "I'm going to be a father, Thor!"

Thor whinnied, sidled, and broke into a canter.

Chapter Twenty-Five

THE COACH BEARING Lady Dickenson, Charles's Aunt Frances, pulled in just after luncheon. Charles had not yet returned to the house. With a faint heart, Nellie stood on the porch to greet her, watching as she gave orders to the footmen and grooms, and sent them scurrying off in all directions.

"Take those to the stables," she said, gesturing to the saddles and riding equipment she'd brought with her. "I want that saddle well-polished before the hunt." She turned to Nellie. "How are you, Cornelia? You look in the pink of health, I must say."

"I am well, thank you. I hope you had a pleasant journey?"

"Does one ever?" She gestured to her groom. "Barker? Have that trunk taken around to the servants' stairs. They will tell you where they have put me. Where has my maid got to? The servants' hall? Someone find her. I must change." She turned back to Nellie. "I trust I am in the blue chamber?"

"Yes, the blue, your usual bedchamber." Nellie was relieved that she'd been forewarned by Catherine. "Grove will see to anything else you might require." Nellie felt the need to assert herself as mistress of the house. "I'll arrange for tea after you've changed."

"Where is my nephew?"

"Charles has gone to assist a tenant with his leaky roof."

"One would think him a gentleman farmer rather than a duke."

Nellie smiled. "He sees it as his role. He's very much liked by all his tenants."

"Well, as long as he takes part in the hunt. The fox hunting community expects it. Both of you must be there."

Nellie firmed her lips. "I shall tell your sister you have arrived."

"Yes, I'll be along to see her shortly." Frances caught her arm as Nellie turned away. She looked suddenly older and fearful. "How is she?"

"She feels better. The new medicine has helped a good deal."

Frances gave a sharp nod and strode through the front door. "There you are, Dove. How are you? Putting on a little weight? We'll have to get you out riding. Nothing like it for the midriff."

Dove nodded serenely and bowed his head. Amused, Nellie knew he would do no such thing.

She climbed the stairs to Catherine's bedchamber, where she rested after her outing in the fresh air. She peeked in. "Your sister has arrived."

Catherine smiled. "That will turn the house upside down. Don't let Frances ruffle you, dear. She's all bluster."

"I'm sure she won't." But Nellie sensed that Frances considered herself more a part of this house than Nellie. The servants all snapped to when she gave them orders. And Frances was well aware of it.

In a few days, the foxhunt would take place on their land. Although Charles insisted Nellie was not to take part, she felt awkward about it. No one knew of her pregnancy. The meet might judge the new duchess harshly.

While it had drizzled the last two days, the morning of the hunt, the skies were a vast blue canopy, viewed with a sigh through Nellie's bedchamber window.

Charles, who had been called downstairs, returned as she sipped her chocolate. He sat on the edge of the bed. "Percy Hanbury's farmhand has just come to see me. Hanbury is the fellow whose roof

I've been helping to fix. It appears he has fallen off it. I must ride over and see how things are there. These people tend to treat their own ills, which isn't always wise."

"The poor man. Will you be back in time to ride out with the meet?"

"I'll endeavor to," he said, kissing her. "But I might be a late starter."

"My, what will Frances say?" Nellie smiled up at him. "Only last night at dinner, she spoke of how important fox hunting was for the community." She bent her head over the cup. "I suspect it was for my benefit."

He placed a kiss on her hair and eased off the bed. "Not as important as a man's life," he said as he left the room.

Nellie gazed after him, thinking of what an exceptional man she had married. Then she called Lilly to help her dress.

After breakfast, she visited Catherine, who confessed to having a bad night. "I am a little tired, Nellie." She took Nellie's hand. "I know you don't intend to ride today. I think in your condition, that's wise. They will go at quite a pace."

Nellie kissed her cheek. "You rest. I will come to see you later in the morning. We can have luncheon together."

As Nellie went down the corridor, Frances appeared, wearing her green habit.

"You aren't dressed for the hunt?"

"I am not planning to ride," Nellie said, stifling her annoyance. She was sure that Charles had told her.

"You must at least make a showing." Frances frowned. "Charles isn't here, and with the host absent, it will look like a dreadful snub. Charles will be embarrassed."

Nellie tensed. "He hopes to join the hunt before the end."

"But what if he doesn't? You know Charles. He would rather fix the man's roof. In his absence, you must act as hostess, and acknowledge the Master, Mr. Doveton Grey."

"Very well."

Frances eyed her. "You really should consider taking part in the hunt in Charles's absence."

"I am against fox hunting. I refuse to witness the killing of an animal in such a cruel fashion."

Frances raised her eyebrows. "Then don't witness the blooding," she said in a more reasonable tone. "Leave the hunt before the fox is caught. Charles will most likely have joined us by then, and no one can be offended."

It was clear that Frances didn't anticipate a refusal. She left Nellie and walked away down the corridor. "You'd best hurry," she called over her shoulder. "Everyone will soon have arrived, and the huntsman will bring the hounds around."

Nellie stared after her. She could refuse. The woman held no sway over her. Her own mother-in-law was in agreement. But was Frances right? Nellie was not yet known by many people here. Would she be viewed as someone who disdained country life? Country people loathed that attitude. Would her absence cause gossip? Her article had embarrassed Charles when his friends discovered it. She would hate it to happen again.

Frances's suggestion seemed a sensible one. Nellie could take part and leave the hunt before the end. She hurried to Catherine's bedchamber to discuss it, but Jane whispered that her mistress slept.

Dressed in her dark blue habit, Nellie stepped out onto the porch. She formally welcomed the elegant Master, Mr. Doveton Grey, who, in a red coat, graciously returned her greeting from atop his white horse.

Men in black riding coats and women in habits hailed her from their glossy thoroughbreds. Nellie explained Charles's absence as the footman carried out a tray of silver goblets and handed the tipple of brandy around.

Frances rode from the stables, leading a horse by the rein. "I've brought you Coventry, Your Grace. Your horse has lost a shoe."

Nellie studied the stocky chestnut. She'd never ridden the gelding but was confident she could manage him.

The head groom hoisted her into the saddle.

Some sixty hounds, herded by the huntsman, milled over the carriageway and the lawns.

Coventry pricked up his ears. Nellie, sensing he was a nervous animal, patted his neck. "It's all right, boy."

The footman collected the goblets. Then the huntsman, controlling the hounds by voice, rounded them up and blew the piercing horn.

A cacophony of sound erupted as they left the house. The horses' hooves struck the gravel, the dogs' barks shrill with anticipation.

Nellie walked Coventry beside Aunt Frances's mount. Reaching the meadow, they urged their horses into a canter, the hounds scampering, some out of sight.

A shout came from somewhere ahead.

"They have a scent," Frances said, tightening her hand on the rein.

Another high-pitched blast from the horn, and the hunt was on. The riders broke from a canter into a full gallop and thundered over the grass. Nellie's mount went with them. The cool breeze whipping around her, she bent over the horse's neck, distrusting the animal's awkward gait.

A fence reared up, and she set Coventry over it. The horse cleared it but stumbled. Aunt Frances, riding ahead, whirled her mount around to view her. She nodded approvingly and rode on.

Frances's horse easily cleared the next hedge. She was a magnificent horsewoman, Nellie had to admit. Nellie followed suit, but Coventry's hooves clipped the top, sending up a shower of privet leaves into the air. They landed safely and rode on. Ahead, the excited barking reached fever pitch.

Breathless, Nellie kept an eye out for a way to escape the pack and ride back to the house. But Frances remained close. Another fence, and this time, Coventry stumbled badly on the other side. Nellie controlled him and received a yell of approval from Frances.

They rode up a grassy hill. Reaching the crest, the countryside stretched out before them, green and lush. The riders clustered below, the red coat of the master amid the dark coats of others. Barking hysterically, the hounds swarmed around the huntsman, who raised his voice to call them to heel.

It was unendurable. With relief, Nellie found what she'd been searching for, a break in the trees to her left. Frances had finally abandoned her and galloped away down the hill.

Nellie slowed Coventry and turned her horse's head toward the trees. She had only gone a few yards when a young hound appeared, running full pelt toward her. Frantic to have lost its way, it ran straight in front of Coventry.

With a shrill whinny, her horse reared. Nellie clung on, but Coventry bolted, heading down the hill toward the other riders. Everyone turned to look, and a shout went up.

Unnerved by the noise, Coventry skidded into a sharp turn. Nellie lost her grip on the rein. She was catapulted into the air. The ground rushed up, and she knew no more.

⇶⇷

PERCY'S LEG WAS broken. Charles sent for the local surgeon and stayed until he came.

"He will be all right, won't he, Your Grace?" Mrs. Hanbury stood clutching her apron with tears in her eyes, the two small children clutching her skirts.

"I think so, Mrs. Hanbury," Charles said, concerned for the man's leg. "He'll have a headache for a few days."

She wiped her eyes with her apron. "Oh, I am so relieved he's alive, Your Grace. I thought I'd lost him."

The bone would have to be set. It seemed a clean break to Charles. Properly treated, he should be up and about on it in a short time, with a pair of crutches. He would stay to watch the procedure. Too many were crippled by bad doctoring.

At least the doctor wasted no time getting here. Jacobs had taken over Chapman's practice, but Charles knew nothing about him. He only hoped the man wasn't a wretched saw bone, and Charles wouldn't have to fight for Percy to keep his leg.

Jacobs examined Percy and made a similar pronouncement as Percy finally came around.

"What happened?" he muttered, a hand to his head.

"You fell off your roof, you foolish fellow," Jacobs said cheerfully. "You have a broken femur, which I'll have to set. A knock on the head, too, but as you're back with us and remember who you are, that's not too serious. All in all, a lucky man." He turned to Charles. "Now, Your Grace, if I can ask for your help? I'm afraid this will be uncomfortable, Hanbury."

The man fainted as his boot was removed. Charles held him steady while the doctor straightened the bone. He went about his work efficiently, impressing Charles.

After it was done, and they left the patient to the care of his wife, Charles praised his methods. "Where did you learn your skills?" he asked.

"The navy," Dr. Jacobs said. "You have to tackle all sorts of wounds on the sea. And it's necessary to learn fast while under pressure."

Charles nodded. "Thank you for coming so swiftly," he said as the doctor prepared to leap into the trap. "Forward any bills to me."

With a cheery farewell, the doctor slapped the reins, and the trap clattered off down the rocky road.

Charles went back inside.

"I'll send over a farmhand to help you until Percy is back on his feet," he told the worried woman.

She fell into a low curtsey. "Oh, Your Grace. Thank you. You are so very good to us."

"Send word to me if there is any problem, Mrs. Hanbury." Charles patted their young boy's snowy head and left.

He rode back to the house, wondering what his son might be like. If Nellie has a daughter, he hoped she would be like her mother. A man could ask for nothing more.

Arriving home, he found he'd missed the start of the hunt. He anticipated as much and turned Thor's head to ride out after them. Crossing the meadow, the distant sound of baying hounds led him on.

He took Thor over two fences and rode on.

A rider galloped toward him. William Faulkner reined in, his face red. He whipped off his hat. "It's the duchess, Your Grace. She's taken a fall."

"Her Grace? She was not to ride today." Charles controlled Thor, who had scented his distress and danced about.

"She took part in it, Your Grace. A young dog spooked her horse."

"Dear God! Lead me to her, man."

Charles nudged Thor into a gallop, his heart beating hard in his throat. They climbed the hill in minutes, and from the top, he saw the horses clustered around the fallen rider. *Nellie!*

Charles could hardly breathe as he rode down to them.

He jumped down, tossed Thor's reins to one of the men, and fell on his knees beside her. She was alive! But she was unconscious. Her face so white, it scared him. What the devil was she doing riding?

"Nellie!" When she didn't open her eyes, he patted her hand. "Her Grace was not to ride today," he uttered savagely, staring around at the concerned faces. "Who changed her mind?" His gaze fell on Frances. "Was it you, Aunt?"

Frances twisted the crop in her hands. "Nellie was not to be there at the kill. She was riding away toward those trees when one of the young hounds got under Coventry's hooves."

"Coventry?" he asked as he examined Nellie for any signs of injury. There was a bruise forming on her forehead. "Why was she riding that feckless animal?"

"Her horse had a loose shoe," Aunt Frances said. "Can I do something to help?"

"Call off the hunt. There will be no fox caught today." Charles hefted Nellie up. His heart attempted to beat its way out of his chest as he carried her limp body in his arms. Her head lolled back against his shoulder, her eyes still closed. For one terrifying moment, he feared he had lost her, but her chest rose and fell. He suffered a surge of relief so strong his feet faltered. He took a stronger hold of her. "You'll be all right, my love," he murmured.

"Bring Thor over here and assist me. Don't just stand there like a statue," he thundered at his hapless groom.

Charles rode home, holding Nellie tightly against him. He thought her face had gained a little color, but still, fear crept in. What if he lost her? *Dear God, he couldn't bear to lose her!*

Why did it take something like this for him to realize how deep and absolute was his need for her? He simply could not live without her. Nellie was his anchor, his passion, his peace.

Charles sat at Nellie's bedside, waiting for the doctor, resting his head in his hands. He'd instructed the staff not to tell his mother until there was good news. Nellie would wake soon, wouldn't she?

Over an hour had passed before she opened her eyes. She reached up with a smile to touch his cheek.

"Nellie, love! You gave me the devil of a scare." He caught her hand and pressed it to his lips.

"What happened?"

"A dog frightened your horse, and you fell."

"Coventry is a nag, Charles, and you should sell him."

"I intend to." He smiled. "The doctor will be here soon. How do you feel, sweetheart?"

She put a shaky hand to her head. "My head aches intolerably." She stretched out her limbs carefully. "I'm a bit bruised in an unmentionable place." Her eyes widened and went dark with distress. "The baby, Charles, have I…?"

"Let's wait to hear the doctor's opinion, darling."

She closed her eyes, and a tear escaped down her cheek. "Oh, I hope I haven't hurt the baby. I should have refused. But I didn't want to embarrass you again."

He smoothed her hair back from her face. "What nonsense. How could you embarrass me?"

"I did once before. When your friends discovered the article I wrote."

"I'd forgotten about it. I wasn't embarrassed. I was proud of you, and I was a damn fool for not telling you at the time. I was angry with Walsh. Jealous of your friendship. I regret it deeply. All the time lost."

"Oh, my darling. I have been jealous, too. But you had no need to feel that way about Walsh. He sought to embarrass me when I failed to invite him back to the salon."

"He'd best stay out of my way, then." Charles raised his eyebrows. "I gather my Aunt Frances was behind you riding today. No need to tell me," he said when Nellie failed to answer. "I could see by her demeanor. She looked contrite, most unlike herself. And she wishes to come and see you. I shall send her packing tomorrow."

Nellie reached up and grasped hold of his sleeve. "Oh, no, you mustn't. Let her come and see me. Your mother might have need of her. You cannot blame your aunt. It was my decision to ride. No one forced me."

He frowned. "Well, I am not ready to forgive Frances yet."

Nellie pulled his head down to hers. "Let's not allow her to upset us," she said with an anxious look. "Not when..." her hand went to her stomach.

"I love you so much, Nellie. When I feared you might have..." He couldn't say the word. He impatiently flicked the tears away. What was wrong with him? He had only cried a couple of times in his life. Not even when they lost Michael or when his father had died. He was ashamed. It seemed so weak.

She reached up to hold his face in her hands. "Oh, Charles," she said, her voice shaking with emotion. "You love me?"

"I do, deeply. I should have told you a long time ago, Nellie." Had he been frightened to even admit it to himself?

"I wish you had because I couldn't tell you how I feel, Charles," she gently admonished him. "I thought you wouldn't want to hear it."

He gazed at her tenderly. "Tell me now."

"I love you with my heart and soul," she said simply. "But I was always aware that I wasn't your choice." She swallowed. "I knew you loved Drusilla, you see, and might have married her instead of me."

His eyebrows shot up in surprise. "Nellie! What nonsense." His gaze shifted to her mouth, and he traced a line over her bottom lip. "I was smitten with you the moment I met you. I wanted to get close to you, but you always held me at arm's length. Beverly told Jason she thought I was in love with you back before we married." He smiled. "But I despaired that you doubted me. You thought I lied to you. That the boy was mine."

"I was foolish not to trust you." She smoothed back his hair from his forehead. "But we knew so little about each other. The man I've come to know would never lie to me. But I know he isn't your son."

He raised his eyebrows. "Marian told you?"

She nodded with a glimmer of a smile.

"The boy's father is a French count," Charles said. "My stupid pride kept me from trying to convince you."

"In the end, I didn't really care if the boy was yours. As long as you were good to him."

Charles jumped up at the knock on the door. "Here's Dr. Jacobs. There was no time to send for Chapman, but I approve of how this doctor treated Hanbury."

The doctor came in with Lilly following. "Twice in one day, Your Grace? I hope I shan't see you again for a while." He walked over to the bed. "Well, Your Grace, you've taken a fall off a horse, I'm told."

"She's with child, doctor," Charles said.

"Might be best if you allow me to examine her. Will you assist me, Lilly?" He opened his bag.

"Please, Charles, do go away," Nellie implored him.

"A footman will be outside the door, Doctor. Should you require me, please send word when you have completed your examination of Her Grace."

At the impatient look from his wife, Charles left the room.

>>><<<

CHARLES AND NELLIE stood in the village church to act as witnesses as Feeley and Lilly were wed. Charles gazed down at his wife. She was radiant at the good news that her baby was growing nicely. His mother was thrilled.

Nellie's mother and father had written to express their delight and hope for a boy.

A happy man, Feeley vigorously shook Charles's hand. "I am indebted to you, Your Grace."

"I shall never have another valet like you," Charles said with absolute truth. "You will be missed."

Feeley chuckled. "I will miss working for you, Your Grace. Indeed I will, but I'm a married man." He cast a warm eye at Lilly, who looked pretty as a picture with flowers in her hair. "And a married man has obligations."

"Be a good husband, Feeley," Charles said. "I wish you well in your new life."

Nellie kissed Lilly goodbye. She was wearing one of Nellie's pelisses and had several other items of clothing in her valise. The couple climbed into the trap, which would take them to the inn. In the morning, they would board the stagecoach for Liverpool and take the boat to Ireland.

Nellie waved goodbye.

"Have you engaged a new lady's maid, my love?" Charles asked. "Barlow tells me you've been inundated with applications."

She tucked her hand in his arm as they strolled over to the curricle. "None of them appealed. Mrs. Bishop, the lady who runs the village store, has a daughter, Lucy. She is a nice girl, Charles, and very willing to learn. As she is keen to go into service, I've decided to engage her."

Charles nodded and smiled to himself.

Epilogue

Shewsbury Park
July 1816.

THUMB IN MOUTH, Bartholomew John Charles, Marquess Pembroke, rolled around the blanket and uttered a discourse on the state of things in general, which made sense only to him.

Nellie cast an indulgent smile at her dark-haired son. "He shall be a great orator in the Lords."

"But of course," Catherine said from her wicker chair, smiling from beneath her parasol. "Like his father, but with his mother's spirit and sense of fairness."

Nellie smiled up at her. "And his grandmother's benevolence."

Peter barked at a raven stalking the grass. It flew onto the branch of a chestnut tree and mocked the dog with a cry, watching him with its yellow eyes.

"Have you heard from your sister, Lady Belfries?"

"A letter came this morning," Nellie said. "Harriet is teething, and the less said about their son, Frederick, the better."

"Still a handful?"

"But his father sees it as a sign of a strong character."

"Jason was a handful, and he turned out well. I believe he and Beverly's little Sarah will be a beauty."

Nellie nodded. "She has her mother's beautiful eyes."

She glanced at her mama-in-law, who had sagged back in the chair. She would have to go inside soon. Catherine grew tired more easily these days. They had been thrilled to have her with them for far longer than expected but knew as Dr. Chapman predicted, she was coming to the end of her life. "Nathaniel and Eliza are to visit us next week with their two girls. It will be good to see them."

"Yes. You know, Nellie. I meant to talk to you about Charles, and I should not let it go too long."

Nellie tamped down the chill, which flooded through her. "About Charles?"

"He and his brother Michael were only ten months apart. They were always very close. Jason was so much younger, he wasn't around for much of that time." She sighed. "They were as thick as thieves. Charles adored Michael. When his brother fell ill, Charles tried everything he could to make him well again. Brought in doctors from abroad, read everything written about the disease, but in the end, none of it helped. It hit Charles very hard when Michael died. He changed from a happy young man to a more sober, cautious one. And then his father died. He had not wanted to believe he would one day be duke. He hadn't been trained to it. Taking the role was hard on him. He takes his position very seriously." She smiled at Nellie. "Why am I telling you now? Because he will suffer when I go. And I wanted you to know how very grateful I am that he has you to turn to, my dearest girl."

"Oh, Catherine, dear," Nellie murmured in a broken voice.

"Now, don't cry, please, Charles is coming. He mustn't see your tears."

Nellie hastily smoothed them away with her hands.

"Well, what have we here?" Charles crossed the lawn to them.

"We thought we'd have tea outside, it's such a lovely, warm day," Nellie said with a smile.

"After such an unusually cold spring," his mother said. "So cold, and those keen east winds!"

Charles sat on the blanket beside them. He raised Nellie's hand and kissed her inky fingers. "Another poem, my love?"

"No, I'm writing an article for the newspaper. I am concerned about the lack of constables on the streets around Covent Garden. The prostitutes are not protected well enough from men's violence. Something must be done."

"Mm? A little controversial, perhaps?"

"Now, Charles," his mother said with laugher in her voice. "You know you shall allow it, as you have all the others that Nellie sent off to the press."

"Too true, Mama." He cast Nellie a lazily seductive look, which always made her want him.

"Bart has fallen asleep." She rose to pick up her sleepy son.

"Mama?" Charles held out his hand to his mother. "Shall we go in?"

She took his arm and leaned heavily against him. "These have been such happy times, Charles."

"Yes, indeed, Mama." His gaze found Nellie's, and she saw the sadness in them. Happy times and sad awaited them. She sighed. But that was life.

⇾⇾⇾❋⇽⇽⇽

AT THE CONCLUSION of the evening, Charles entered Nellie's bedchamber. She turned to look at him from her seat before the mirror.

"You may go, Lucy," he ordered Nellie's new maid. He stood for a moment, his eyes meeting hers in the mirror. She cast him a playful smile while continuing to brush out her long locks. She began to plait it.

"Don't."

"Don't?" Nellie asked huskily.

He slowly shook his head. "Uh-uh."

His love and devotion for Nellie was rooted in his soul. As the hot need rose in him, he released a slow breath. He could never get enough of her. When he was away from her, he thought about this. The special time they had together, when he could assuage the passion he felt for her, which brought him alive. Made life worth living.

"I find myself in urgent need of you, Your Grace," he said, eyeing his provocative, passionate wife, who was always intent on pleasing him, as she did now.

She pushed back her heavy tresses and rose, casting him a wicked look. "Do you, indeed?"

He scooped her up in his arms and carried her to the bed and placed her on the turned-back bedclothes. While watching the pleased smile teasing her lips, he stripped off his cravat and shirt. He was aware of being much aroused as he removed his breeches. "I've been thinking of this all evening."

"That's why you let me win at cribbage." Nellie's eyes were warm with delight and affection.

His gaze roamed over her. The neckline of her nightgown slipped down over one creamy shoulder, and her full breasts jutted through the satiny material.

"You won," he said, his voice a low growl, as he placed a knee on the bed. "Because I was distracted by lustful thoughts."

"That should happen more often." Her grin, cheeky and inviting, heated his blood. "I enjoy beating you at cards. It happens so rarely." She ended the words on a little cry as his teeth grazed her collar bone. "And the end result," she said breathlessly, as he gently rolled her over onto her stomach, "Is most certainly to be wished for."

His hand moved slowly down her delicate spine and swept over the flare of her hip to take a firm hold of her rounded bottom. He lowered his head and took a small bite.

"Charles!" Nellie wriggled.

He chuckled. A quick gesture and her nightgown and peignoir were on the floor. She lay in an abandoned pose beneath him, on her back now.

Charles drew a nipple into his mouth and then took the other as she clutched his head and moaned. His kisses trailed down, he dove into her navel, producing a delighted shriek, then kissed a path over her rounded stomach to her soft, damp core.

As he kissed and teased her hot center, Nellie arched and screamed, her body convulsing.

He pushed her legs apart and slid slowly into her warm, slick body with a sigh of satisfaction.

With a mew of pleasure, Nellie gripped his shoulders.

Charles withdrew, then surged back, fighting to keep it slow and steady while his need for her became almost unbearably intense. He could hold on no longer, murmuring her name, he thrust hard and came in an explosive climax.

As he settled at her side, their breaths slowing, he acknowledges the love he felt for Nellie was deep and true. Nothing he felt in the past could come close to this. It scared him a little, and he fought to push away the feelings of vulnerability, knowing how blessed he was. He'd never expected this gift.

"I wonder if we made another baby?" Nellie's voice sounded heavy and sated. She nestled against him, half asleep.

"A daughter who takes after my beautiful wife."

He stroked her hair away from her cheek and pressed a kiss there. Nellie pregnant again would worry him, but the concern was soon lost in the flood of joy coursing through him at the thought of his son. They would have more healthy children, God willing.

About the Author

A USA TODAY bestselling author of Regency romances, with over 35 books published, Maggi's Regency series are International bestsellers. Stay tuned for Maggi's latest Regency series out next year. Her novels include Victorian mysteries, contemporary romantic suspense and young adult. Maggi holds a BA in English and Master of Arts Degree in Creative Writing. She supports the RSPCA and animals often feature in her books.

Like to keep abreast of my latest news? Join my newsletter.
http://bit.ly/1m70lJJ

Blog: http://bit.ly/1t7B5dx
Find excerpts and reviews on my website: http://bit.ly/1m70lJJ
Twitter: @maggiandersen: http://bit.ly/1Aq8eHg
Facebook: Maggi Andersen Author: http://on.fb.me/1KiyP9g
Goodreads: http://bit.ly/1TApe0A
Pinterest: https://www.pinterest.com.au/maggiandersen

Maggi's Amazon page for her books with Dragonblade Publishing.
https://tinyurl.com/y34dmquj